WITHDRAWN
FROM THE
ISLINGTON
LIBRARIES

35p

2

1

16

Books that   ve been
            to the
[1124]

Beef
Wellington
Blue

Also by Max Davidson

The Wolf

Beef Wellington Blue

Max Davidson

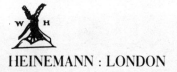

HEINEMANN : LONDON

William Heinemann Ltd
10 Upper Grosvenor Street, London W1X 9PA
LONDON   MELBOURNE   TORONTO
JOHANNESBURG   AUCKLAND

First published 1985
© Max Davidson 1985
SBN 434 17520 X

ISLINGTON LIBRARIES
LIBRARY &
ACC. No.   N 660924
CLASS No.   F
DATED.

Photoset by Deltatype, Ellesmere Port
Printed and bound in Great Britain by
Biddles Ltd, Guildford

For André and Fiona

Part 1

1

Westminster

Islington
Libraries

1

'Who's the broad?' asked Mumford. He had never told me he was a Bogart fan.

'Talking to Carter?'

'Yes.'

'With the tight skirt?'

'Yes.'

'And the legs?'

'Yes.'

I eyed her casually, pretending to admire the panoramic view of the Thames behind her. She was a not-so-natural blonde and looked about thirty, or it may have been forty. It makes no difference to a man like me, rising fifty-three and 22 stone with it, but I guess she wanted to be given the benefit of the doubt. Her make-up was assiduous and her clothes discreetly flattering. Whatever was inside the paper, the wrapping was immaculate, an advertising man's dream. Drape her across the bonnet of a new sports car and nobody was going to ask about miles to the gallon. Only a certain self-consciousness marred the overall impression. Her charms would have been greater if she hadn't cosseted them so strictly, sweeping her hair impatiently out of her face as it was caught by gusts of wind from Lambeth, and maintaining a severely upright posture. She was the sort of woman middle-aged men said they wouldn't throw out of bed, but never expected to get into it.

What she was doing with Carter was a mystery. Junior Cabinet Ministers usually prefer safer escorts, women who will look at home in the kitchen with oven-gloves but use the

3

bedroom for sleeping. Carter had no reputation for being adventurous with women, quite the reverse: you expected to see him flanked with posses of civil servants, not socialising with the opposite sex. Of the members of the new Government, he was regarded as more dependable than colourful, a possessor of 'bottom' rather than 'side'. The conventional wisdom credited him only with decency, diligence and dullness, and those labels stuck to him like limpets. He might be a real wow in his private life, but nobody had bothered to find out, so his image of uninspired competence was never challenged. This stereotype was to prove a grotesque misreading of Carter's character, but I was as much in thrall to it as everyone else. To my eyes, the pairing of him and the leggy women was an incongruous one, and the incongruity was reflected in the woman's nervous bearing. She held a glass of wine in both hands as if afraid of dropping it, and nodded her head too emphatically as Carter pointed out various landmarks on the far side of the river. It was probably the first time she had come to the House and mingled with politicoes over a lunchtime drink on the Terrace. Legs or no legs, I felt a bit sorry for her.

Mumford winked leeringly. 'Better than Carter's usual, don't you think?'

'I didn't know he had a usual.'

'Mrs Carter, I mean.'

'Isn't she a dental surgeon?'

'No, she's in orthopaedics.'

'I knew it was one or the other.'

'Trust Carter.'

'Trust Carter.'

'Are you two at it again?' boomed Geoffrey Hammond behind us, waddling back from the bar with three large whiskies. 'You hacks never let up. Who have you got your knives into this time?'

We let the jibe pass. Lobby correspondents are immune to this sort of banter from Members of Parliament. It reflects the cynical professional amusement with which we view each other's activities, without which the House of Commons would

4

be incomplete. The cynicism is part of the furniture of the place – as familiar as Big Ben, only centuries older.

'Who's the woman with Carter, Geoffrey?' Mumford asked. His bluntness would have seemed unsophisticated if he hadn't been a professional journalist, paid to find out these things.

Hammond peered down the Terrace over his little piggy spectacles and snorted. 'Never seen her before. Legs a bit of all right.'

'We noticed.'

'Probably his private secretary at the Department. Civil servants can wear anything nowadays. If not, she's his mistress. It comes to much the same thing. Who cares, for God's sake? She's a woman, not an opinion poll. Legs a bit of all right. Lucky Carter.'

He took a gulp of whisky and glanced at us in that odd coy way of his, begging us to indulge his tired one-liners. We smiled politely, but no more. He had lost weight since the last operation and the short wheezy sentences were the only vestiges of a once powerful political intellect. It was sad to see him hanging on to his seat in the House so stubbornly. He should have retired before the election, not come back to tell his rambling stories about Winston and Nye and be pitied by the callow new intake of lecturers and merchant bankers. After his outspoken years, I couldn't imagine him enjoying the grey political twilight where not even his opponents would be rude to him.

We drank a toast, half ironic, half sentimental, to parliamentary democracy, and sat in silence for a few moments looking across the Thames to St Thomas's Hospital and enjoying the familiar scene. Then Mumford started plying Hammond with questions. What was the rationale behind the new Cabinet? Was the Prime Minister going to start cautiously or push the radical elements in his programme through quickly? Why had so-and-so been given Industry rather than Transport? Why was there no Housing Bill in the Queen's Speech, as promised in the manifesto? Would there be a mini-Budget in the autumn? Hammond answered frankly but long-windedly and, after listening to his bitchy indiscretions for a while, I gradually switched off. This sort of material was all right for Mumford, because his readers were interested in it. In the better parts of London, they read his elegantly crafted columns over Sunday breakfast and on Monday pronounced his opinions as their own. My own paper was less, shall I say, cerebral; its most junior sub would have struck out the word without hesitation. The volume of political coverage depended on extraneous factors. If the pin-up girl was 35–24–36, I might get all of 300 words. If she was big on top, I'd be down to 100. If she had a 38-inch bottom as well, my copy would be spiked. That's what I tell people anyway. On a paper like mine, you need to make jokes like that just to survive.

As Mumford and Hammond talked on, I ran an eye over the other people on the Terrace. The usual parliamentary circus was there – MPs and Peers, dowdy wives and well-dressed mistresses, chattering officials with half-pints of beer, wide-eyed constituents from Derbyshire, Wales and Sussex. The midsummer sun was in its firmament and gleamed down on us from the Lords end of the Terrace, where the red and green marquees – red for the Lords, green for the Commons – fluttered in the breeze like beer-tents at a country cricket match. Every face I saw seemed to be smiling, and there was a palpable gaiety in the air which contrasted with the sleepy progress of the Thames beside us. Without obvious razzma-tazz, a beginning-of-term party was in full swing. The bitterly fought election campaign was finally over, the people had given a decisive verdict, and the Queen had ridden in state to open her new Parliament and pray for God's blessings on its deliberations. Democracy was alive and well in SW1 and even the vanquished had something to celebrate. I saw a senior Minister from the outgoing administration walking down the Terrace with a renewed spring in his step, as though he had forgotten how good life could be without red boxes and chauffeur-driven cars and trade delegations from Korea. He nodded without animosity at the man who had been given his portfolio in the new Government and whom I had last seen

6

savaging him on television two weeks before. It was that sort of day. The occasion, the weather and the setting were all too idyllic to be interrupted by politics.

Mumford and Hammond were still deep in their discussion about the new faces in the Cabinet, so I shifted the position of my chair slightly to get a better view of Carter and his friend, who were now leaning against the parapet, looking across the river. In the water below them, a boat-load of tourists from Westminster pier gawped up and clicked cameras, and looked indignant at the sight of Members of Parliament enjoying themselves. One wag shouted something facetious which got lost in the wind, and Carter raised his glass ironically in salute as the boat swung round to make the journey down to Greenwich past the distant dome of St Paul's. Then he and the woman turned away from the river and stood talking to each other about fifty yards from where I was sitting. I couldn't catch what they were saying, but it promised to be excellent silent comedy.

Legs, or whatever the woman was called, still didn't seem very sure of herself. Her perfect physical poise couldn't conceal her nervousness in Carter's presence. She laughed unconvincingly at the dry little ironies with which he always peppered his conversation, interrupting once or twice when he wasn't expecting it and remaining silent when he seemed to want her to talk. I had the impression that, although they enjoyed each other's company, they weren't relaxed about being seen together in public. Anyone but a Fleet Street hack would have had the manners not to stare at them, but I was too old for such niceties and it was the Fleet Street hack in me who spotted something which higher-minded people might have missed: the band of gold around the fourth finger of the woman's left hand. It was so delicate that it needed a trained eye to pick it out at fifty yards' range, but it was there all right and it increased my interest in the woman. As Mrs Legs, she had greater news value for my prudish, sex-obsessed readership.

What happened next had my fingers itching for a typewriter.

Carter suddenly moved a fraction closer to Legs and said something to her in a lowered voice. I couldn't make out what it was, but you didn't need binoculars to see its effect on the woman. Her face reddened immediately and she said something back to Carter which simply produced a shrug and a slight shake of his head. Then, without warning, she turned and marched off down the Terrace, passing quite close to where I was sitting. She seemed very agitated and, if I'd been writing the story up in the paper, I would have said she was choking back tears, because that's the sort of stuff people pay good money every morning to read. The woman was actually too composed to choke back anything, but she was upset all right. Her pace quickened as she reached the steps leading down from the Terrace into the House and, within seconds, she was out of sight completely. Carter made no attempt to follow her, but began chatting to a backbench colleague who was entertaining some constituents at a nearby table.

What had he said to her? I couldn't imagine. It looked like an old-fashioned pass, with Carter being given the bum's rush, but I just didn't believe it. The sixth sense for which I was paid to frequent the House, picking up the political vibrations and drinking indiscretions out of Members, told me that Carter wouldn't be so unsubtle in a thousand years. His career had been marked by an almost monkish reluctance to blot his copy-book, and I could remember one of his colleagues bitching that he preferred reading Hansard to the company of women. Why should he waste his energy on such a fool's errand with the House due to sit in twenty-five minutes? I didn't believe it.

It struck me on reflection that Legs hadn't shown annoyance with Carter himself, but shock at something he had said to her. Her hurried departure reminded me of an incident on the Terrace years ago, when a Member called Barrington told me he had put £1,000 on a certainty in the 2.30 at Plumpton. When I assured him that the animal was out of training and would do no better than third, the man had reacted in an identical way to Legs, rushing off to try and lay off his bet. I doubted if there was

8

a horse involved here, but it might be something similar and I just hoped the explanation wasn't too banal, like Carter telling the woman her mascara was running. These mini-dramas added spice to the dog days at Westminster and I shared this one with Mumford and Hammond, who had been too absorbed in their discussion to notice it.

'Interesting,' said Mumford. 'She just did a bolt, you say?'

'Right.'

'After Carter had said something to her?'

'Right. She didn't even finish her drink.'

'Must have been serious. Perhaps Carter made a pass at her. Cabinet Minister Offers Love: Woman Flies in Terror – you could run that one.'

'No, I don't think it was that. It looked more like he told her some news she wasn't too wild about.'

'It's really perfectly obvious, my dear fellow,' Hammond chortled. 'Waterworks.'

'Sorry, Geoffrey?'

'Woman had to go to the lav. It's the only explanation if you stop to think about it. Now can we talk about something else, please?'

I smiled wryly at Mumford and we abandoned the subject. It was annoying to leave an unfinished bone, but Hammond's only topic of conversation was politics and that was what our editors paid us to talk to him about. As Mumford fetched more whisky, I asked Hammond how well his vote had held up at the election. I knew this would keep him happy, for he was one of those Members with safe seats who take immense pride in doing better on their own 'patch' than national trends indicate and in pushing up their majorities in bad years as well as good. He purred a little at my question, then started a long spiel about percentage swings nationally and locally and the effect of boundary changes in his area. I knew I wouldn't be expected to contribute to the conversation for the next ten minutes, so I sat back in my chair and let the sun beat down on my face.

As Hammond talked, I slowly became aware of a figure

standing in the shadows to our right. He must have just come on to the Terrace, for he was looking tentatively around him and seemed to be alone. He stood rooted to the spot for a short while and I thought he was about to leave altogether when he caught sight of the back of Hammond's head and made his way slowly towards us. When he got within ten yards, it dawned on him that he might be intruding on a private conversation and he came to a standstill again. Then something about my appearance reassured him – my cuddly 22 stone perhaps, or my friendly journalist's smile. Shedding his inhibitions, he came up to our table.

'Do you mind if I join you?' The voice was pleasant, but unassertive. He sounded like a tennis player looking for a partner in the club-house, sure of his second service but a bit intimidated by everyone else's steel rackets.

Hammond twisted round to see who it was, shielding his eyes against the sun which shone powerfully from behind the newcomer's head. 'Is that Christopher? I can't see a thing in this bloody light. Come round this way a bit. That's better. I *thought* it was Christopher. You can certainly join us, young man. Have you met Bob Mumford? Bob Mumford, Christopher Jackson. Chris is our new Member for somewhere in the Midlands with a funny name. That's right, isn't it, Chris?'

The man nodded shyly. It was a cue for him to talk, but he seemed diffident about boring strangers with details of his constituency. It was a rare form of restraint and I liked him for it. Hammond put his hand on my forearm.

'This is someone else you should meet, Chris. Christopher Jackson, John Wellington.'

'Pleased to meet you, John.' A gossamer smile flickered across the man's face as we shook hands. 'Aren't you also –'

I gave a low snarl of warning. 'Yes, I am also. John Wellington, also known as Beef Wellington. Congratulations on being the thousandth person this month to remind me of the fact. With a name like mine and a weight problem, you give the wits in the House a field day. The really original ones call me Boots as well. As a matter of fact –'

I was about to make further sarcastic comments on the vexed subject of my nickname when Hammond interrupted. He had heard my views on fattism before and, seeing that Christopher had wandered on to sensitive ground, covered up the gaffe with some characteristic banter.

'John is simply the worst lobby correspondent in the House, Christopher. Terrible drivel he writes. If he offers you a drink, tell him Uncle Geoffrey said you weren't to talk to strangers. You must never let him quote you. These fellows always get it wrong. Write it down for him if you have to. He won't mind, he's got a friend back at the office who can read for him. Don't get upset if he writes something rude about you. He's rude about all of us. Only does it to boost circulation of that dreadful lavatory-paper of his. But if he says you're going to be the next Prime Minister but six, steer clear of him for about a fortnight. He'll get the message, and the Whips will let you off with a warning. Whisky?'

'An orange juice would be fine, thank you, Geoffrey.'

'*Orange* juice? Are you sure? You'll be telling me next that democracy means not having to drink alcohol. Dreadful balls you youngsters talk sometimes.'

He struggled off to the bar, puffing heavily. He could become very loquacious when people laughed at his jokes, but the effort of cracking them exhausted him. I couldn't tell whether Christopher had laughed out of politeness or because he hadn't heard the jokes before and found them funny. It had never really registered that there might be people who hadn't heard Geoffrey Hammond's jokes. They were part of the House's background music: after a time, you forgot that the tunes had words to them. I wanted to have a quiet word in the newcomer's ear and say that it would be kinder not to laugh at Geoffrey, that he might live longer if people didn't encourage him to do his star turns any more, but I restrained myself. However jaded you become, a fresh face always commands a certain respect and Christopher's was the freshest face I'd seen in the Commons for years. He looked no more than twenty or twenty-one and his chin was as smooth and uncreased as the virginal blue suit he was wearing. I remembered now seeing him on television on election night, stepping modestly up to the microphone to thank the returning officer after defeating an incumbent Cabinet Minister. He had looked callow under the television lights, although one studio expert had commented on his intellectual brilliance and another had said something patronising about how nice it was to have young blood in the House. I don't usually feel protective about politicians, but in this case I couldn't help it. He was so green that someone would try to take a lawn-mower to him sooner or later. I just hoped for his sake it was the right person.

Mumford still had Carter's woman on the brain and he started chatting to Christopher about Carter in an oblique way, feeling his way gradually with him and not resorting immediately to the sort of blunt questions with which he had plied Hammond. It was Christopher, curiously, who provided the bluntness. Almost as soon as Carter's name was mentioned, he blurted out: 'He's the best man in the Cabinet by a mile.'

Mumford and I glanced at each other, taken aback by the lack of equivocation. Then Mumford continued, giving his words his usual deceptive coating of saccharine.

'Why do you say that, Chris? I'm interested.'

'Well, don't you agree?'

'I'm a journalist. I'm not in the business of agreeing or disagreeing.'

'I'm sorry, I'd forgotten.' I could see him wondering whether he should be making such sweeping generalisations to strangers from the press, but his convictions overcame his doubts. 'I just think it's obvious, that's all. He's the only one in there who doesn't fudge issues the whole time and who has a concrete vision of the future. Because of his unpretentious background, he really understands ordinary people and he's about the only political figure at the moment who can generate confidence and a sense of purpose. I know he's only forty-three, but in my opinion he should be Prime Minister already.'

Again Mumford and I exchanged glances. This was the closest thing to an honest opinion we had heard in the House for

12

years. It was the sort of candour which got young MPs into trouble if they weren't careful about it. I wondered what punishment the Whips' Office would devise if they heard of this disloyalty to the present Prime Minister: a paddle in the Thames in concrete boots or a few years on the European Legislation Committee? The boyish hero-worship would have been affecting if he hadn't made such an odd choice of hero. I didn't know Carter well, being imbued, as I said, with all the conventional prejudices about him, but he had always struck me as a careerist who had opted for the inside rails. I didn't doubt that he was aiming for the very top, but I never expected him to get there by projecting a concrete vision of the future, whatever the phrase meant. It sounded aesthetically grim, but I avoided saying anything facetious about architectural styles in the third millenium. If Christopher wanted to talk in clichés, I wasn't going to correct him. It would do his political career no harm, and might help it.

'You seem to have a lot of faith in Carter,' I said. 'How have you got to know about him?'

He blushed. 'I was his researcher for two years when he was in Opposition. You mustn't think that's the only reason why I –'

'Why you what?'

'Why I think so highly of him. I worked for him because I admired him. I don't admire him because I worked for him. There's a difference.'

'I can see that.'

'And he didn't help me get selected as a candidate, if that's what you're thinking. In fact, he advised me not to put myself up as a candidate until next time round, because –'

'Because you were too young?'

'Yes.' Again his cheeks went an intriguing shade of red. 'I suppose you find me rather naïve?'

I opened my mouth to say something, then stopped. The trouble with naïve people is that they ask naïve questions which cynical people find hard to cope with. I should have said straight off that I found him bloody naïve, that his attitude to Carter was positively pre-pubescent, and that if he carried on

13

drinking orange juices he'd get a headache. But how could I? He was only a boy, and I felt protective in a strange kind of way.

'You're young,' I said, trying to invest the word with the right mixture of avuncularity and menace. 'You're new to this place and I imagine you'll have to do some adjusting.'

He looked at me suspiciously and I wished I'd chosen a better word. If he admired Carter for not fudging, the prospect of making adjustments himself can't have been very uplifting. Mumford saw I was getting bogged down and intervened smoothly.

'About Carter, Chris. What do you know about his private life?'

'Very little, I'm afraid.'

'Oh?'

'You see, he likes to keep that side of things entirely separate from what he does in politics. I agree with him about that. You can't mix the two. I've been to his house several times, of course.'

'Of course.'

'His wife, Sophie, is a doctor. In orthopaedics. You probably didn't know that.'

'Orthopaedics? Really?'

'She's a good person, a really good person. She cares enormously about her work. They only have one child, a boy. He's about fifteen now.'

'What about his sex life?'

'Whose? The boy's?'

'No, Carter's.'

'Well, I don't – he's married to Sophie, who's a doctor.'

'What's that got to do with it?'

'Well, nothing, I suppose. She –'

He stopped, looking flustered and rather unhappy. For all Mumford's patina of sophistication, when he was hot on the scent he could be as subtle as a bull-elephant negotiating drinking rights at a water-hole. On this occasion, he had overplayed his hand badly. The boy's nose had begun doing rabbit-like twitches as soon as he heard the word 'sex', and I

14

could see his left leg shaking like a piston under the table. He looked over his shoulder for help, hoping that Hammond was on his way back with the orange juice, and was obviously disappointed to see him still stationed at the bar trying his cumbersome charms on the barmaid. I thought he was about to make an excuse and leave, so I put him out of his misery by telling him about the mysterious Mrs Legs and the incident I had witnessed earlier. This reassured him that there had been a semi-respectable purpose in Mumford's questions and he relaxed again, although he couldn't help us unravel the mystery. Carter was a man of great integrity, he said, who put his family as high as his country and who certainly didn't 'sleep around'. This last whispered phrase emerged after so much coy dithering that even Mumford got the message and dropped the subject. Any hypothetical inquiries about Carter's hypothetical sex life would have to be pursued with a more forthcoming source.

Our casual small-talk had become uncomfortable and we were all relieved when Hammond returned from the bar. Although his absence had allowed Mumford and me to pump Christopher in peace, the pumping was such hard work that it was best negotiated in stages. For once Hammond's undemanding badinage came as a tonic. 'Sorry to keep you – they had to send up Victoria Street for the orange juice. I'd check that you've still got your wallet if I were you, Chris – you never know with these comedians. If you're not sure about anything you've said, go and talk to a lawyer immediately.' The jokes were sadly predictable, but they were a good substitute for conversation and Christopher still laughed at them dutifully. His laugh was an octave deeper than his speaking voice and quite attractive in its way, like the healthy gurgling of water down a plug-hole.

Just before 2.30 we wandered back into the House in time for the start of the sitting. Hammond had to meet a constituent, so we took a slight detour via the Central Lobby, arriving there at the same time as the Speaker's procession. This held us up for a minute or two, because everyone freezes in deference as the

Speaker enters the House with the Mace carried before him, and the policeman in the Central Lobby shouts 'Hats off, strangers!' as the procession comes into view. The instruction is directed at the members of the public gathered to watch the spectacle, in case any of them have forgotten their manners and are wearing a hat indoors. It dates from a time when people owned both hats and manners and is now strictly redundant, although the policeman who shouts the instruction removes his own helmet as he says the words, to escape the charge of using empty symbolism in a built-up area. A nice touch.

As the procession passed, I instinctively watched Christopher's face. You could call this a journalist's hunch if you like, although my instincts were more those of a father watching his son's reactions to a pantomime in the hope of re-experiencing the lost spontaneity of his own youth. Either way, I wasn't disappointed, for the reverential intensity with which the boy – as I increasingly thought of him – gazed at the procession was quite out of the ordinary. It was not matched by any of the tourists who had gathered to view the spectacle and whose faces showed only that polite curiosity with which people observe the local customs of foreigners. They looked with interest at the dignitaries in the procession and you could see them thinking 'How cute!' or 'Comme c'est drôle!' or something Japanese, as they noted the various paraphernalia laid on by the costume and props department: the white gloves, the knee-length breeches, the Speaker's wig and gown, the Serjeant-at-Arms' flimsy-looking sword, the Mace itself. But they were not much moved, as Christopher so obviously was. His face buckled a bit as the Speaker passed, and he stood with exaggerated erectness as though fighting an instinct to drop to his knees in prayer. He must have seen me staring at him, for he apologised for his display of emotion as soon as the Speaker had passed out of sight.

'I'm sorry, John. You've probably seen all this hundreds of times before.'

'Once or twice.'

'You must remember that it's comparatively new to me. I get

very moved by this sort of thing.'

'I can see that.'

He blushed and put his hand confidentially on my shoulder. 'It's the great love affair in my life.'

'What is?'

'Parliamentary democracy.' He grinned sheepishly. 'I love it so much I could –'

'You could what?'

'I don't know. Die for it, kill for it – one or the other. I feel so elated just being in this building, let alone being an elected Member and representing –'

'You'll get over that.'

'But I don't want to get over it.'

'You should. See a doctor and he'll give you a sedative.'

He took his hand off my shoulder and stepped back as if I had slapped him. My jibe was meant to deflate rather than wound, but it had cut deep into something tender and I regretted it. The boy's prattle was naïve but harmless, no worse than the garbage I had talked when I had first come to the House as an 11-stone tyro and called Members sir. I had been brutal, but I knew that others would be more brutal, that the House was no place for blushing innocents and that it would soon make that clear to him in its inimitable way. I told myself I was only protecting him against later disillusionment, although there was also – why deny it? – another reason for my sourness. Chris Jackson was beginning to bug me.

Seconds later, we went our different ways. Christopher scuttled into the Chamber to hear the resumption of the debate on the Queen's Speech, and I ambled back to the Press Gallery at my leisure: at my age you know in advance what speakers are going to say, so there's no need to hurry. I couldn't say I'd made a new friend after my final *faux pas*, but I resolved to watch Christopher's progress with interest. Although I was used to seeing new Members struggling to find their feet in the House, this complete rawness of his was different. It suggested an almost frightening vulnerability and started tiny alarm-bells ringing at the back of my head. How would he manage? Would

17

he even survive at all? I think he must have got under my skin a bit because, when I got home at 10.30 and Jenny asked me about my day, he was the first person I mentioned. Her snap judgment on him was typically forthright.

'He sounds cretinous,' she said, curling up in her armchair with a mug of coffee. She loved these end-of-day post mortems more than any other time we spent together, and would dig herself in for at least an hour's gossip about the House before we went to bed. 'Were you rude to him?'

'A little.'

'I'm not surprised. How old is he?'

'Twenty-eight. I looked it up. He looks at least eight years younger.'

'How ridiculous! Why do people vote for someone that age? From what you say, he ought to be still at school. And how can he possibly think Carter ought to be Prime Minister? He's the most colourless, faceless one of the whole lot. Well, isn't he, John?'

'Absolutely. Christopher just seems totally infatuated with him.'

'You mean, like a schoolboy crush?'

'More or less. He used to work for him. Says he's got a concrete vision of the future or some balls like that. By the way –'

I started telling her the story about Carter and the woman with the legs, toning down the legs part slightly. It was the sort of mystery she adored trying to unravel, for the House's machinations fascinated her at second remove and she embraced the little excitements of my career even on its downward slope. Being Mrs Beef Wellington wasn't quite like being a leader-writer's wife and there was no room in my tacky column for the snippets of stream-of-consciousness elegance she had once hoped to contribute to my journalistic output. But she had long since stopped being frustrated with my penny-dreadful prose, and there was no condescension in the interest she took in low political intrigue. With a few imaginative flourishes, she elaborated a theory about Carter and his friend which involved

18

a sudden fall in the Yen, a Swiss bank account and a secret trade agreement with Nigeria. I didn't believe a word of it but, as always, I loved watching the animation on her face as she weaved her extravagant theories and made sharp character observations about the people involved. She should never have been a solicitor, I thought, not for the first time. She should have been an actress or written thrillers or followed some other semi-reputable profession like my own.

I felt particularly fond of her that night because she forgot her calorie check. Don't ask me why, but she had made it her mission to reduce me from 22 to 20 stone and would question me minutely at the end of each day on my food and drink intake, then produce a calorie chart and a calculator and fire in pedantic supplementaries. How many chips, roughly? How much butter on my toast, roughly? The questions were not just tedious, but embarrassing. I didn't like lying but, when all the calories had been totted up, the truth wasn't very appetising either. As I fell asleep that night, I was grateful to Christopher and Mrs Legs for providing a diversion.

2

What was it about that Session of Parliament that I found so deadly? It was no different, on the face of it, from the twenty-one previous sessions which I had chronicled in my wine-shot prose. All the usual ingredients were there: leadership crises, monthly rows over the economy, dissension in Government ranks, dissension in Opposition ranks, plots, arguments, cock-ups, jokes, plenty of jokes. Every day was different, and every day there was something which, with a little exaggeration, you could call a story. It wasn't like being an obituaries editor and waiting weeks for someone half-way interesting to snuff it. Things were happening all the time. It was only for me that the shifting pattern of life in the House suddenly became motion-less and stultifying.

I saw no similar boredom among my fellow hacks in the Press Gallery. When we reassembled that autumn, after the summer recess and the weary slog round the party conferences and the cheap seaside hotels, everyone else threw themselves back into the swim of things with the chatter and bustle of second-year students at university. There remained something jaded in the hauteur with which they looked down from the Press Gallery on the undignified happenings in the Chamber beneath, waiting for a moment of special idiocy or a crass speech to seize on and lampoon. Yet, however profound their cynicism about the House's proceedings, they still plied their trade with the enthusiasm of people who wouldn't willingly have worked anywhere else. I saw in most of them that strange, forlorn addiction to Parliament which I had suffered myself for so long and which I had mysteriously mislaid in some cavity between the summer and autumn of that year. Without consciously trying to kick the habit, I found that by mid-November I had booted it almost out of sight. It was no longer just a physical effort to heave myself out of the Press Bar to phone copy through to the paper: it required mental determination, like listening to Wagner played very slowly by a provincial symphony orchestra.

There was nothing unusual, of course, in being disenchanted with the House. It was something we all went through from time to time, during those dull nocturnal hours when three or four bored Members would perch on the olive-green benches trying to spin out a debate, or at some great parliamentary set-piece when every word rang hollow and you asked yourself what you were doing listening to it. Even the Members, the ones with the speaking parts, questioned the value of their existence sometimes, so why shouldn't an ageing spear-carrier in the Press Gallery? Doubt is the first privilege of democracy.

There was more than doubt, though, in my depressed state of mind that autumn. Doubt can be shrugged off, dissolved by rational argument or drowned in alcohol. When one of my fellow hacks gets fed up with the House and leaves to work somewhere else, making me question whether I should do the same, I always console myself that he is deserting the capital for the provinces, and I believe it. If it was simply a lack of confidence in the House's institutional usefulness that was depressing me, I could have got over it quickly. But there was something else. I can't describe it and, if I could, there mightn't have been a problem. A psychologist would probably have talked about a crisis of identity, and certainly the fact that I was always being cast in clownish roles contributed to my *malaise*. The weight of other people's expectations of me – I was fat so I ought to be jolly, a journalist so I ought to be cynical – had a sometimes crushing effect. Was there a decent, serious, wafer-thin man locked up inside and struggling to get out, or did I just believe there must be one because of the old maxim? And was it even worth going into it in that convoluted way? For the

21

moment, let's just say Beef Wellington had the blues.

My journalism should have suffered from this sudden listlessness, but didn't. To be brutal, I practised the kind of bad writing which so little reflects its author's moods that it can operate on auto-pilot. I was a hack writing for a paper whose editor never fussed about split infinitives or reliable sources of information. He just wanted little splashes of political colour to reassure his readers that there was a world beyond bingo and that his correspondents were out there in the thick of it, ready to report on the great events if they ever threatened to push sex off the front page. With an editor as easy to satisfy as Brian Sparks, it wasn't difficult to keep churning the stuff out through the numbing boredom of that autumn. On 14 November indeed, after one of my weightier scoops about a Cabinet Minister whose dog had gone missing and turned up in the back garden of the French Embassy, Brian even telephoned to congratulate me. When I had to tell him the next day that I had got it wrong and that a cat, not a dog, had been involved, he didn't seem to mind about such a detail. The story had read better with a dog, he said, and the cat wasn't going to serve a libel writ, was it? He was a very professional man.

He looked rather surprised when I turned up in his office one morning later in the month and asked for ten minutes of his time. He wasn't much used to dealing with his political correspondents in person, preferring to sit alone in his room doodling on blank sheets of paper and barking instructions to his minions down the telephone. But he welcomed me cordially enough and, after waving me into one of his black leather armchairs, poured out a generous shot of whisky.

'Now, Beef, what's your problem?'

'It's like this, Chief. I'm bored.'

'Bored, Beef?'

'Yes, Chief.'

As usual, our conversation slipped quickly into the rhythms of comic opera. Brian was not only high on being called Chief (he had seen *Citizen Kane* too often) but used my nickname scrupulously, making rhyming couplets inevitable. My reference to boredom seemed to puzzle him. He sounded as if he had heard the term before, but couldn't see its relevance to a correspondent on a fun-loving family paper like ours. He put one end of a green felt-tip into the corner of his mouth and began gently masticating it.

'I don't want to intrude, Beef, but if we're talking about a woman problem here –'

'No, Chief.'

'– some seven-year itch or what have you, then I can't help. Jenny's not getting any younger, you're not getting any younger, you've both got to take the rough with the smooth. Am I right, Beef?'

'Absolutely, Chief, and thanks for the shrewd words of advice. But you've missed the point. It's the work I'm bored with.'

As I said the words, I again felt as though I was talking to a foreigner unfamiliar with my language. Brian's workaholism was a Fleet Street legend and nobody could remember him taking anything as self-indulgent as a holiday. He looked at me suspiciously, as if I was trying to sell him a second-hand car with three wheels, then poured a whisky for himself.

'What's wrong with the work? Don't I *pay* you enough?' It was a knee-jerk response, as cheap and unsympathetic as I would have expected. 'You've got no business being bored, Beef. You are the number one political correspondent on a big national newspaper. You know the House of Commons the way Lester Piggot knows Epsom race-course. If people want to find out what's really going on behind the scenes at Westminster, then you're the one they read. They don't want heavy political analysis over breakfast or when they're commuting to work. They're looking for gossip and atmosphere and a bit of a laugh, and that's why they like the stuff you write. At the end of the day, they trust you. Beef Wellington is one of the best by-lines on my paper. It has a ring to it, it makes people feel they're not being sold short, it gives them something they can –'

'I don't want to work in the House any more.'

'Say that again.'

'I said, I don't want to work in the House any more. Sorry, Chief.'

'Bloody hell.'

He was shocked now, not just puzzled, and I understood his reaction because I had shocked myself. The thought of leaving the House hadn't been in my mind at all when I walked into the room. I just wanted to grouse about my general boredom and talk him into giving me a sabbatical doing features or on the home desk. A change of scenery might freshen me up a bit, I thought, and put some more zest into the system before it packed up completely. But just as the first mention of divorce in an unhappy marriage is often unpremeditated, a sudden cry for help at the height of a blazing row, so my plea to be released from my drudgery at the House caught me on the hop as much as him. I wasn't at all sure it was what I wanted, but I was glad I had spoken out because I could now confront the possibility that it might be.

At first his sarcasm was biting. 'What do you want to be instead, Beef? Table-tennis correspondent? Editor of the fashion page? *Ballet* critic? You and Your Stars with Beef Wellington?' Then the thought dribbled into his brain that a lighter touch might be required, and he took his felt-tip out of his mouth and tried to be fatherly. It was ludicrous, because he was five years younger than me, but his adoption of a paternal role with sub-editors had given his performance of the part a certain polish, and he did his best to be reassuring. I don't think the thought of losing a valued political correspondent had many terrors for him. Whatever he said, people didn't buy our paper for its political coverage, and he would only have to whistle outside his door for my successor to come running up from the sports desk. What upset him was disloyalty in a member of his precious team. In his cock-eyed arrogance, he took this as a personal affront, so he started methodically talking me out of my plan.

In the end, he won easily enough, although not without fighting dirty. He even had the gall to produce the letter which an old dear in Bridlington had once sent him, raving about our

24

'magnificent' paper and mentioning my 'hilarious' column in the same breath as our 'invariably tasteful' nudes. The letter was part of the paper's folklore and was invoked as a talisman by the Editor when circulation wobbled or morale was flagging. Its authenticity was doubtful, and there was one theory that it was a hoax by the author of the cookery column, whose wife lived in Bridlington and who, for some reason, was credited with a sense of humour. But nobody dared challenge it to the Editor's face. As soon as I saw him fumbling for it in the top drawer, I knew that the big guns were being lined up and that I had better concede gracefully. In the end, I was glad I did. My resignation had only been half-heartedly tendered and it wasn't difficult to be persuaded that life away from the House might have boredoms all of its own. I even regretted having made this public parade of my difficulties. What could a crappy editor say that would make a dull debate in the House any more gripping or persuade me that the Westminster soap-opera still had an underlying importance? My frustration with the place was a symptom only, part of a general restlessness, not simply a dissatisfaction with where I happened to work. It was a problem of the heart and mind and, if I wasn't going to drown in my own apathy, I had to rediscover the lost thread of enthusiasm for myself.

At home, Jenny spun her own theories to account for my depression. It was lobby correspondent's menopause, she said, and I would get over it. Or it was religious *Angst* and I would get over it. Or it was dieter's depression and I would get over it. Everyone always got over everything in Jenny's world, because she was a fighter and anti-apathy in a big way, like a gym mistress with heart. She showed her heart by going easy on my diet for a while, questioning me less about my calorie intake and allowing me the odd glass of wine in the evening to wash down the lettuce. This armistice in the weight war proved strangely successful. My weight stabilised at 21 stone and, although it didn't dispel my depression, I at least began going into the House with a little more enthusiasm. The phase hadn't yet passed, but I had a glimmer of hope that it was one of those

25

phases which would. That very week, providentially, the Government Chief Whip had a brush-up with a bouncer at a Mexican night-club in Bayswater.

It was a bloody silly story, like most of my exclusives. None of the serious papers touched it for three days and even the other tabloids were slow on the uptake, because the management of the night-club was as keen as the Government to play the story down. For once, though, my source was impeccable: an old poker-playing friend called Eddie Butler, who liked to relax in style after minting it in the City and who was sitting next to the Chief Whip when the incident happened. Eddie didn't hear what the bouncer said or what was said in return, but he saw the fists fly and, even if I'd doubted him, the Chief's bruised jaw the next morning was all the corroboration needed. The story would have been a bit thin for front-page purposes, but then a bright junior reporter of ours discovered that the father of one of the club's strippers had once cited the Chief Whip as co-respondent in a divorce case. There was no evidence that the two things were connected, but you're not a journalist if you can't misuse the word 'ironically' and juxtapose paragraphs in suggestive ways. One thing led to another and, by the end of the week, there were ritual calls for the Chief Whip's resignation. Nobody seriously thought he should go, but that didn't inhibit the bayings of protest and he eventually had to make a personal statement to the House, explaining that his argument with the bouncer had simply involved a misunderstanding about the validity of his American Express card. True or false – and nobody dared call him a liar – the statement was immediately hailed as a masterpiece of humbug by the connoisseurs in the Press Gallery. Everyone congratulated me on starting a good hare running, and the whole episode lifted my spirits a bit. However often you tell yourself that anything can happen in politics, you do sometimes doubt it and any spectacular new proof is invigorating. There were only two weeks to go before the Christmas recess, and I began contemplating them with less despondency.

In the House, the Government was having a bumpy ride. Its

honeymoon with the voters had been the shortest on record, and a fortnight after its summer triumph opinion polls showed it trailing ten points behind its opponents. The sensible conclusion was that the electorate hadn't realised what it was voting for and that a prosecution under the Trade Descriptions Act was called for, but the Government didn't see it that way. Ministers were miffed that they weren't the popular darlings they thought they were, but they made the usual confident noises about a mandate and pushed their manifesto commitments through the Commons with a regimentary precision suggestive of paranoia. They had a majority of 48 for their Education Bill, a majority of 48 for their Transport Bill and, yes, a majority of 48 for their Energy Bill. On the second reading of the Social Services Bill, the majority dropped to 47, but nobody took much notice because this was the night when my story about the Chief Whip broke and, if he had left one of his flock behind in the lavatory, that was understandable. Otherwise, whatever the opinion polls were saying, the Government meant to keep an unrelenting grip on its Commons majority.

One of the Government's few success stories, surprisingly, was Carter. Having seemed at first a fraction lightweight for a Cabinet Minister, he assumed the mantle of office confidently and without fuss. Although his Department wasn't handling anything controversial, the Prime Minister was said to be impressed by his grasp of detail and his unwavering support in Cabinet for the Government's economic strategy. Being still shackled by the conventional wisdom, I couldn't myself imagine what he saw in Carter, but the man certainly had the ability to inspire admiration from improbable sources and, since this is one definition of a successful politician, I decided to observe his progress more closely. I even wrote that he was a rising star, not because I believed it or because I meant him any malice, but because political correspondents are expected to behave like racing tipsters and he was as good as anything else in the paddock.

As for Christopher, I hardly saw him. He became almost

27

indistinguishable in the sea of new faces and made no early bid to set himself apart from the herd. From time to time I would pass him in a corridor, walking with his head uplifted in wonder like a novice monk strolling in the cloisters, but we never stopped to talk. Our paths didn't cross again properly until mid-December, when he delivered his maiden speech in the House. It wasn't the sort of side-show my paper covered but, because of our meeting in the summer, I drifted into the Gallery to listen when his name appeared on the annunciator screen. As a rule, maiden parliamentary speeches are a lowly art form, something between ballroom dancing and raffia-work. They always start with over-the-top tributes to the new Member's predecessor, then take the House on a Cook's tour of the constituency's natural beauty spots before getting on to anything of substance. Tradition prescribes that they should be uncontroversial in content and shouldn't be heckled or inter-rupted by other Members – an interesting example of the House's institutional memory for, in the nineteenth century, Disraeli's maiden speech was jeered to a standstill and he had to resume his seat shouting, 'The day will come when you *will* hear me!' Nowadays, the House is more overtly polite, although it is often only a sadistic fascination with the new Member's stage-fright which keeps his colleagues glued to their seats. It was a similar ghoulishness, I suspect, which made me wander in and listen.

The Chamber was thinly populated, forty Members at most. It was nearly seven and there were too many counter-attractions to make the debate any longer a lively one. Many of those who remained had notes laid on the benches beside them and were obviously only waiting to catch the Speaker's eye themselves later in the evening. A few loitered by the doors at the far end of the Chamber, gave Christopher's speech a few minutes to catch fire and sauntered off to dinner when it didn't. It was a harsh verdict, I felt, for Christopher began compet-ently enough and spoke clearly and fluently without consulting his notes. Most maiden speakers aren't fully House-trained and forget to observe the rules of parliamentary debate (addressing

28

all remarks to the Speaker, never using another Member's name, and so on), but Christopher had it all off pat. Important-sounding phrases like 'my Right Honourable friend' and 'the Honourable Member for West Dorset' dripped effortlessly off his tongue. Although no Disraeli, he had the glib polish of someone who has belonged to all the right university debating societies, and the rawness of his speaking voice was only betrayed by his tendency to slip into a falsetto register when emotional. It wasn't the delivery of the speech which most struck me, however. It was the content. Quite simply, it was dreadful.

Just why it was so dreadful isn't easy to express. Maybe when I choose that word rather than another I'm being too much influenced by what happened between us later. The speech certainly wasn't half as dreadful as hundreds of other speeches I'd had to listen to. It was quite intelligently argued, it was coherent and its prescriptions for the ailing economy, though unoriginal, were at that time respectable. You could even say it was a good speech, provided that you made the necessary qualification and said it was a bad good speech, with 'bad' being the operative word. 'Bad good' is actually a better description than 'dreadful' because, in an odd way, the speech's badness and goodness were so intertwined that they were hard to distinguish. They both derived from Christopher's extraordinary naïveté, the quality in him which had struck me in the summer and which the intervening months had done little to eradicate. Naïve people can sometimes be very attractive, of course, and I can't say I was unattracted by the good intentions which shone like Christmas tree lights through that speech. But the attraction only lasts until you begin to cringe, and I cringe quickly, even for a hack. After five minutes, I'd had more than enough of his confident young certainties and, as he began a sentence 'The only way' for the third time, I clattered out to the bar.

It was unlucky, in the circumstances, that we should run into each other the next day in the Ways and Means Corridor, which runs between the Members' Lobby and the Library and is a favourite place of consort between lobby correspondents and Members. I had gone down there in search of a quote from some obliging Minister which would lend my soggy prose a bit of body, when I saw Christopher approaching. He was the last person I wanted to talk to but, when you're too bulky to fade into the background or tie up your shoe-laces, you get used to handling such encounters. I leant against one of the wooden lockers which line the corridor and manufactured a crooked smile.

'Well, Christopher?'

'How are you, John?'

'Down a stone since the summer. Otherwise fine.'

'You're looking well on it.'

'Thank you. My tailor's really pleased with me.'

'Oh, good.'

He dug his hands deep into his pockets and looked uncomfortable, as I had intended. Fat jokes are like Jewish jokes, you see, in that only fellow sufferers really understand them. He shifted from one foot to the other and changed the subject.

'I did it,' he whispered, leaning confidentially forward.

'Did what?'

'Made a speech in the House. I was very nervous, which is why I left it for a few months. But yesterday's debate was quite low-key, so I –'

'I know. I heard you.'

'Did you really? You know, I *thought* I saw you in the Gallery. I looked for you again when I sat down, but you'd gone.'

'Yes, I'm sorry about that. There was a lobby briefing at seven.'

'What did you think of the bit you heard?'

'You were, er, quite impressive.' I sweat when I tell lies, so I was trying to edge back towards the truth. 'You didn't consult your notes once as far as I could see. That's very unusual for a maiden speech.'

'Thank you.'

'And you were perfectly audible.'

'Thank you.'

30

He hesitated, a bit like an actor who's been congratulated on remembering his lines but hungers for some chunkier praise, then changed the subject abruptly, too proud to beg just as I was too proud to flatter. We swopped gossip idly, then he told me how much he'd enjoyed my scoop about the Chief Whip. When I showed surprise – the publicity had embarrassed his Government and others in his Party had been cold to me afterwards – he again leant towards me.

'The thing is, John, that I'm out of favour with the Whips right now.'

'Really? What did you do? Wear a Carter for Prime Minister T-shirt in the Smoking Room?'

'I wish I had, now you mention it.' He grinned mischievously. 'No: my big crime was to abstain on the Social Services Bill last week.'

'Very courageous of you,' I sneered. 'I noticed the Government majority was down. Why didn't this great act of rebellion get into the news?'

'I don't really know. There were distractions, I suppose.'

'Did you actually tell anyone from the Lobby that you weren't going to vote?'

'Not specifically. I thought someone might notice my name wasn't on the division list and ask me about it.'

I shook my head in disbelief at this further evidence of naïveté. 'Only the Whips read those things, Christopher. Journalists aren't going to go through all the names every night. In any case, you might have been paired. Hundreds of people are paired every week and don't vote.'

'That's true.' He looked disconsolate for a second, then smiled. 'Anyway, I did it, that's the main thing. When the Division Bell went, I just sat in the Library for quarter of an hour without moving a muscle. It felt really terrific in an odd way. I got an awful bollocking from the Whips the next morning.'

'I'm not surprised. You're mad. What's the point of being a martyr if you don't get a headline out of it?'

He thought hard about the question, wondering how far such

31

journalistic cynicism could be trusted, then admitted I was right. After explaining at length his reservations about the Bill and the delicate pirouettes of conscience which made him abstain rather than vote against it, he promised to let me know next time he was planning a one-man guerrilla attack on the Government. As we parted, he suddenly asked if I could come to dinner at his house the following Monday. I wasn't prepared for the invitation and, since I'm bad at impromptu excuses where food is concerned, I found myself accepting.

3

I could tell at once it would be an evening that everyone would want to forget. The tall willowy girl who opened the door of Christopher's Pimlico flat seemed unfamiliar with obesity on my scale. She ran her eyes incredulously over my physical dimensions and raised a timid pair of eyebrows in greeting.

'Mr Wellington?'

'That's right.'

'I'm Sandra Jackson. Won't you come in?'

I followed her into the hall and peeled off my overcoat, which she hung up in a stripped pine cupboard crammed with tennis rackets and old newspapers. I could see her squinting in the mirror to see if there was as much of me as there seemed, and I appraised her less ample person in return. I don't know why, but, until she opened the door, it hadn't occurred to me that Christopher might have a wife. If he was too young to be a Member of Parliament, then he was certainly too young to be married. I found myself wondering what kind of woman could settle for so very immature a man. Someone equally immature, or a woman with mothering instincts who didn't want the hassle of having babies? This girl didn't really belong to either category. She was grave-looking and subdued and wore a severely cut dress which concealed any curves on her trim, wholesome figure. Her features were pleasant in a Home Counties way, but there was no obvious warmth underneath. She seemed tense rather than exuberant at the prospect of company, so I showed her my front teeth and wheeled my small-talk gingerly into action.

'Am I the first?'

'Yes, you are.' She smiled back shyly. 'But the others are late, so don't worry.'

'Is Christopher home?'

'He's around somewhere.'

'Good.'

We exchanged opinions about the weather, then she led me into the living-room, a modestly furnished expanse of blues and greys. Some well-chosen English watercolours and a few middle-of-the-market antiques completed the quiet but blatant display of good taste. Christopher was standing at the far end of the room, looking out of the window and sipping a tomato juice. He turned when he heard us and bounded clumsily over towards me.

'John,' he said, clasping my hand in both of his, like a bishop on television. 'Good. Excellent. I'm so glad you could make it. You're a very welcome addition. The numbers would have been all wrong otherwise, because of Sheila. You single men are a tremendous asset sometimes.'

I looked thoughtfully at the carpet and shuffled my left foot in deliberate embarrassment. Christopher's gaffe was understandable, but some perverse feeling of devilment made me keen to exploit it. His wife read my thoughts quicker than he did.

'You *are* single, aren't you, Mr Wellington?'

I looked appropriately coy. 'Actually, I'm afraid to say that I'm not.'

'I'm so very sorry. We would have asked your wife, of course, if we'd known.'

'That's quite all right.'

'We'll get it right next time.' She turned forlornly to her husband and tugged gently at his sleeve. 'Christopher dear, didn't you think of asking if there was –'

'No, darling. I'm sorry. My fault.' He flushed, then looked at me rather accusingly, as if I'd pulled a fast one on him. 'I didn't think you had a wife, John.'

'Don't worry about it, Chris.'

'You don't seem the marrying sort somehow.'

'What do you mean?'

'You just don't.'

I looked at him politely, waiting for him to continue but knowing he wouldn't. The crooked logic that made him suppose me a bachelor obviously contained as many insulting assumptions as my own surprise at finding him with a wife. He couldn't say that no woman in her senses would marry a 22-stone man, because it was graceless and illiberal, but I could see him having the thought and blushing at his own prejudice. I'm ashamed to say I was beginning to enjoy his embarrassment, when the other guests started arriving.

They were a predictable assortment, the kind of political colleagues young Members are expected to curry favour with. I was pleased to see Geoffrey Hammond among the early arrivals, although he was half-drunk already and leaning heavily on his wife's arm for support. He gave me a rollicking grin and asked Christopher the way to the whisky with a directness that took the younger man aback. The other guests I knew mainly by sight. Sheila Lovell was a broad-bottomed Yorkshire woman who chaired the Select Committee on Environment. She had been in the House for thirteen years and would have been Housing Minister, or so it was said, if she hadn't held uncompromising views and known too much about the subject for other people's comfort. She must have been used to fending off spare men laid on by diligent hostesses, because she smiled when she saw I was her 'pair' for the evening and seemed relieved that the two of us couldn't credibly be expected to get any sort of act together. Jim Tyndall and Tony Nugent were also there. They had been elected at the same time as Christopher and had earned notoriety in the House for their sycophancy at Prime Minister's Question Time, jumping in with searching questions like 'Will my Right Honourable friend accept that he has the backing of the entire country for his courageous course of action?' I was amused to see how closely their wives duplicated their brittle, transparent ambitions. Both women were wildly overdressed and hung on their

35

husbands' most fatuous pronouncements with an uncritical imbecility which would have put me off my prawn cocktail if the *sauce Nantua* had been less mouth-watering.

It was as I was demolishing the last prawn that the final guests arrived. I heard fulsome apologies being made in the hall and Christopher and his wife saying it didn't matter in the slightest and what a pleasure it was to see them at all, and then the Carters came through the door into the dining-room. I was half-expecting them, but my pulse quickened slightly all the same, now that a bigger political fish had swum in among the minnows.

From the first, Carter affected the busy Cabinet Minister manner at which he was becoming so adept. He didn't do anything obvious like walk in carrying a red despatch box, but the slight stooping in his shoulders was intended to remind us of the great burdens he had to bear in his Department. He sat down next to Linda Nugent, who started fluttering, and exhaled gently, releasing all the cares of office upon a discreet tide of breath. Then he took off his spectacles, wiped the lenses with a little pink cloth, and put them away in his breast pocket before addressing himself to his food. It was an understated performance, but an effective one.

His wife entered less demonstratively, gliding almost un-noticed into her place between Tony Nugent and me. I had never met a female orthopaedist before and was intimidated at the prospect. Women in worthy professions suspect fat men of self-indulgence and can say savage things to them at dinner parties which put them off their food, so I scanned her closely for any of the tell-tale signs of an intolerant personality: narrow eyes, blotchy cheeks or a nose like an over-ripe carrot. Finding nothing more objectionable than an excess of mascara, I quickly took a liking to her. Although not beautiful, she combined affability with dignity, and I particularly liked the way she said 'I *do* like your column, Mr Wellington', like a minor member of royalty. Admittedly, she got the name of my paper wrong, but a compliment is always a compliment in my profession and we were on John and Sophie terms in no time. I noticed she didn't even count the potatoes I was eating, which was rare for a medical person.

The conversation over the chicken Marengo was about politics, the same subject, coincidentally, that had been discussed during the first course and had dominated the pre-dinner small-talk. My own efforts to raise the tone by discussing England's chances of regaining the Ashes were firmly squashed by Christopher, who obviously wanted a serious symposium to develop on the major topic of the day. Everyone knew what the topic was. A sensational Gallup poll that morning had given the Government only 18 per cent support – an all-time low – so the atmosphere at dinner was a bit doom-laden and everyone expressed earnest opinions about how Party confidence might best be restored. Tyndall kicked off by saying that there was no need to panic, because voters were cretins or, as he put it, volatile, and there was bound to be something good at the end of the tunnel, if only one soldiered on and looked for it and didn't deviate from the one true path. It was extremely important, he said, pursing his brow and trying to sound original, not to put *short-term* popularity before *long-term* achievement – a view supported by his wife, who gave a bird-like nod of her head and flashed her teeth at Carter to show that she wasn't just a pretty face. Her teeth were so prominent that she wasn't even a pretty face, but maybe that's an unchivalrous observation. After that, we all had to listen to Nugent agreeing with Tyndall and his wife agreeing with him. It was promising to be the non-debate of the year when Geoffrey Hammond suddenly looked up from his wine-glass and said that everyone else had got it arse about face. People ought to remember 1971 and 1962 and 1954 and, for that matter, 1949, before they started talking about tunnels, and that he didn't care what anyone said but he thought we had the best bloody electorate in the world and, if the Prime Minister didn't listen to the signals they were sending, he was the biggest bloody fool in SW1. This was also thought-provoking stuff and, if his wife had been as dutiful as everyone else's, that would have made it 4–2 with everything to play for. But Izzie

Hammond wasn't that sort of woman. She just said, 'You're pissed, Geoffrey' – which was pure consensus politics, because nobody was going to disagree – and told us to ignore him, which we did.

Sheila Lovell then had a go at the Press. If newspapers weren't so biased and morally spineless, she said, glowering fiercely at me, and so quick to splash bad news over the front page, then nobody would think there was an economic crisis at all. It was like sex, wasn't it? People only got steamed up because the media encouraged them to. Among ordinary working people like her constituents, among *real* people, the Government wasn't at all unpopular. Only the other day at her surgery, a bricklayer had come in and told her that this was the best Government since the war. That was a far more representative opinion than anything that was said in Fleet Street – whereupon her voice rose an octave or two and she threw me a look of defiance challenging me to defend my prostituted profession. It wasn't something I normally did, but I felt I had to chip in with something and was gingerly cobbling together a theory about the merits of a free Press when Carter interrupted. He had been silent for some minutes, listening a little condescendingly to what his backbench colleagues had to say, but now judged it was time to weigh in with his own views.

'I'm not sure,' he said, 'that the time hasn't come for some slight change in emphasis on the Government's part. What do the rest of you feel?'

It was a typical Carter pronouncement, the double negative affording perfect protection against misinterpretation by unsophisticated minds. He hadn't said he was sure the time *had* come for a change, because he wasn't – or, if he was, he wasn't going to state as much quite so baldly at this early stage in the discussion. All he had said was that his mind was open to the *possibility* of change, which was different – although, of course, once one understood the code, it came to much the same thing. As someone who earned his living from chronicling these little fissures in party ranks, I was intrigued that a Cabinet Minister supposedly loyal to the Prime Minister should make such a revisionist observation and I waited with interest for him to continue. He wiped his mouth with his napkin, noted with satisfaction that he had reduced everyone else to an expectant silence and went on smoothly.

'You see, I don't myself believe that 82 per cent of the electorate can be wrong. Geoffrey's quite right about that.' He nodded courteously at Hammond, who was now inelegantly slumped over the table. 'Either we're not getting our policies across properly or the policies themselves need some re-appraisal. If we shrug off our unpopularity too lightly, we won't deserve ever to be popular. You can govern without consent for some of the time but, if you make a habit of it, the whole exercise becomes dangerously undemocratic and people start questioning the legitimacy of your mandate.' He paused, sensing that this was rather a mouthful for the lesser brains around the table to digest, and retreated for a moment from seriousness. 'This is very nice wine, by the way, Christopher.'

'Thank you. It's only Oddbins, I'm afraid. Sandra got it.'

'Congratulations, Sandra. Your taste is impeccable – in wine as in everything else.' He smiled at her down the table, but she blushed and looked away. I had a vague impression that she was trying not to giggle, although I couldn't imagine why. The exchange of pleasantries had given everyone an opportunity to weigh up what Carter had said, but nobody seemed anxious to follow him or put forward an alternative point of view. After several seconds' silence, it was Linda Nugent who spoke.

'I don't think any of us would want to disagree with you, Secretary of State.' She really enjoyed that bit. 'But Tony always says – may I, darling?'

'Of course, darling.'

'Tony always says that democracy means being ready to do the *un*popular thing. Don't you, darling?'

'That's right, darling.'

'And I agree with him – for what it's worth.' She giggled and turned to Tyndall. 'What do you think, Jim?'

Tyndall nodded his head gravely. 'You're absolutely right, Linda. Government by opinion poll is political suicide.'

39

'I should say it is,' added his wife. 'Apart from being morally wrong.'

'Apart from being morally wrong, of course.'

'And cowardly.'

'And cowardly.'

'And stupid.'

'And stupid.'

Their double-act was getting oppressive when, with the succinctness of the very drunk, Hammond leant across the table towards me and whispered loudly, 'What fucking turnips!' Tabloid journalists aren't supposed to waste words and, unparliamentary or not, his economy of language impressed me. A sober man could have plundered the *Dictionary of Insults* for an hour without finding anything so effective. Janet Tyndall burst into floods of tears, her husband rose to his feet shouting 'Nobody calls Janet a turnip like that!', and Sheila Lovell banged the table with her fist and bawled 'Cut it, Geoffrey!' This made Christopher's wife stop serving the profiteroles and she looked desperately towards her husband, who dithered and looked helpless. In its own kitsch way, it was all quite exciting, and tempers were so high that a fight might have broken out if Izzie Hammond hadn't acted so forcefully. She told Geoffrey a few blunt truths which reduced him to a surly red-faced pulp, then took Janet into the next room to mop her up. Jim Tyndall followed them out. Those who remained were so embarrassed that Carter decided the moment had come for him to play a more assertive role. He put down his wine glass and, without warning, proceeded to unveil an Alternative Economic Strategy.

He didn't call it that, of course. He wasn't so vulgar, so reckless. Because of my presence, he framed his remarks in an elaborately coded form, almost as if he was addressing a public meeting, not a few fellow guests at dinner. He got his message across in the end, but by a complicated, tortuous route. If you hadn't followed his auxiliary verbs and double negatives carefully, you might even have thought he was endorsing the Government's present economic policies, so fulsome was his praise of the Prime Minister and the Chancellor. He was almost too fulsome – and that was the point. His listeners became suspicious of his superficial enthusiasm and rumbled it, as they were meant to. Although many of his comments had the ring of orthodoxy, when every word was taken into account, his underlying heresy gradually became clear: that, if he were in charge of the economy, he would be handling it very differently. Even Linda Nugent understood his real meaning. I could see her reddening at the thought that her own staunch pro-Government line might have appeared politically naïve. She looked anxiously at her husband for reassurance, but he was too busy listening to Carter to notice. I wondered cynically how soon he and Tyndall would be modifying their opinions to make them consistent with Carter's, and poured some cream over my profiteroles to help me concentrate.

For nearly ten minutes, Carter explained his ideas for refurbishing the Government's economic strategy. He made constant references to fine-tuning, but nobody believed them. We all knew by now that a radically different programme was being advocated and listened to each new proposal in a state of some suspense. The atmosphere in the room was prickly, not least because Carter had a subtle, compressed way of express-ing himself, which would have made the going tough if he hadn't been so articulate. Theatre critics would have called it a high definition performance and gone overboard about his stage presence; the star quality was undeniable. Apart from an awkward hiccup when Linda Nugent asked what M3 was and we all had to pretend to know, he kept his listeners totally transfixed. I had never seen him perform like this before, and my opinion of him rocketed. There was nothing novel, of course, in a Cabinet Minister letting his hair down in private and dissociating himself from the albatross of collective responsibility. The political animal couldn't survive unless his instincts for self-preservation were properly developed, and only Ministers with a death-wish support unpopular Governments unreservedly. Carter's political footwork was something special, though. It was as adroit as any I had seen, and I understood for the first time why a younger man like Christopher should think so highly of him.

Looking at Christopher's face now was a revelation. He had told me all about his admiration for Carter, so I can't say I was surprised at his look of settled devotion or the reverential way he kept nodding his head at the great man's pearls of wisdom. It was the fervour and intensity of his emotions which really startled me: any weaker word than 'love' would be quite inadequate to describe them. It was not a sexual love, indeed like all Christopher's emotions it had a distilled, bodiless quality which was ultimately asexual. A better comparison might be the hero-worship bestowed on footballers or pop-singers: charming in a ten-year-old, understandable in a teenager but, in a man of thirty, a matter for a psychiatrist. Maybe because I'm paid to mock politicians rather than idolise them, I get these things out of perspective, but I found this flowering of pagan idolatry in SW1 unnatural and disturbing. You can call me prudish, but the expression of foolish adoration on Christopher's face shocked me profoundly. Members of Parliament are supposed to be constitutional equals and conduct rational debate with their peers, not drool over each other's words like poets at a literary *salon*. What would Edmund Burke have had to say about this one-man political fan-club, I wondered, or Bagehot? It was too depressing to speculate.

I was still quietly shuddering when a bell rang in the hall to signal a Division in the House. Christopher's flat was only just within the eight-minute Division Bell distance, so the Members stopped talking immediately and charged off together. They promised to return later and left me ensconced with their wives and an assortment of French cheeses. Tyndall made a puerile quip to the effect that the latter were in greater danger than the former, which everyone seemed to find hysterical, and then they left. Linda Nugent turned to me and fluttered.

'Don't you find it thrilling being a fly on the wall?' she whispered. 'Listening to all this important talk and hearing the Secretary of State – *such* a clever man – thinking aloud about the economy? I do. I love it, I really do. What people out there

don't realise' – she waved in the general direction of Victoria –
'is how terribly human politicians are underneath it all and
how desperately concerned to find the right answers. Not just
for us, but for our children too. Don't you agree?'

I nodded glumly and asked Sandra as politely as I could if
she had any brandy to help the cheese down. I could see I was
going to need it.

4

By nine minutes past ten, Geoffrey Hammond was dead. The exact time was easy to establish, because the Speaker had ordered the doors of the Division Lobbies to be locked at eight minutes past and Hammond and the others at the dinner party had only just made it, squeezing past the door-keeper at the last minute chivvied on by exasperated Whips. They were walking up the lobby towards the division clerks' desks to give their names when Hammond suddenly stumbled and fell on the carpet. Everyone at first assumed a drunken stupor and Tony Nugent muttered something humorous, at which several younger Members giggled. Then one of the Whips tried to help Hammond to his feet and realised from his bulging purple face that it was something more serious. Another Whip was dispatched to fetch Dr Parfitt, a bluff Opposition Member from Cornwall who had just voted in the other lobby, but by the time he arrived it was too late. Ten minutes later, after the Speaker had been notified, the body was whisked discreetly out of the House and taken away in an ambulance.

It was Christopher who brought us the news. He burst into the dining-room and stood panting in the doorway, having obviously run all the way from the House, before blurting it out. One of those dull, sickening silences descended and we all glanced instinctively at Izzie Hammond who, by a cruel coincidence, had just been telling us about Geoffrey's passion for fly-fishing and saying how glad she was that this would be his last Parliament and that there would be no more constituency jumble sales or late-night sittings to contend with. Like

44

the formidable woman she was, she calmly put down her coffee-cup when Christopher had finished his report and half rose to her feet to leave. Then the effort of fortitude became too much and she collapsed back into her chair.

'Dammit!' she said in a cracking voice, angry at the tears which she tried to suppress but which suddenly welled up in her eyes. Then she decided it was better to release them and, putting her arms around me (I was her oldest friend present), cried for several minutes on my shoulder. Sandra poured her a brandy and hovered unhappily in the background, while everyone else maintained a respectful silence. When Carter and the others got back from the House a few minutes later, they saw that Christopher had already delivered the news and stood by the door with obvious awkwardness, shuffling their feet and scratching their ears and looking at the patterns on the carpet. For men accustomed to making decisions, they agonised terribly over the etiquette of bereavement. Should they leave or stay, trot out clumsy platitudes or say nothing, respond emotionally like Izzie or display stoicism? Such questions fell quite outside their normal parliamentary business and, although everyone coped as best they could, they were never comfortable. When Sheila Lovell eventually took Izzie away in her car, the sense of relief was palpable. The men took off their jackets and threw themselves down in chairs, and the women gravitated nervously towards their husbands. Carter was the first to say anything.

'What a bloody mess!' he said gloomily, pouring himself some coffee. 'We all knew he was going to go one day soon, but it's still a shock when it comes. I saw the Prime Minister in the Chamber afterwards. He was really very upset. I think he and Geoffrey used to know each other quite well and go to Lord's together, or something like that.'

Tyndall lit a cigarette and looked morose. 'I've never seen anyone die before,' he said, staring vacantly at the table-cloth. 'I didn't know Geoffrey well, thank God, but it was ghastly all the same. It all happened so suddenly, that was what was so frightening.'

45

'How absolutely bloody life is!' Nugent exclaimed, resorting to a philosophical folksiness that jarred. He put his arm round his wife's shoulder and stroked her cheek with his hand. 'Isn't life bloody sometimes, darling?'

She nodded agreement dutifully, then started whimpering like a constipated spaniel, which embarrassed everyone into silence. Sandra and Sophie began quietly clearing the plates off the table and Christopher helped them in his clumsy way, picking up crumbs of food with his fingers and depositing them in an ash-tray. I wanted to get back to the House and pick up some reactions to Hammond's death, but I felt too lethargic to move. Bad news at the end of a big meal can leave you as drained as a dry sponge and this was very bad news because, in a strange, unsentimental way, I had liked Geoffrey Hammond a lot. He was the sort of larger-than-life Member who had been common on the backbenches when I had first come to the House, but was now a rarity. He had coarsened with drink and age, of course, but then we all coarsen, even if we call it mellowing, and not all of us begin coarsening from such a high starting-point as he had.

Carter suddenly raised his head and looked at me across the table. I had never noticed before what piercing blue eyes he had. They were small and hooded, like a reclusive tropical bird's, but you couldn't mistake the intellectual force behind them.

'Do you think the Press will say anything about Geoffrey's drinking?' he asked, sounding casual but obviously anxious I should give the right answer.

I shook my head and managed a half-smile. 'No way. The Street of Shame doesn't have many principles, but that's one of them. People may say that Geoffrey sometimes seemed disillusioned with politics, which is the same thing, but that's as far as anyone will go.'

Carter nodded his head thoughtfully, then we all spent a few more minutes agreeing what sterling qualities Hammond had had and how sorry we all felt for Izzie. Nobody immediately asked the question which some of us had privately started

46

wondering, but I knew it wouldn't be long in coming. Under the British constitution, dead MPs need to be replaced by less dead ones, and nobody is so eminent that his death isn't swiftly followed by calculations about his successor. It was Tyndall, predictably, who first raised the question of the by-election.

'I don't want to sound callous,' he said, sounding precisely that, 'but how safe was Geoffrey's seat?'

There was a fractional pause as people wondered if it was proper to discuss this so soon, then scruples were efficiently overcome.

'Very safe,' said Nugent firmly. 'Must have been. He's been around for thirty-odd years, don't forget.'

'Wasn't it one of the safest in the country last time round?' Christopher asked. 'I thought I heard him saying something like that.'

'In that case, we should be able to hold on to it,' said Tyndall. 'If it's more than a twenty thousand majority, that ought to be a big enough cushion, whatever the opinion polls say. There won't be much of a turn-out at this time of year, and there should be some personal votes.'

Carter suddenly coughed and looked scholarly. I noticed he had put his glasses back on.

'I think you'll find that Geoffrey's majority was about 32,500,' he said smoothly. 'And that was on a 75 per cent poll. We'd need a colossal swing against us, something like 45 per cent, to lose it.'

Everyone else was silenced by this erudition, and I decided it was time to leave. I thanked Sandra and Christopher and drove home in the rain, feeling as black and cheerless as the weather. The favourable impression which Carter had created earlier had been quite dissipated, and all my old cynicism about him and his type returned with interest. How callous he had sounded, how coldly, inhumanly pedantic! I had somehow guessed that he would have all the figures in his head, but I still loathed the calm way he produced them. If I'd been him, I would have waited another hour, or at least until the corpse was cold. It would have made him seem more statesmanlike –

47

which if I'd been him, I would have wanted.

I really hated Carter that night but perhaps, looking back, I was too hard on him. All the papers the next day showed exactly the same dispassion. They noted that Hammond's death precipitated the first by-election of the Parliament, but said little of his political achievements. In the tabloids, needless to say, there was the usual spate of humbug and irrelevancies. My own paper launched a mindless attack on the Government for dragooning sick Members through the division lobbies when it already had a majority of fifty, and one of our competitors asked its readers to grapple with the trenchant question: Would He Have Died if the House had Sat Normal Hours? Only the quality papers recorded the principal features of Hammond's career: his impassioned, sometimes mercurial oratory; his blistering sarcasm at Question Time; his Private Member's Bills on prison reform and road safety; the brilliant future he had mysteriously frittered away in the fifties and sixties; the time he called the Prime Minister a mendacious dog and was suspended from the House for refusing to withdraw the allegation; his love of ceremony and his implacable hostility to televising Parliament; his *bons mots* about other politicians and their shortcomings. It was all wrapped up in a couple of well turned paragraphs, but it didn't really capture the man and, when I sat down the next day to write my Thursday column, I had a feeling in my gut what it ought to be about.

'Death of a Backbencher', the sub-editors headed it, a cheap whodunit title to engage readers' hearts and minds and take their eyes off the model on the opposite page. If it had been called 'Geoffrey Hammond: a Tribute', nobody would have read it, because Geoffrey had no national constituency and had never sought one. He was virtually unknown outside Westminster and the West Midlands market town he represented, and I had to spend the first quarter of my piece explaining who he was. It wasn't the most promising way to start an obituary, but after that it was all plain sailing and my main problem was what to leave out rather than what to include. If I hadn't been writing for a family newspaper, I would have loved to put in his description of the Tyndalls as 'fucking turnips', if only because a lifetime's devotion to talking frankly and choosing words with care was concentrated in that phrase, which would have been an apt memorial to his whole style. But I desisted. In cold print, '******* turnips' didn't have the right ring at all, and Geoffrey wouldn't have liked the twee little asterisks, for he was a plain man underneath all the camp and viewed the coy prurience of the popular Press with unmitigated contempt.

Several times as I was drafting the article, I wondered just what Geoffrey would have wanted me to say about him. That he was a politician of star quality who didn't achieve the prominence he deserved? Or just that he was an engaging old soak with whom I'd drunk more whisky than most people get through in a lifetime? It wasn't easy to strike the right balance between sentiment and irreverence because, like most people you like but aren't so strongly attracted to that you can't see their faults, the memories Geoffrey left were complicated and ambivalent. I couldn't decide whether to say that, if the other 649 MPs were more like Geoffrey, Parliament would be a better place, or that, if there were 650 Geoffreys in the House, the country would be in the biggest shambles since the Romans dropped in to civilise us. In the end, I said both, which sounds supine but is what my readers expect, the Beef Wellington style being an equivocal one and not very conducive to definite opinions.

I spent nearly four hours on that piece, my longest continuous period of employment for fifteen years, and ended up tolerably pleased with it. Jenny liked it anyway, and Izzie wrote to say how much it had meant to her, and that was all the reward I could have asked for. Or so I thought. About a week later, however, as I was eating an early lunch at home before leaving for the House, the telephone rang. It was Brian Sparks, my editor. He didn't normally ring me at home and I assumed he wasn't asking about my diet, so I cradled the receiver cautiously in my hand and adopted my most affable manner. If he wanted to fire me for the *lèse-majesté* of being bored with my work, I wasn't going to go out without a fight.

'It's you, Chief,' I said sweetly. 'I'll just put this pizza back in the oven, if you don't mind. Now, how's things?'

'Fine, Beef, fine. Listen –'

'Circulation still holding up, I see. That nude horoscope was a great idea. Mine nearly came true yesterday, but the long-legged blonde didn't show, so I had to make do with Jenny.'

'Very funny, Beef. Now look here –'

'Too bad that goalless draw at Wembley last night, wasn't it? Robson should have scored with that header in the first half, then we'd have had a hatful. I thought that Swedish referee was *pathetic*. He should –'

'Yes, Beef, it was a penalty. I know. Do you have a minute or two?'

'Sure, Chief.' His tone was so mild that I decided to give him a chance. 'What's the problem?'

'It's you, Beef.'

'What about me?' I looked suspiciously at the ear-piece and wondered if he really was going to fire me.

'You remember you saw me a few weeks ago and were whingeing about working in the House?'

'Sure.'

'Are you still feeling that way?'

'So-so.' I paused, and I could hear him breathing heavily at the other end of the line, waiting for me to commit myself one way or the other. 'Put it this way, Chief. If you want me to go out to Australia and report the Perth Test and do an article on proportional representation in Fiji on the way home, then I'm bored up to the back teeth. If you're lining me up a retirement cottage in Shepton Mallett, then I want to hang around a bit.'

'Very good, Beef.' He chuckled in his awful nicotiney way, then stopped. 'As a matter of fact, it's something between the two.'

'I thought it might be.'

'I enjoyed your piece about Geoffrey Hammond last week –'

'Thank you, Chief. You know what they say: the only honest politician's a dead politician.'

'– and I was wondering whether you'd like to do the by-election for us.'

'What do you mean, "do the by-election"?'

'I mean, go up to the constituency while the campaigning's going on and send in some reports. Just a few hundred words a day, of course. There's a lot of other, er, news to fit in.'

'Sure, Chief, I understand.' I held the receiver against my chest for a moment and tried to puzzle out the situation. The normal coverage of by-elections on our paper was derisory. The news editor simply got on the telephone and commissioned some opinion polls and the political staff wrote emotion-packed stories about the percentage swings. Talking to actual voters, especially in safe seats like this one, wasn't really our style, a fact of which I reminded Brian.

'I know that, Beef, but –' There was a long silence and I would have thought he had hung up if I couldn't still hear his dry, crackly breathing. 'I think this may be quite a special by-election somehow. It's got that feel about it. Could be a big upset.'

He didn't sound convinced by his own theory, so I remonstrated. 'Come on, Chief. The Government had a majority of 32,500 last time. They're not going to lose that.'

'No, I know, I know.' He hesitated. 'The point is, Beef, that I thought you might enjoy doing it. It would get you out of the House for a few weeks and you did say that's what you wanted. You've been getting stale and you need a break, so I'm offering you one. That's all.'

I believed him. Up to now, I'd had to remember that he might simply be drunk or floating some half-baked idea just for the heck of it, but the sudden kindness in his voice was convincing and characteristic. He wasn't a complete shit, and he had a reputation for doing members of his staff special favours to keep them happy. Now that I saw it for what it was, the offer was too generous to refuse. We agreed that I would leave London in early February and stay in the Wopsley constituency for three weeks. Wopsley wasn't Fiji, but it promised to be different and I psyched myself into thinking I

51

would enjoy it. I don't know if I was convinced, but I was certainly smiling when I told Jenny the news later in the day.

'Wopsley?' she asked disdainfully, curling her lips down and her eyebrows up. 'Where's that?'

'Somewhere between Birmingham and Wales. It was Geoffrey Hammond's old constituency.'

'And they want you to go up there and cover the by-election?'

'Right.'

'How bloody silly!' She threw back her head and started laughing in that wild, mirthful, Irish way which I loved so much. 'You'll be hopeless, darling. You haven't been further than Annie's Bar to get a story for the last twenty years. What are you going to do up there? Stay in a bed and breakfast and chat up local shoppers all day? How ridiculous!'

She looked me up and down and started giggling even more helplessly. I couldn't see what she found so hysterical, but I admit I was an improbable roving reporter. Flesh in any quantity is by nature sedentary, and Jenny knew my aversion to exercise better than anyone. When her mirth subsided, she changed her tune and looked at me sharply, pretending to be fiercer than she was.

'You're not going to spend the whole time eating and drinking, are you, dear?'

'Of course not, dear.'

We both laughed at that one.

Part 2

2

The Provinces

5

'Geoffrey Hammond?' The whey-faced woman behind the counter looked doubtful. 'No, I don't remember the name. Was he an actor?'

'In a way,' I said. 'He played character parts, but he's dead now.'

'Oh dear, I am sorry. Cancer, was it?'

'Heart.'

'Oh dear.' She put my pork pie and Mars bar in a paper bag and counted out my change coin for coin in a slow, meticulous fashion you would never see in London. Then she allowed herself a pinched smile. 'Enjoy your stay in Wopsley, sir.'

'Thank you, I will. Could you point me in the direction of the cathedral, please?'

'Surely, sir. Turn left at the end of this street, then walk along that street till you get to Sainsbury's. Then left at the lights, up the hill and it's about a hundred yards from there.'

'Thank you, I'm obliged.'

I walked out of the shop into the pale February sun and wondered what to make of the Wopsley Woman. I'd only been there six hours, but she wasn't the first person to have shown complete ignorance about Geoffrey. Would he have been disappointed, I wondered, if he'd known how shallow an imprint he'd left on his constituency after thirty-two years? It's a long time to be the local rep at Westminster, and you're not human if you don't expect some gratitude for the fêtes you've opened and the babies you've kissed and the motorways you've tried to stop and the running battles you've had with

55

local bureaucrats. Geoffrey had been a conscientious Member, who had enjoyed unravelling his constituents' problems and writing rude letters to the housing department of the local council. I had already met some, usually older, people who remembered him with affection, but they weren't the majority. For most of the burghers of Wopsley – most of the twenty I had canvassed, anyway – Westminster seemed a long way away and politics a side-show: at best, a watchable soap-opera, at worst, an irritating distraction from the compulsions of daily life.

I had arrived before the main by-election circus. Polling was still three weeks away, only two of the parties had selected their candidates and there wasn't another journalist in sight. The windows of the neat limestone semis which lined the main road from Birmingham weren't yet displaying political posters and I doubted if many of them would. It was the heart of winter and the town was hibernating so snugly that I had a sneaking suspicion it hibernated twelve months a year. The fellow guests at my hotel were mainly retired people, staying there indefinitely at reduced rates, and a travelling rubber-goods salesman called Tomkins on the floor above was the only reminder of the unacceptable face of provincialism. He called me 'horse', put his arm obsequiously round my shoulder the first time we met and wore shiny black shoes without laces. If he'd been booked in for longer, I would have had to review my accommodation arrangements, but he was due in Glasgow in three days and had a woman in tow called Doreen who looked a handful, so I decided to risk it. The hotel was pleasantly situated on the river running through the outskirts of the town, and its menu showed a promising awareness of the needs of a working journalist.

Wopsley town centre was everything the name suggested, and the walk to the cathedral was cheerless and depressing. Even the wintry sun lent no answering warmth to the faces that I passed, and I couldn't have had a cooler reception if the mayor had declared a Wopsley War on Fat. People are supposed to be friendlier north of Watford and positively garrulous when you get past Birmingham, but there was little sign of it. The line of shoppers queuing for a bus outside the supermarket looked no different from their counterparts in Hackney or Ealing; surly, impatient and uncommunicative, stamping their feet to keep warm in the cold, but otherwise motionless. The post-war buildings in the pedestrian-only shopping centre were as grey and featureless as the age in which they had been designed. I passed an Odeon, a Chinese take-away, a few tacky shoe shops, two bookmakers side by side, a maternity shop, a funeral parlour and a Woolworth's, turned left at Sainsbury's as directed, and trudged slowly up the hill past a municipal car-park and a cramped row of Victorian workers' cottages in need of restoration. A few wizened faces peered out at me from behind dingy lace curtains and withdrew hastily as I got closer, alarmed by my bulk. I could smell the damp slowly rotting the walls of the cottages and was glad I wasn't a candidate, having to look concerned and produce a pat solution on every doorstep.

The cathedral wasn't up to much either. The late afternoon sun bathed its walls in a certain *fin de siècle* splendour, but the architecture was unremarkable and only the spire gave any hint of spirituality, pointing skywards with the massive certainty of an umpire's finger. The journey wouldn't have been worth it in overcast conditions, but it was a clear day and, from the cathedral's commanding position at the highest point of the town, you could see the constituency's various elements spreading out into the distance: factories and smog to the north, farmland and villages to the south and west, the motorway and a sprawling series of housing developments to the east. It was a psephologist's dream, a hotchpotch of all the ingredients which are supposed to reflect socio-economic trends but which never quite coalesce in the way the experts expect. If I hadn't been around long enough to know that politics wasn't a science but a blood sport, I might have panicked at having to interpret this mass of humanity for my readers. It's sometimes comforting to be just a hack journalist with a mission to entertain and, with this objective, I was looking round the square for a colourful

57

local personality to interview when a noise behind me made me turn round. It was a priest, wheeling his bicycle out of the cathedral porch. He stopped when he saw me and gave a goofy smile.

'It's a magnificent vista, isn't it?' He belonged to the generation who use that word. 'In the summer, you can see as far as Wales, you know.'

I opened my eyes wide and tried to sound impressed. 'Wales? Really?'

'Yes. It's extraordinary, because it must be nearly thirty miles away and we're not all that high up here. It's something to do with the light, they say, and the way it's reflected off the top of the hills. Or is it refracted? I never remember. Have you been up the spire?'

'No, I'm afraid I –'

'Oh, you should, you really should. You'll find it's quite out of the ordinary. The vista from there is even more exceptional than here. It inspired Wordsworth to write a poem which people say is rather marvellous. Do you know Wordsworth?' I think he must have seen my lack of enthusiasm, because he suddenly peered at me more closely and got the message that he wasn't talking to a mountain goat. He stopped and blinked apologetically. 'There isn't a lift, I'm afraid. You'd have to walk. It was three hundred and twenty-three steps at the last count. I don't know if you –'

'Thank you,' I said. 'I have moments of great athleticism, but not usually three hundred on the same day. Are there postcards of the view from the top?'

'What's that you say? Postcards? Yes, certainly.' He looked startled by my Westminster sarcasm, which I hadn't yet toned down for the country, and began making strange twitching movements with his left hand, like a kleptomaniac in a delicatessen. 'Won't you come through into the porch? I think you'll find there's a goodly selection.'

I followed him, bought a couple of postcards and, after listening to him explain why the transept was unique in English church architecture, re-emerged into the square. The priest put on his bicycle-clips, wished me a pleasant stay in Wopsley and was getting on his bicycle before I remembered what I was doing there.

'Do you vote?' I asked.

He stopped, with one leg resting on the handle-bar and the other on the ground, and swivelled round awkwardly to look at me. 'What's that you said?'

'Do you vote? Are you a voter?'

'I'm not on the General Synod or anything grand like that.'

'No, I meant Parliament. Are you registered in this constituency and, if so, are you going to vote in the by-election?'

'Excuse me a moment.' He lifted his leg off the handle-bar and rested the bicycle against the wall. I noticed that his voice had dropped a little in volume. 'I thought that's what you were asking, but I wasn't sure. The short answer is that we're allowed to vote, but that that's where the trouble begins. I say, you're not a journalist or anything, are you?'

I shook my head. I didn't like lying to a priest, but it seemed prudent. 'A humble travelling salesman, I'm afraid. In rubber goods.'

'I imagined it was something like that. You have the manner of a peripatetic person.' I took the insult smilingly on the chin and he leant towards me. 'You see, a lot of people think that priests should remain above the hurly-burly of secular politics and, of course, they're quite right in one sense.' His voice dropped again. 'There is, however, a man called Campbell. He will be standing in the by-election and I shall vote for whichever candidate seems likeliest to stop him. If ever the Devil took human form and stood for Parliament, he would stand on exactly the same principles as Campbell. I could tell you –'

He obviously could tell me, because he drew himself up to his full height to dramatise his announcement and was about to explain the diabolical nature of Campbell's appeal to the Wopsley voters when one of his flock greeted him from across the square. He returned the greeting and beetled off, leaving the gargoyles above my head to grin down at my frustration.

59

Back at the hotel, I telephoned my first copy through to the paper and wrote Jenny a postcard. To my readers I said, 'By-election fever is sweeping through this vibrant community', and to Jenny, 'Good news in the weight war. Have climbed to the top of Wopsley spire this afternoon.' Something about the country air was already making lying easier.

6

Was it a success, you will want to know, my busman's holiday in Wopsley? Did all that bracing country air breathe new life into my tired bones and the rolls of sagging flesh which encased them? Did the Beef Wellington blues evaporate in the humane, heartwarming atmosphere of the West Midlands? Did I discover a better, cleaner, saner, more honest, world away from the Westminster madhouse? Did my encounters with real people restore my lost faith in humanity and remind me of the eternal verities held in trust by the common folk? Did the *svelte* philanthropist inside me burst out of his lacklustre elephant's skin and astound the world with his freshness and generosity of spirit? The short answer is no, and the long answer is unprintable. Wopsley was a five-star hole and I couldn't wait to get out of it.

Campaigning began in earnest the following week. The main parties completed their selection processes bloodlessly, and there was the usual string of oddballs and also-rans. As this was the first by-election of the Parliament, the cranks were out in force and, when nominations closed, there were nineteen names on the ballot-paper. Charlie Denver, the Government candidate, huffed and puffed and said the deposit ought to be raised to £2,000 to keep out the riff-raff, but nobody took any notice and the Press were exuberant at the spectrum of eccentrics on offer to the voters. If the four main candidates got out of control and started taking themselves seriously, we could devote our columns to profiles of their more frivolous rivals. It was the free Press's perfect response to political humbug.

The media darlings were the two dogshit candidates, the pro-dogshit candidate and the anti-dogshit candidate. The latter was called Campbell, funnily enough, which cleared up The Mystery of the Outraged Priest, even if it shed ambiguous light on Church of England environmental policy. The candidates gave themselves grander names, of course, but everyone knew what they were talking about and they campaigned with such vigour and originality that the tabloids, with no originality at all, tagged the by-election the Wopsley Dog-fight. On the face of it, the pro-dogshit candidate had the harder political product to sell, but he ran a cunning smear campaign in the columns of the local newspaper, alleging that Campbell was not just anti-dogshit, but anti-dog as well, in favour of £100 dog licences and public vivisections and other acts of barbarism. This produced angry denials from Campbell, who protested that he had adored dogs ever since he was a boy and had taken his uncle's collie, Ben, for walks in the New Forest. When challenged to produce documentary evidence of this, he prevaricated, saying sadly that both Ben and his uncle were now dead, thereby dividing voters equally between sympathy and suspicion. The fate of his campaign was in the balance when, with great enterprise, he borrowed his neighbour's Alsatian and took it canvassing with him. At first, this looked like certain political suicide, for Alsatians rarely suffer from constipation, but he outwitted his would-be-obituarists by investing in a Pooper Scooper, an American device for defusing these problems at source. Press-hounds spent long days tracking him, hoping to take the photograph which would destroy his whole campaign, but their efforts were in vain. Campbell trotted earnestly behind his dog, guarding against all eventualities, and his public-spiritedness might have won the day if the Alsatian hadn't suddenly turned vicious and snapped at a four-year-old child. This 'moral outrage', said his opponent in a gleeful press release the next day, was irrefutable evidence that Campbell was not a dog-lover, since a genuine dog-lover would have walked the dog properly and not kept him on so tight a leash . . . And so the arguments continued, attracting not just heavy press coverage but large side-bets on the two candidates. All the other politicians could do was grit their teeth, avoid saying anything controversial about dogs and praise the virtues of a pluralist democracy. I don't normally waste sympathy on politicians, but my heart bled a drop or two as they repeatedly tried to discuss disarmament and the economy only to be side-tracked by questions about the proper use of choke-chains.

The four main parties had all chosen candidates of the type known as 'young and thrusting'. Two – Denver, the favourite, and John Beeston for the main opposition party – were under thirty, and the other two – Tony Bavin for the SF and the Democrat Jill Appleby – were only just over. When it came to thrust, there was little in it; they all campaigned with the brash certainty of political virgins, gripping complete strangers warmly by the hand and using up a year's supply of *bonhomie* in a day. I think the selection committees must have calculated that the way to take a sleepy place like Wopsley by storm was to wake it up first but, if so, they had blundered. A boring old fart would have romped home without breaking sweat, but youth looked too much like inexperience and the attempts to campaign aggressively irritated the senior citizens in the shopping centre. You could see them looking suspiciously at the various campaign-mobiles and the young people riding on them with big megaphones and rosettes the size of soup-plates. 'Young know-alls' was the most frequently heard comment, with 'noisy buggers' a close second. It proved what I had suspected from the first: that razzmatazz and Wopsley were as incompatible as weight-watching and chocolate éclairs.

For all the energy, it was a strangely passionless campaign. Wopsley was light years behind the times and, because news of the Government's unpopularity didn't seem to have reached it from London, there was none of the agonising about future policies that the pundits had predicted. Voting habits in the town were about as volatile as cold mashed potato and, after early opinion polls had given the Government candidate a lead of between 30 and 40 per cent over his nearest rival, nobody

63

expected to catch him. The usual tactical voting ploys were tried, but without conviction. Denver's opponents each produced canvass returns to show that they, and they alone, could beat him, but they announced their carefully massaged figures so sheepishly that the Press just fell about laughing. When I pointed out to John Beeston that, on the basis of the parties' combined canvass returns, 62,000 electors had pledged 198,000 votes, he went crimson and nearly burst into tears. 'I think that's an extremely mischievous use of statistics, Mr Wellington,' he said slowly, flannelling hard as he tried to find a suitable fig-leaf. 'The people of Wopsley are, er –' Since he couldn't finish the sentence, we tried to help him. 'Cretins?' offered Tony Daly of the *Post*. 'Liars?' asked a local reporter. 'Two-faced? Three-faced? Sensibly undecided?' others chipped in quickly. 'No, no, *no*,' he said in irritation. 'The point I am making, if you will *allow* me, gentlemen, is that the people of Wopsley are, er –' Again he hesitated, fatally this time, allowing a wag at the back of the room to produce the killer punch. 'More numerous than they appear?' he asked in a sweeter-than-sweet voice which reduced the rest of us to hysterics and Beeston to an apoplectic rage. 'Balls to the lot of you!' he shouted, and stormed out of the room. He wasn't very good with journalists; he thought they were serious people like himself.

These moments of naked, idiotic humanity were Wopsley's only form of pleasure but, fortunately, there were several of them. As well as John Beeston's tantrums and the antics of the dogshit candidates, history will record the 1957 tandem on which Tony and Mrs Bavin did their canvassing together and the French farce of Jill Appleby's sex life. This came to light when, on the same day, a bank clerk called Baker and an estate agent called Butcher both claimed to have had a tempestuous affair with her in the Celestial Hotel in Ibiza in 1980. On the following day, they both retracted within an hour of each other, saying that they must have got the wrong Jill Appleby, but doubts remained in people's minds and the town's older residents were reported to take a dimmish view. I distributed several tenners to local gossips to dredge up some more muck and satisfy the public's right to know, but I never got to the bottom of the story, which was a pity. It meant I had to write about the issues, which is the last thing my sort of lobby correspondent wants.

Although the Baker/Butcher episode raised my hack's adrenalin a notch or two, my country sabbatical failed to rejuvenate me. The dank mid-February weather enveloped the town in a shroud of sullen indifference, and stumping round interviewing people was an unrewarding chore. As I'm not in the market for votes, I don't have to be nice about the man in the street, and the man in the Wopsley street was dull, very dull. He might fascinate other Wopsleians, but his charms for a Londoner were limited. It's all a matter of perspective; you see things differently depending on which side of the fence you're standing. Back at Westminster, my boredom with the House had been caused by its parochiality, its clubbiness, its obsessive political in-fighting; here I found the reverse attitude to politics just as irritating. When voters told me how little Parliament meant in their lives, I took the rebuff personally, as if they were · sticking pins in my solar plexus. My lifelong assumption that, in however banal a capacity, I was at the centre of events was being challenged at every street-corner, in every pub and on every housing estate, and my wounded self-esteem made me correspondingly bitter towards the burghers of Wopsley and their own narrow preoccupations. I kept wanting to begin my reports, 'Here, in the arsehole of the West Midlands . . .', and having to find some politer way of saying the same thing. 'This unhurried market town' became my pet euphemism and I wrote about the 'down-to-earth' qualities of its citizens, without adding that down-to-earth meant buried ten foot under. Overt condescension is taboo in a family newspaper, you see, so you have to patronise your readers with subtlety. It was with dark relish that I reported that the town's only noteworthy citizen in seven hundred years was Mayor Abel Tucket, a candle-maker at the time of the Civil War who had lent the king a horse, or a donkey (historians differed), and whose statue still stood in the market-place, mounted on a horse with donkey's ears to satisfy both traditions. When I added that none of the present candidates was likely to supplant Mayor Tucket's reputation as Wopsley's most famous son, but that the town's reverence for donkeys appeared to be as great as ever, I got into deeper water. All the candidates started giving me the brush-off, calling me Beef in loud voices and deliberately walking fast when they were campaigning, so that I couldn't keep up with them. It was typical of the grim, humourless spirit in which the whole campaign was fought.

A week before polling, the bookmakers stopped offering odds on the result. The general apathy and the absence of an effective challenger made Denver's position look impregnable. Even so, the usual circus of high-powered politicians and journalists came down from London over the final weekend of the campaign. They dipped their toes in the electoral water, got some free publicity and made appropriate democratic noises about the joys of the hustings, without necessarily knowing what hustings were. They seemed to think that, if they pressed enough Wopsley flesh, they could become honorary Wopsleyologists and talk authoritatively about the state of local opinion, but their considered pronouncements weren't worth waiting for. Those you expected to say that the opinion polls had got it all wrong said just that, and those you didn't didn't. The ones in government thought the Government was doing well despite the world recession, and the ones not in government said that the world would end in eighteen months if fingers weren't pulled out immediately in Whitehall. It was all as predictable as the effect of beer on the shape of a man's stomach, but the rituals still had to be gone through and for a few days the place was swamped by national political leaders talking to shoppers for the benefit of the television cameras. They smiled bounteously, but their eyes couldn't conceal their terror of meeting someone with vociferous opinions of the wrong sort who would spoil the whole show. The quality Press were no better. I saw Bob Mumford strolling through the town looking completely lost until I rescued him and took him off to lunch. 'What a hole!' he muttered several times over his Beaujolais, as he asked me all the questions about Wopsley he should have been asking the residents. 'But, Bob,' I said, 'you should visit some of the new housing developments here and see these things for yourself.' He blanched before he realised I was joking.

The only political big-shot whose visit interested me was Carter. He was billed to address a rally in the Town Hall the night before polling, and he arrived early in a Government Princess to do a walkabout in the shopping centre. I tried to look like an inconspicuous member of the welcoming crowd outside Sainsbury's, but he recognised me at once and exchanged a few words of greetings before plunging into a crowd of shoppers. With him was a bodyguard, a civil servant and also, to my surprise, Christopher. He burst into a smile on seeing a familiar face in the crowd and shook me limply by the hand.

'I've enjoyed your articles, John,' he said, with his usual stiff, rather forced courtesy. 'You don't seem to think very much of this place.'

'Damned right I don't,' I muttered, not wanting to give unnecessary offence to the people queuing for the bingo behind me. 'I'm surprised you've bothered to come at all. Not many of your lot have been up from the House, and I don't blame them. It's sewn up for your man Denver, so why waste your time? You're not going to lose the seat and another fifteen or twenty on the majority won't make any bloody difference.'

My cynicism bit as hard into him as ever and he went immediately on the defensive, taking a step away from me and turning a delicate shade of red.

'I just felt I should, John. Geoffrey was a personal friend and my patch is only fifty miles from here, so it would have been churlish not to come. Anyway, I've got to. I don't have much choice, do I?'

'How do you mean?'

He looked at me in surprise. 'Haven't you heard about my promotion? I've been Carter's PPS since last Monday.'

67

'Have you now?' I nodded thoughtfully and offered some tepid congratulations. Parliamentary Private Secretaries are the lowest form of Government life, being proverbially no more than unpaid Ministers' valets, but the posting at least offered Christopher an opportunity to consummate his political love affair with Carter. I could imagine him carrying the great man's briefcase devotedly around the House and trotting after him into the sunset, in search of the concrete vision of the future he had talked about. It was rather a waste of young talent, but I refrained from making a comment to that effect and said smoothly, 'I'm pleased for you, Christopher. You'll be able to take a look at government from the inside and see if it's as bad as everyone says.'

'It's interesting you should say that, John', he said softly. My sour jibes were still making him defensive, but he seemed anxious to tell me something. He opened his mouth to continue, then glanced through the crowd of shoppers to where Carter was glad-handing a fat woman in a turquoise raincoat and realised his services as an acolyte might be required.

'I think duty calls, John. Listen, can we meet for a drink in half an hour?'

'Sure.'

'I'll be free then because Carter has a private engagement he doesn't need me for. Where shall we go?'

'The Swan?'

'Where's that?'

'Just down there on the right, past the record shop.'

'Oh, I see it. I'll meet you there at six.'

He loitered for a fraction of a second, not sure whether to shake hands or not, then shot off into the crowd of ghouls who were beginning to form around Carter. When he reached his master, he stood obediently behind him waiting for further instructions, like a dog returning a stick. Others might have been charmed by this devotion, but again I felt waves of nausea rising slowly within me. Instincts stronger than my instinctive distrust of politicians told me that no good could come of this and made me shudder with apprehension. I didn't know what

68

Christopher wanted to talk about, but I had a vague suspicion. When we were established at a corner table at the Swan half an hour later, I pre-empted him.

'Don't tell me, Chris. I can guess.'

'Guess what?'

'What you want to tell me. Carter's been rather unsporting, hasn't he? He's said that he wants your candidate in the by-election to do badly. Right?'

'Yes, but how did *you* know?' His nose began twitching. 'Have you been talking to him?'

'No, I just guessed.' I gave a smug, worldly, middle-aged smile. 'I have been about a bit, don't forget.'

'Yes, I know, John. But still . . .' His voice tailed off, and he looked at me with the sort of adoring reverence he usually reserved for Carter. For a terrible moment, I thought he was going to come out with a 'cor!' or a 'gosh!' or a 'wow!' or some other term of approbation culled from a schoolboy paperback, but he remembered in time that he wasn't a boy, but a person of consequence in the adult world, and said 'How interesting!' instead. It was a brave attempt to sound grown-up and detached, but it didn't fool me. I could see he wasn't just interested by my show of political acumen, but absolutely riveted by it, so I spent a few self-indulgent minutes explaining myself.

During my time in the House, I began grandly, sounding as if I'd personally thwarted the Gunpowder Plot and been on Willie terms with Gladstone, there had been about eighty by-elections. Half of them had been boring and changed nothing, and the other half, although not exactly thrilling and also changing nothing, had all been The Most Important By-Election Since The War. There had been cliff-hangers and landslides and unspeakable yawns, but they all had one thing in common. Although MPs publicly supported their own party's candidates, in private there were always some who hoped their party would suffer a setback. If, say, they belonged to the minority wing of the party, then they wanted a signal sent to the party leadership – and what better than a humiliating by-election defeat? – that the party was out of touch with the voters. There was nothing machiavellian about this, I went on, astonishing Christopher that I knew such a long word; it was just common sense applied in a cynical and roundabout way. In a word, it was politics. As for Carter, if he really believed that the Government's economic policies were taking it up Shit Creek without a return ticket, then he needed the political ammunition to convince his Cabinet colleagues. A resounding raspberry from the burghers of Wopsley would do nicely, wouldn't it?

'I can see that, John, I can see that.' He was nodding agreement, but looked more agitated and unhappy than I had ever seen him. 'That's more or less exactly what Carter said to me yesterday. He didn't say "raspberry", but then he wouldn't.' He smiled bravely, then the nervous pallor returned to his cheeks. 'We didn't discuss it at all because he had a meeting to go to, but it's been worrying me in an odd way ever since. Obviously, I can see that it's a *logical* position to adopt, but I still find it rather –'

'Devious?'

'Yes. And for him to come all the way up here and support this man Denver when he secretly wants him to do badly is just, well –'

'Hypocritical?'

'Yes.' He looked relieved that I had supplied the vital words and not him. It must have hurt him even to have thought such things about Carter, and the vulnerability of his position struck a dull, faint chord somewhere within me. I now realise that I shouldn't have listened to it. I should have seized the opportunity of his disenchantment with Carter to drive that woolly, adoring nonsense out of his head for ever. I should have said, 'Carter *is* devious, Christopher, and you're a bloody fool not to have seen it earlier,' but I fluffed my lines. The old avuncularity returned to dispel the sourness, and I tried to reassure him by reminding him of some basic facts of political life. Principles weren't everything in politics, I said, or rather they were everything if he insisted (for he had winced visibly at my pronouncement), but they couldn't be pursued in isolation from the real world. The modern party system meant that politicians had to accept the concept of give-and-take, had to support policies they were tepid about in order to implement others they really believed in, had to keep a lower profile at some times in their careers than at others, had often to say one thing and believe something slightly different, had to trim here and fudge there, had to make calculations of personal advantage if they ever wanted to achieve anything. I became almost passionate in my pragmatism and slowly won him over to my point of view, dispersing his doubts about Carter and restoring his faith in the older man's vision. If anything, my homily strengthened it, because I reminded him that political visions could only be achieved if the prophets of the visions had cunning as well as conviction, and that Carter had both. I didn't share this Messianic view of Carter, of course, but it seemed to bring such serenity to Christopher's face that I felt no shame in reinforcing it. How could I have been so bloody short-sighted?

When I had finished, he thanked me for my advice and said with a coy, virginal smile that I had *half* reconciled him to Carter's attitude towards the by-election, but that he still hoped the Government didn't lose the seat altogether. After that, he fell silent and started fingering a beer-mat on the table. Nearly thirty seconds passed, then he suddenly looked up at me and blurted out: 'I'm not really a very good politician, am I?'

What could I say? I remembered my Latin teacher distinguishing between questions expecting the answer no and those expecting the answer yes, and wished he had mentioned that real life wasn't so simple. I would have preferred not to answer, but I could see from Christopher's anxious face that he hadn't meant it rhetorically, so I floundered and said: 'You're learning, Chris.'

'Thank you.'

'You could be very good at it one day.'

'Thank you very much.'

It was spineless but effective. My half-truths made him less

71

tense and he stopped playing with his beer-mat. I don't usually regard tact as a virtue, but this time it paid off, because Christopher was more communicative when he relaxed and he proceeded to pass on some interesting gossip about Carter.

At last Thursday's Cabinet, he reported, speaking in a strangulated whisper in case Wopsley should get hold of this high political drama, Carter had 'come out'. During preliminary Budget discussions, he had argued that the Chancellor's whole approach was wrong and that bolder economic measures were needed urgently. This was exactly what he had said at Christopher's dinner before Christmas, but it ran counter to his previous endorsement of the prevailing orthodoxies, so other Ministers had been taken aback. When he had finished speaking, twenty-two pairs of eyes had instinctively swivelled to look at the Prime Minister. What would he make of this blatant revisionism from someone who had previously been unwavering in his support? Not very much, it seemed. According to Christopher, the PM's eyes suddenly glazed over and he spent the rest of the morning brooding in the ominously detached way which was the hallmark of his displeasure. His summing up of the Budget discussions made no reference to Carter's views and, when they passed each other in a corridor later, he cut him dead.

Christopher recounted this like a television soap-opera, with the Prime Minister cast as the villain and Carter as the fearless, tough-talking hero. I couldn't take such a simplistic view, but I was still stimulated by the story and found it perfectly plausible. Everyone had been predicting that the Cabinet consensus wouldn't survive the economic crisis, and now it sounded as if Carter had decided the present strategy was unsustainable and made a calculated bid to be the leader of the alternative school of thought. It was a high risk move, which confounded the stodgy image of Carter I had held before, and I wondered whether he would use some discreetly coded language in his speech that evening to stake out his position more clearly. There is no more entertaining sight in politics than a Minister booking his place in the lifeboat as the Government is about to sink, so I broke the habit of a lifetime by arriving at the meeting five minutes early.

The hall was only half full and I could see red-faced party officials glowering crossly at the empty seats. They must have hoped for a bigger turn-out, although Wopsley in February was incompatible with mass hysteria and I myself was surprised to see so many. The faces in the audience were respectful rather than enthusiastic; a few had the shining confidence of party zealots but the rest were plainly agnostics, there to listen quietly to what was said and make up their own minds in the safety of their homes. When Carter arrived with Denver, they ignored the efforts of the party hacks to orchestrate a standing ovation and remained firmly seated, which I liked. Wopsley's apathy wasn't entirely a bad thing.

After some words of welcome from the chairman and a short contribution from Denver, Carter rose briskly to his feet and started delivering a prepared speech. It began blandly enough and, if his secret ambition was for Denver to lose the seat, he was too subtle to score own goals to achieve it. After a few minutes, he even started scoring goals at the other end, making neat side swipes at the Opposition parties which sent little ripples of mirth around the hall and brought big smiles to the faces of the party loyalists. The woman next to me, a farmer's wife by the look of it, with two large rosettes pinned to her mountainous chest, wriggled with pleasure at hearing her prejudices so wittily restated, and a man on the other side of the hall had to be restrained from clapping loudly at all the punch lines. I could see Christopher sitting on the rostrum behind Carter looking rosily down at the audience. His man was performing as expertly as ever.

A sudden gust of expensive perfume from my left made me turn my head. If it wasn't coming from the effeminate-looking man at the end of the row, then it had to belong to the woman sitting on her own in the row behind, with a hat pulled down over her eyes. She was quite decorative and, as Carter had just begun a sentence, 'Inflation is caused by several different factors', I decided to concentrate on the counter-attraction.

Within seconds, I had recognised her: she was the same woman I had seen on the Terrace with Carter the previous summer. Her presence in Wopsley was most intriguing and, if Carter said anything original about inflation in the next five minutes, I was far too engrossed to make a note of it.

She wasn't a Wopsley voter. You could tell that at once. Whatever the town's other qualities, cosmopolitan poise wasn't among them and this woman had poise or she had nothing. Everything about her posture exemplified the quiet refusal to sacrifice dignity for comfort which is believed, by those who care about such things, to embody breeding. Nor, I decided, was the woman a political animal. Her face wasn't animated by a pleasure in public debate and, when Carter scored points off the other parties, she was alone in not registering amusement. The conclusion was inescapable: she wasn't there to listen to his speech, she was there to listen to *him*.

Then it happened. Even more abruptly than on the Terrace the previous summer, the woman got up and bolted. She didn't wait for a convenient hiatus in the speech or shuffle out during a round of applause so as not to draw attention to herself. She just vanished. One minute she was sitting there apparently focused on Carter, and the next she was gone, attracting furious stares from the party hacks as she swept out through the hall. It was too good an opportunity to miss. I'm no greyhound, but I was outside the hall in pursuit before Carter could finish his sentence. He may have been about to say something earth-shattering, but I was willing to risk it.

7

Outside it was raining, a dull drizzle which you could only see in the headlights of the passing cars but which lent a treacherous black gloss to the pavement. The queue outside the chip shop on the other side of the road, which normally stretched round the corner into Queen Mary Street, had concertina-ed sharply as Wopsley's ungilded youth huddled together in pairs under the awning of the chemist's, holding each other's hands and puffing at shared cigarettes which glowed fitfully in the dark. It was an unpromising setting for an intrigue, but I looked up and down the road for my prey, then saw the right pair of legs disappearing towards the main square under a blue-green umbrella. I pulled up my collar and set off after her.

She was walking quickly but in perfect equilibrium, as if competing in an egg-and-spoon race. Had she once to parade around a room with a book on her head, I wondered snidely, and, if so, what had her etiquette teacher told her about dealing with run down hacks hot for a story? Once she glanced over her shoulder, and must have seen me taking a rapid interest in the Victorian terraced houses on display in an estate agent's window. She should have guessed that no house-buyer in his senses would have been out in a night like that, but she showed no suspicion and maintained the same steady pace without looking round, which was lucky. Inconspicuousness is not one of my qualities.

I guessed where she was heading before she got there. Only one hotel in Wopsley would do for so sophisticated a visitor, and the Crown was directly on her route. Its best-in-town reputation rested on a star it had once had in a guide-book long out of print and, like the town itself, it had seen better days. The ivy on the front wall had a diffident aspect, as if uncertainty of long tenure made it grow cautiously, and Scimitars and Saabs populated the car-park where Bentleys would once have dominated. I watched from the other side of the road as the woman went into the front foyer, waited ten seconds exactly, then followed her. The hotel had one of those revolving doors which discriminate against the overweight and, by the time I had struggled through, my chance seemed to have gone. The foyer was deserted except for a dozy reception clerk with a walrus moustache, and I assumed the woman had gone upstairs to her room. Then I noticed a hotel bar to the left of the foyer and smelled – or did I imagine it? – a lingering scent of perfume coming from that direction. Exhausted by the half-mile walk, I brought my heavy breathing under control and ambled in the direction of the liquor.

The woman was sitting alone at a table in the corner, looking vacantly through the lace curtains into the street. A glass of white wine sat untouched in front of her, like a stage-prop someone had put there to lend authenticity to the scene. Without it, one would have wondered what she was doing there, while, if the glass had been half empty, it would also have seemed wrong, for she didn't look like a dipso, just someone killing time before going to bed. I went across to the bar and ordered a whisky, then heaved myself up on to a stool where I could observe her without being too obvious about it. It was a bit risky, but it worked. She glanced at me only once, appeared to meditate briefly on the excesses of modern life, then stared out of the window again, leaving me free to spy on her at leisure. We were the only customers in the bar, so there wasn't much background to fade into, but you can get away with murder in these situations if you pretend to be a lifelong friend of the barman, so I instinctively tried it.

'Have one yourself. Bob.'

'Thank you, squire. I'll have a Scotch if I may.'

He was a tall, red-faced man who seemed to take his responsibilities in life seriously. He called me 'squire' because he respected the conventions of his trade and knew it was the proper form, and he took no offence at my own pretence of familiarity. Bob might even have been his real name, although he looked more like a Graham or a Bruce from the rather flash check tie he was wearing. I tipped him a vulgar amount and ran doggedly through the gamut of Wopsley small-talk.

'Terrible night out, Bob.'

'Raining, is it?'

'Just a drizzle, but the wind's up again.'

'We'll have more snow at this rate.'

'That's all we need.'

'Last lot only melted Monday.'

'Terrible.' I paused and lit a cigarette. Conversational tempo in Wopsley never rises above *andante*, and pauses are compulsory. It's quite soothing when you get used to it, but you have to be careful not to fall asleep in mid-sentence.

'Quiet in here tonight, Bob.'

'Always is on Wednesdays.'

'Many up for the by-election?'

'One or two.'

'Which way's it going to go, then?'

'Denver. By a mile. Don't you reckon?'

'Sure.'

Another pause. Bob – I had now decided he was more likely a Charles or a Walter – lit a cigarette of his own, a more expensive brand than mine, and leant sideways on the bar.

'About yourself, sir.' It seemed he had also had second thoughts; I wasn't really a 'squire' and he had worked that out. 'Will you be staying in town long?'

'Till Friday morning only, I'm afraid. Wopsley –'

'Has limited attractions for a man of the world, sir. I understand.' He gave a melancholy grin, which I hadn't thought possible. 'Up for the by-election, I suppose?'

'That's right.'

'Television?'

'No. Press.'

'I imagined as much, sir. I couldn't remember seeing your face before.'

For nearly ten minutes we meandered on like this, constructing a dialogue out of tiny mumbled fragments and adjusting so well to each other's rhythms that the pauses seemed more like deliberate variations in pace than breaks in our chain of thought. And, all the time we talked, we gazed across the bar at the woman and let her charms work invisibly on the faculties we did not expend in conversation. I thought it was only me at first, but the barman's face was too unused to deception to hide its emotions and I noticed that a certain expression of wistfulness came over it whenever it was pointed in her direction. Who could blame him? If you're a middle-aged man in Wopsley, reduced to impotently contemplating the forbidden fruits from behind a glass of whisky, it's a bonus if the woman you're ogling is something special. I would probably have been ogling myself if I hadn't been puzzling so much about the woman's identity. Who was she? And what the hell was she doing in Wopsley?

The next move wasn't going to be easy. Something about the woman warned me that she wouldn't tolerate social liberties and made me coy, which was unusual. When you're a journalist, you're used to button-holing strangers, asking them rude questions and harassing them if they fail to oblige you. A hectoring manner and sharp elbows are professionally indispensable and, if you're not unconscious of social rebuff, you become immune to it. I'm not normally squeamish about being told that something is none of my business, because everything is Fleet Street's business and the things that people think aren't our business are usually more our business than anything else. But still I hesitated. The woman's superior manner, coupled with the fact that I didn't even know her name, made failure not just probable but potentially humiliating. When I finally dragged myself off the bar-stool and tried to walk across the room towards her in a manner akin to a saunter, my lack of inner confidence must have shown, for she rumbled me

78

immediately. She viewed my approaching figure with a mixture of alarm and disgust and, when I got within six feet, snapped: 'Go away, creep.' What was I supposed to say? It was an impossible line to follow, so I pretended I hadn't heard it and tried to look the reverse of a creep by smiling affably. From her sophisticated manner, I had expected some concessions to tact but, when she followed her opening gambit with an acid 'Nothing doing, fatso', I was completely nonplussed.

'You've got it all wrong,' I protested in an embarrassed whisper. 'I'm not trying to pick you up or anything like that.'

'Then why are you slobbering over towards me?'

'I just wanted to talk to you.'

'What's the difference, for God's sake?'

'There's a lot of difference. I –'

'Go on, piss off, creep.'

'I'm a journalist.'

'Really?'

'Called Wellington. John Wellington.'

'Really?'

To my relief, the second 'really?' was less aggressive than the first and she looked me in the face for the first time. Before, she had been talking to my body, begging it to go away and stop offending her aesthetic senses, but my name rang some bell and aroused her curiosity. I thought she might even ask me to join her, but the spark of interest in her face flickered and went out and she turned her head abruptly away.

'Please stop pestering me, Mr Wellington. I'm not in the mood.'

It was obviously my marching orders. 'In the mood for what?' I might have asked in different circumstances, keeping the conversation alive and parading my gift for slick repartee. But not with this woman. She had made her wishes too clear to make it profitable to dispute them, so I nodded cordially and retreated to my stool at the bar.

'Commiserations, sir,' whispered the barman, with a leery wink. 'It was worth a try.'

'It wasn't what you're thinking, Bob,' I began, then ran out

79

of energy to explain. The woman's bluntness had infected me. 'Mind your own bloody business, Bob.'

'Yes, sir.'

'And stop staring at me in that ridiculous way.'

'Very good, sir.'

He blushed and began washing up the glasses, leaving me to lick my wounds in peace. What a farce! I thought. Why had I ever thought Wopsley would make such a refreshing change from the House? At least in the House, you knew exactly where you stood. People either ignored you or they abused you in the same light-hearted vein as you abused them. There was never anything as raw or barbaric as the treatment I had just received. I glowered darkly at the woman in the mirror behind the bar and wished I had never set eyes on her. All I had established from our conversation, if you could call it that, was that she wasn't English. Something about her short vowels, the 'a' in 'fatso', the 'o' in 'slobbering', wasn't quite correct and, since the rest of the ensemble was immaculate, I was sure it wasn't careless pronunciation. Was she French? I couldn't see it. A French woman would have sent me packing with even greater *élan* and certainly wouldn't drink wine in an English bar. German perhaps, or Swiss? It was possible, but no more. Danish maybe? Now there was a possibility. The idea attracted me more than the others for some reason, and I had just decided that she was called Eva Olafsson and had trained as a karate teacher, when the action started.

My brain must have been asleep that evening, because it hadn't occurred to me that the woman was waiting to meet someone. I had assumed she was staring out of the window because that's where people do stare when they have nothing better to do, particularly if the room's interior contains nothing more sightly than a chronically overweight journalist. But then the woman's body stiffened, and she leant forward and made a parting in the curtains to get a better view of the street. I peered in the same direction, saw the headlights of an approaching car, then heard the car slowing to a standstill and its engine being switched off. Before I could move, I saw the familiar figure of

Carter coming through the revolving door into the foyer. It was an exhilarating development, but I couldn't stay where I was, so I took the only safe line of retreat into the gents', missing Carter by seconds. I locked myself in, sat down and breathlessly plotted my next move.

Right now, I was trapped. Whatever the reasons for Carter's rendezvous with the woman, my reappearance would cramp both their styles and only invite further abuse. It was fifty-fifty anyway that the woman would mention her brush with me to Carter and make him suspicious. 'A journalist called Wellington, you say? Fat man with big lips? And he's in the gents' now?' I could imagine Carter's sharp, insistent questioning, and didn't suppose he would be exchanging soft somethings with the woman for too long if he knew I was in the vicinity. My only hope was that she would be too preoccupied with the matter in hand to remember me. But what was the matter in hand and how could I find out? Common sense still pointed to an amorous intrigue. Why else should a woman with expensive perfume and a man like Carter arrange a clandestine meeting in a Godforsaken place like Wopsley? Yet the very obviousness of the possibility made me fight it, if only because a simple tale of adultery would be scant reward for my efforts; in my pigheaded professional pride, I wanted a front page splash out of all this, not a snide paragraph in the gossip column. You can call it wishful thinking, but it was wishful thinking reinforced by instinct, for, as on the Terrace the previous summer, I had a gut feeling that something more than sex was involved, and this time I meant to get to the bottom of it. My scope for action was restricted while I was in the gents', but my brain began really humming and I had just constructed a provisional theory to cover the sequence of events, in which Eva Olafsson, the Danish karate expert, had become Natalia Poporova, a KGB agent, when there was a knocking on the door of my cubicle.

'Are you all right, sir? You've been in there for twenty minutes.'

I froze and tried to sound constipated. It's not an easy role, requiring a small and very precise vocal range, but I think I pulled it off. 'I'm sorry, I –'

'It's George, sir.'

'George? I don't think –'

'You've been calling me Bob, sir.'

'Oh yes, of course. Thank you, George.' How could I have missed that name? It was obvious when you thought about it. 'I think I'll be all right, thank you, George. I'm having slight trouble with the old waterworks after an exhausting few days. That's all.'

'I understand, sir.'

'Listen, George.' He's dependable, I thought, and he's bored; what better stooge could I ask for? 'I wonder if you could tell me something. Is the lady still there? The one in the grey dress.'

There was a short silence, and I could hear him simpering with delight at what he imagined was my predicament.

'The lady is very much still there,' he whispered pompously, then got a giggling fit. 'I fancy your chances in that direction are declining, sir.'

'Why?'

'I fancy madam has other fish to fry, sir. In a manner of speaking.'

He was chuckling aloud now and sounded so insufferably amused by the situation that I couldn't stand it any longer.

'I know exactly what you're talking about, George,' I said sharply. 'Madam is having a drink with Mr Carter, the Cabinet Minister. Is that right?'

'Indeed, sir.' The deflation was total.

'Now please get out of your head this ridiculous idea that I'm trying to jump into bed with the woman, and listen carefully for a minute.'

'Very well, sir.'

'I am not a journalist, but a private detective. I work for Witherspoon and Hodges, 373 The Strand, and I am up in Wopsley on professional business. Is that understood?'

There was a long silence before he whispered 'Yes', but I think he was suffering from shock rather than disbelief. Anyone who thought a man of my dimensions made a habit of picking up strange women in hotel bars obviously had a fertile imagination, and I didn't doubt that George read old-fashioned books where private detectives really existed. The wilder my inventions, the more likely he was to treat them as gospel, so I laid in on good and thick.

'My name is Parnassos,' I began, speaking softly but clearly, as though it was vital for him to commit every detail to memory. 'Solomon Parnassos. My father was Greek, and my mother an Austrian Jew. I was born in Cyprus and came over to England after the war. I worked in a bookshop in the Charing Cross Road for five years, then I ran messages for a security firm. There've been some ups and downs since then, but I've been on this present assignment for eighteen months. The lady in the bar is a member of the exiled Hungarian aristocracy. Her name is Countess Constanze Boruschti and she may or may not be in receipt of stolen jewels to the value of £5 million. That's what I'm here to find out. Is that all quite clear?'

I could hear him panting heavily at having to digest so much information so quickly, but eventually he stammered, 'Boruschti . . . jewels . . . £5 million', and promised his assistance in any way I asked.

'Good,' I said. 'Now go back to the bar, George, and keep me in touch with any developments. Don't for God's sake try to eavesdrop on their conversation or do anything silly. One or both of them may be armed. All you are to do is let me know when Mr Carter has left the bar. Don't worry about the lady. I think I can handle her on my own.'

'Very good, sir.'

There was a pause while he mustered his courage, then he was gone. I began laughing quietly to myself, intoxicated by the ludicrousness of the situation, and I was still chortling when George returned a minute later.

'Come quickly, Mr Parnassos!' he shouted in a hoarse whisper, rattling the door of my cubicle. 'They both left the bar a short while ago. I don't know where they went.'

I followed him back into the bar, remembering to flush the

83

unused toilet after me, and we ran through into the foyer, which was deserted. I heard a car engine starting up outside and got out into the street in time to see Carter's official car disappearing round the corner. There were two other men in the back seat – Christopher, presumably, and a Civil Service minder – I assumed the woman was still in the hotel. I turned to George, who was looking abject now the excitement was over, and put my hand on his shoulder.

'If the Countess is staying in the hotel, George, I have to know her room number. Perhaps you could ask that clerk at reception for it.'

'Very good, sir.' He trotted off eagerly and returned in less than a minute. 'I forgot to check, sir. Was it Boruschti with an "o" or an "a"?'

I gagged, then remembered. 'Neither, George. She'll be staying under an assumed name, you can be sure of that. You might find out what name she's using at the moment. It could be important when the case comes to court.'

'Will do, sir.' His face lit up at the word 'court', as if the prospect of appearing in the witness-box at the Old Bailey was being dangled physically in front of him, and I would have felt ashamed of myself if I'd been that sort of person. I watched from a safe distance as he held a whispered discussion with the reception clerk, then waited anxiously as he padded back across the foyer.

'Wiseman,' he announced under his breath. 'Mrs A. Wiseman. And a bloody obvious pseudonym too, sir, if you'll excuse the French.'

I excused the French and smiled. 'And the room number, George?'

'Two hundred and eleven, sir. On the second floor, just next to the lift.'

'Thank you, George. You've been most helpful.'

I left him looking gratefully at a £20 note, small compensation for his duping, and got into the lift. It ground and creaked its way up two floors, complaining vociferously at my bulk, then deposited me in a corridor so plushly carpeted that I was able to steal up on room 211 without a sound. I knocked gently and was surprised when the door was opened immediately. I had expected to have to stick a foot in the crack and argue the toss for five minutes before gaining admittance, but my reception was instant.

'Come in, Mr Wellington,' said Mrs A. Wiseman, smiling graciously as if I was an old friend. 'I was hoping you would come up for a chat.'

8

For a few seconds I stood motionless in the doorway, completely taken aback by this welcome. Everything was suddenly moving much too quickly, as if the fatuous intrigue I had dreamed up to satisfy poor George had developed a life of its own. I just couldn't reconcile this politely smiling woman with the harridan in the bar downstairs, and I peered cautiously past her in case she had an accomplice waiting to mug me as I walked into the room. Seeing nothing suspicious, I accepted her invitation and was waved into an armchair next to the window. The room was as dowdily furnished as the rest of the hotel, but a television and a small fridge showed that some concessions had been made to the twentieth century and, from the fridge, the woman produced some whisky miniatures.

'You are a whisky drinker, I think, Mr Wellington? You drank whisky in the bar, I noticed.'

'You are very observant,' I said in a flat voice, noticing that the woman's foreign accent was slightly more pronounced than before. She was holding so many of the cards that I would have to play a waiting game until she had shown her full hand. I wouldn't have been surprised if she'd told me what I had had for lunch the Monday before last, so great was her psychological ascendancy.

'I'm sorry I was so rude to you earlier,' she went on, realising from my look of bemusement that her volte-face needed explaining. 'I'm not normally so discourteous, but there are times when one must have privacy. Don't you agree? He was due in about ten minutes, and we had to be alone or it was

86

pointless. He doesn't like journalists very much, I think. You will understand that.'

I nodded and smiled at her for the first time. She was still several moves ahead of me, but there's something strangely titillating about conversations where things are left unsaid because the other person trusts to your common sense. I was flattered by the woman's assumption that I would know who 'he' was and appreciate why journalists were vermin whom grown-up people didn't like. She sipped demurely at her whisky, as prim and proper as a Sunday schoolteacher with a cup of tea, and went on talking smoothly.

'You got out of the bar very fast when he arrived. I didn't think you would be able to move so quickly.' Her cool grey-green eyes ran thoughtfully over my body and came to rest on my torso. She studied it for a second, then looked at me sympathetically. 'You have a weight problem, I think, Mr Wellington.'

'It's not as bad as it looks,' I said with a straight face. 'I can still see my knees in the mirror.'

'I'm sorry?'

'I said, I can still see my knees in the mirror.'

'I don't quite understand.'

I started explaining the joke, but she stopped me impatiently, irritated that I should make light of such a serious matter. 'You have a nickname, don't you, Mr Wellington? When you told me your name in the bar, I remembered reading —'

'Beef,' I said glumly. 'Beef Wellington is my professional name. Somebody thought it up about fifteen years ago when I began losing my figure, and after that it stuck. It's a pun, but it's not very funny and I don't like it. Please call me John. It's a nicer name and easier to remember.'

'Thank you, I will —' She was about to say 'John' but held back, not quite ready for that particular hurdle. Then she stretched out her hand for me to shake. 'I am Anna Wiseman. You may remember my husband Peter.'

My brain stalled in neutral for a moment, befuddled by too

87

much whisky, and I couldn't think who she was taking about. Peter Wiseman sounded like a middle-aged actor, but I couldn't put a face to him or remember what films he had been in, if any. Then it suddenly came back to me, so clearly that I wondered how I could have been so slow on the uptake. Peter Wiseman! The name rang such a loud bell and was linked so closely to Carter's that all the jigsaw-pieces seemed to be falling into place at once. Wiseman had been a friend of Carter's and, although I remembered other details only hazily, I was sure about one fact because it had got into the newspapers. It seemed wise to make a diplomatic reference to it.

'Your husband's death must have come as a great shock, Mrs Wiseman,' I said gently. 'He was still very young.'

'Yes,' she said, after a respectful pause. 'Peter was young, and it was a shock, but I am over the worst of it now, thank you very much.' She gave what was meant to be a brave smile, but the serenity of it so outweighed the sadness that the effect was sanguine rather than melancholy. I remembered that her bereavement hadn't stopped her chasing after another man, a friend of her husband's, and felt my sympathy for her drain sharply away. She must have noticed the hardening in my expression, because she suddenly stopped smiling and said: 'You are right, Mr Wellington. I didn't love him all that much. We would, I think, have got divorced one day. But his death was still a shock.'

'Of course.'

'I had to identify the body after it was found. It wasn't very pleasant.'

'I'm sure.'

'It was horrible.' She shuddered and cocooned herself for a while in the memory. Nothing approaching a tear got to the surface, but her face became very black indeed and she stared hard into her whisky as if some physical relic of her husband was in the glass. I waited deferentially, not wanting to press for more facts until the time was ripe, and my patience was rewarded when she gave a final shake of her head, knocked back the whisky and went over to the window to draw the curtains. Then she asked me if I had half an hour free.

'As long as you like, Mrs Wiseman.'

'I didn't want to talk to a journalist earlier, but now I do. You are a very persistent man, I think. When you are hot on a story, you don't give up.'

'Not if I can help it.'

'But are you also discreet? I want our conversation to be off –what do you say?'

'Off the record?'

'That's right. Is that understood?'

'Certainly.'

'Good. Then where do you want me to begin?'

She asked the question teasingly, coquettishly almost, as if she wasn't used to dealing with journalists but was fast warming to the experience. I also noticed she was getting slightly tipsy. She had taken off her shoes, which her etiquette teacher can never have recommended in the presence of a middle-aged alcoholic, and, whereas before she had sat very upright on the corner of the bed, she now reclined sideways like a Roman courtesan in a B movie. Her alluring, mildly decadent posture might have deflected a lesser man from his task, but I have always regarded sex, like Prime Minister's Question Time, as an overrated pastime, so I was able to resist her charms. Her story was in any case too compelling to be interrupted. When I suggested that she begin as near the beginning as possible, she fell upon her narrative like a seasoned raconteuse.

She was Dutch, she said, born Anna van Dok in Leyden in – she was about to give the date, but stopped coyly, in what I was sure was a deliberate bit of teasing. After studying at Leyden University, she had gone to Rotterdam and worked for a commodity broker's as a secretary. There she had met Peter Wiseman. He had been over from London on a business trip and had taken her out to dinner a couple of times, in fashionable restaurants with candle-lit tables and waiters in tailcoats. She had found him extraordinarily charming, she said bitterly, giving the word the darkly ironic emphasis with

which only hindsight could invest it, and had been completely
bowled over by his English gallantry and sense of humour. He
hadn't told her he was already married or that he had two small
children and, when she found out a year later, he had said he
didn't think it was particularly relevant. Again the knife
seemed to turn, and she mouthed the word with a venom which
issued incongruously from her languid position on the bed.
After their second dinner together, she went on, they had made
love in Peter's hotel room. It was 21 July, a Wednesday, and the
hotel had been called the Saturn, room 374. Peter had worn
blue pyjamas, which she had thought hysterically English, and
had smoked a cigar afterwards.

I nodded politely, affecting an interest in these erotic
minutiae which had implanted themselves so deeply in her
mind, and glanced ostentatiously at my watch, hoping she
would get a move on. If we had been talking on the record, I
would have been taking down the details slavishly, knowing
their power to thrill my readers with their macabre precision,
but off the record they were irrelevant. I was impatient to get to
the point where Carter appeared, and she must have sensed my
impatience because she suddenly moved the narrative up a
gear.

At the point where she resumed, she was married to Peter
and living in a converted Victorian farmhouse on the outskirts
of Maidenhead. Several years must have intervened, time for
Peter to have got divorced and remarried and for her to have
been initiated into all the Anglo-Saxon rituals: Sunday lunches,
country walks, summer holidays in France. She left it all out,
but it was easy to imagine. It was a Wednesday – why did
everything that mattered in her life happen on a Wednesday? –
and John and Sophie were over for dinner. John who, I thought
for a second, then remembered. So few people used Carter's
Christian name – he wasn't one of those cuddly politicians with
whom everyone affects intimacy – that it came as a shock. At
that time, he had just been made a Minister of State in the
Foreign Office and was, she said, quaintly missing the idiom,
above the moon at his appointment. He had talked brilliantly

90

over dinner about political prospects for the next decade and, although politics didn't interest her, she could remember thinking how idealistic he was compared with Peter, who had been tired after work and had just made cynical remarks all evening. John's eyes were so luminous, though, and his voice had the most extraordinary resonance, as if –

'Wait,' I said, beginning to be suffocated by the romantic gloss she put on everything and fearing she was about to descend into trivia again. If she told me what colour John's pyjamas were as well, I was terrified I would laugh aloud and be thought unsympathetic. 'Can we track back a little, please, Mrs Wiseman? I'm particularly interested in this friendship between Peter and Carter – sorry, John. They had a bit about it in the papers when Peter died, as far as I can remember. Weren't they friends at Oxford or something like that?'

'Yes, that's right. It went back a long, long way.'

'What college were they at? Do you remember?'

'Jesus, I think.' She looked as startled at my choice of significant details as I had at hers. 'Or it may have been Corpus Christi. It was certainly something very religious, which was funny because neither of them were like that at all.' Some bawdy secular memory seemed to flash through her head and she gave a guilty little smile. 'Of course, they hardly ever talked about Oxford.'

'Why "of course"?'

'Do you really not know?'

'No.'

'Well, well.' She looked at me playfully. 'I knew it was quite a well kept secret, but I would have thought that a journalist like you, who works in the House of Commons and keeps his ear close to the ground –'

'What is it?'

'What's what?'

'What's the secret, for Christ's sake?'

'Ah, Mr Wellington.' She was playing hard to get, and I had blundered by asking the direct question. A more oblique approach might have winkled it out of her, but I had fluffed my

91

chance. Her face took on the affected air of mystery which was her most exasperating mannerism, and she said simply: 'It's not very important and it's a long time ago, but I don't think I should tell you. If you were a real journalist, you would find out in no time.'

It was a gauntlet and there was no point in refusing it. She might clam up completely if I badgered her about this side-issue, so I let the matter pass and returned to the main theme, steering as clear as possible of pyjama colours and the significance of different men's eyes. 'Didn't Carter and your husband have a professional connection of some sort?'

'That's right. After Oxford, they set up a business together.'

'What sort of business?'

'Oh, something very grand-sounding. Management consultants: does that sound right? They were very clever young men and they wanted to get rich in a hurry. They called themselves Carter and Wiseman, which Peter didn't like at all. He wanted it to be Wiseman and Carter, because he worked harder or said he did. But John said it had to be Carter and Wiseman because C came before W in the alphabet and it sounded better. Aren't men silly?'

I nodded sagely, content not to argue about meaningless generalisations, and drew her back to particulars. 'What happened to the business?'

'I think after about ten years they sold it, or it got taken over by another company. Peter wanted to work in a different area and John had gone into politics by then. He was first elected when he was only thirty. That's very young, isn't it?'

'Some get in even younger,' I said, remembering Christopher. 'But it's not always a good idea. Did they remain good friends after that?'

'Oh yes, very much so. They saw a lot of each other until about two years ago. John was best man at our wedding.'

Her eyes misted over at the memory and, to my annoyance, she launched into another romantic interlude. How they had had to get married in a registry office because Peter was

92

divorced and her church wouldn't sanction a church wedding;
how she had worn a pale blue dress made of satin and brocade
and had had two bridesmaids, Marie, her youngest sister, and
Stephanie, Peter's cousin; how they had gone to Jamaica for
their honeymoon and eaten mangoes and waterskied and made
passionate love under palm trees to the sound of crickets and
the sea lapping gently on the beach . . . It was nearly ten
minutes before I could get her off this schmaltz, she enjoyed
wallowing in it so much. She had got as far as the plane back
from Jamaica with Peter and you could tell a mile off that he
was about to say something wounding which would cast a
shadow over their entire relationship and make her wonder if
she'd made a terrible mistake in marrying him, when my
patience ran out and I interrupted her in mid-sentence.

'Why are you telling me all this, Mrs Wiseman?'

'Aren't you interested? I thought –'

'I'm interested in more recent events, to be quite honest. I'd
like to hear more about your husband's death and about
Carter's role in everything and about what the hell you're doing
in Wopsley right now. Isn't that what you wanted to talk to me
about? All this earlier stuff is very interesting and you've
obviously led an, er, fascinating life, Mrs Wiseman, but, well,
it's all over now, isn't it?'

'Ah, Mr Wellington.' She looked me sadly up and down as if
I was fifteen years younger than her, not fifteen years older.
'You're not very astute, are you? You work for a daily
newspaper, so you think the here and now is everything. Can't
you see that all these small things that took place ten years ago
had a great, a very great influence on what happened last year?'

'I would know that better,' I retorted, 'if I had the slightest
idea what did happen last year.'

There was a long silence. I thought for a moment my
bluntness had angered her, but then she nodded her head,
acknowledging the justice of my point, and went into a trance. I
could see her mind covering a lot of ground very quickly and
several times she furrowed her brows intensely, revealing
wrinkles I hadn't seen before and making me realise how much

nearer forty she was than thirty. Then she looked at me hard, the sort of look you give the drivers of adjacent cars at traffic-lights to assess how quickly they will accelerate when the lights go green. If I'd known what she was hoping to see, I could have moulded my face to order, but the best I could do was exude a general beneficence and try not to squirm under her gaze. In the end, I easily passed the examination she had set. The strange thing about fat men is that, although women shun us physically, they are happy to trust us absolutely in other contexts. We are so obviously real, corporeal, earth-bound beings that we reassure them. Our girth suggests that we won't run away in a crisis because we won't be able to, and we look so physically absorbant that people assume we can retain secrets as easily as carbohydrates. Neither prejudice has any founda-tion in my case, but I have long attracted people's trust on fraudulent bases and I did so again here. Mrs Wiseman completed her examination, found no reason to withhold confidences and resumed her narrative. She left out the emotional embroidery, as I had requested, and got straight to the point.

'My husband died on 8 May last year. He was out walking his dog at night in a road near our house when he was knocked over by a passing car. It was assumed it was a drunken driver because nobody came forward to claim responsibility.'

I nodded. I remembered the details now, because it was this aspect of the case which had attracted publicity.

'Peter died on the way to the hospital. He was dead before I got to him, thank God. His injuries were appalling.'

There was a pause, a period of respectful remembrance, then she took another gulp of whisky and, looking me straight in the face, said:

'John Carter was driving that car.'

9

Let me digress. When I proposed to Jenny twenty-one years ago, it was September and we were in Brighton. I was down there to cover one of the party conferences and Jenny was then a Party person, although she later outgrew that. We had met only a few times before, but the chill sea-breeze proved oddly inflammatory and we dined out together every night that week. On the last night, I had two whiskies before the meal and put the question in stammering, convoluted form during my second helping of trifle. I don't know why I was so frightened, because I was then only 13 stone 10 and was said, by people who usually got these things right, to have a brilliant future ahead of me. I was frightened, though, and, when I had asked the question and had to endure Jenny pondering it gravely in silence, my knees started knocking together under the table, as if I was the hero of a trashy novel staring down the barrel of a gun.

I say this, not out of sentiment, but to show that there are silences and silences and that, like women, they are generally pregnant or not pregnant. The silence that filled the room after Anna Wiseman had said these words was nine months gone, as taut and uncomfortable as that fifteen-second eternity in a Brighton restaurant twenty-one years before. I could hear a train rumbling in the distance, even though the hotel was more than a mile and a half from the station, and from the next room the sound of a stiffly bristled toothbrush being slowly rubbed against someone's teeth. I could easily have broken the silence by saying 'You're joking, Mrs Wiseman' or 'Did you just say what I thought you said?', but I don't believe in pretence

95

between consenting adults, and it would have been pure pretence to suggest I hadn't heard her properly or thought she was just guilty of a little Dutch humourism. She had meant what she said all right, and her face was vibrant with emotion as she watched my reaction. Triumph and apprehension were written on it almost equally, triumph at the success of her bombshell and apprehension at how I would react. I had erred on the side of haste earlier in the conversation, so now I bided my time, letting the full significance of her allegation sink in and considering possible responses. The silence reached a crescendo, if that's imaginable, and she broke it by going over to the fridge and dispensing more whisky. I nodded my thanks, said 'You're making a very serious charge, Mrs Wiseman', by way of a holding answer, and slumped pensively back in my chair.

Journalists are not fools. If we sometimes appear naïve, it's only because the assumptions we make about our readers' intelligence are insultingly cautious. We ourselves are not naturally credulous, being knaves rather than gulls in the human comedy, and, although we love good stories and tell them with gusto, we only believe them about twenty per cent of the time; in the end, our cynicism easily eclipses our penchant for romantic fiction. Now I admit that Mrs Wiseman's bald statement about Carter gave me a definite *frisson*, like the smell of a leg of lamb rubbed in garlic when it's just out of the oven. It was a climax to my inquiries which I had secretly yearned for, the gigantic once-in-a-lifetime scoop which I needed to confound my boredom with politics and lift the depression into which Westminster and Wopsley had thrown me. In the will-o'-the-wisp part of my being that ached to escape from the predictabilities of daily life – the deadlines, the lobby briefings, the long hours in the Press Gallery, the gossip with Members, the hard, senseless drinking – I wanted desperately to believe her. And yet I couldn't. The idea of an eminent politician driving out to Maidenhead to run over a man walking his dog was too preposterous. I wouldn't have dared include such an absurdity in my cock-and-bull story to poor George, and I was

96

damned if I was going to be more trusting than him. Rather than a climax, I felt I had now reached an anti-climax, with the woman leading me up the garden path to nowhere, for some twisted reason bedded deep in her crazed romantic psyche. The more I thought about her allegation and all the teasing that had preceded it, the angrier I got. When I finally spoke, I was bitter and sarcastic.

'How long have you been living in England, Mrs Wiseman?'

'About ten years now. Why?'

'Haven't you heard about our law of slander yet?'

The room was dimly lit, but I think she blushed when I asked the question.

'How do you mean?' she asked in a subdued voice, knowing damned well what I meant but playing dumb, the way people do when they're feeling defensive and want you to do the talking.

'I mean you'd better be careful what you're saying. Mr Carter's a senior Government Minister. He might even be Prime Minister one day. You can't go around saying he bumped off your husband just because he won't sleep with you tonight. I take it that's what you were hoping for?'

It was a shot in the dark, but she winced and I knew I'd got it dead on.

'You are very cruel, Mr Wellington. Only a journalist –' She groped for something cutting to say, then realised that seasoned hacks don't cut up easily and abandoned the search. 'But you're wrong about John, and I'm right. He did kill my husband.'

'How do you know? I suppose he ran him over and left his photograph next to the body, just to make it easier for the police? And you found the photograph before the police and protected Carter, because you loved him and hoped he would marry you now that your husband was out of the way? And I suppose the dog knew it was Carter who had done it and was going to tell the police, so you put some cyanide in his Winalot? Come on, Mrs Wiseman. We're in Wopsley, not Hollywood.'

'You're being childish, Mr Wellington.'

97

'*I'*m being childish?'

'Yes.' She paused, seemed to toy with being very rude indeed, then simmered down. 'I know that John killed my husband because he told me.'

'When?'

'Last summer. Just after the election.'

'Where?'

'On the Terrace of the House of Commons. He asked me there for a drink.'

I gripped the arm of my chair and stared at her. In the pit of my stomach, I was conscious of that sinking sensation you experience half-way through an argument, when you know you've lost but have to argue on to save face. It was beginning to look as if I might lose this argument, but I'd never been keener to lose an argument in my life, so I was more elated than defensive.

'Tell me,' I said, trying to sound as if the question mattered less than it did. 'How did you react when Carter told you he'd killed your husband? Were you shocked or had you suspected it all along?'

'I was shocked, of course.' She lowered her voice and I had to lean forward to be sure of hearing the next bit. 'To be quite honest, Mr Wellington, I just panicked. I couldn't believe what John was saying to me, and I couldn't bear to go on talking about it there, in the middle of all those people. I was afraid I would get hysterical or something. So I just ran.'

'You left the Terrace in a hurry, you mean, and didn't come back?'

'Yes. What's the matter?'

She was staring at me and I realised I was panting heavily, as fat news-hounds do when they get a meaty bone thrown in front of them. I tried to control my breathing by taking gulps of whisky, but it wasn't easy because my brain was on time and a half. Of course, I thought, still playing devil's advocate, she might be bluffing. She might have remembered seeing me on the Terrace and made up the rest of the story to tie it all in. I couldn't be certain of anything, although she was fast con-

98

vincing me of her case. If I wanted hard facts, I had to sift deeper, so I slowed down the tempo of questioning and attacked some of the missing links.

'Tell me about you and Carter. You love him, don't you?'

'I *loved* him, Mr Wellington.' She altered the tense deliberately, and it wasn't the moment to challenge her. 'Not any more. Not after this evening. But once, yes.'

'Were you his mistress?'

'Does it matter?'

'Of course it matters. I write for a tabloid, Mrs Wiseman, not the bloody *Times*.'

It was a weak joke, and it fell even flatter when I had to explain what a tabloid was. She looked a bit nauseated, as if she'd learnt she was sharing her room with a gangrenous skunk, but she gave the answer I was looking for.

'We had a short fling – is that the expression? – about three years ago.'

'How short?'

'About nine months.'

'So not all that short?'

'It passed in no time.' She smiled ruefully. 'He was in opposition then, of course. He had more time for the important things in life.'

'Like sex?'

'Don't be cheap, Mr Wellington.' The rap over the knuckles was savagely administered, then she continued in a more detached voice. 'After Peter's – after Peter died, I hoped we might be able to make a success of it again. This was before I knew that John had killed Peter. When I learnt about that, I thought the two of them must have had a fight about me, so I tried to get in touch with John again. But he wasn't interested. He didn't return my calls and his bloody Department kept him working twenty-four hours a day, so I gave up. Then I read in a newspaper that he was going to speak in Wopsley tonight. I booked in here, left a message with his secretary for him to meet me in the bar downstairs after the meeting, and went along to listen.' She stopped and looked at me. 'Were you at that

99

meeting?'

'Yes.'

'I remember you now. There was a fat man in the row in front
of me. I didn't think there could be two –' She tailed off,
remembering her manners just in time. 'Wasn't it boring, that
meeting?'

'Well –'

'Whatever sort of people go and listen to that nonsense?
John's speech was so bad that I just got up and left half-way
through. He has become very ambitious, I think.'

'He was always that.'

'No, it's more serious now. He's getting near the end of the
race and he thinks – *I* think he thinks – he's going to win it. Do
you think he will?'

I shrugged and felt genuinely indifferent. The significance of
that particular rat-race had completely receded in the last
half-hour.

'He might,' I said. 'But not as a convicted murderer.'

'Good.' I hadn't thought of Anna Wiseman as a cruel woman
until I saw how she smiled at my comment. 'Very good. He was
cold to me this evening, very cold. I wondered how I could ever
have loved such a cold man. His eyes –'

'I understand.' She was about to get maudlin again, so I
stopped her dead. When I wrote up the story I could make up
as much slush as they wanted, but right now I had to be
purposeful and direct. 'Listen carefully, Mrs Wiseman. You
may well be right and John Carter may have been driving the
car which killed your husband, but we still have a long way to
go. In the first place, why did he kill him? From what you say,
he didn't do it because of you, so what other reason can there
be? In the second place, how are we going to prove it? We can't
just go on something he said to you on the Terrace six months
ago, because he'll deny it. What did he say to you, by the way?
Do you remember his exact words?'

'Not his exact words.' She pursed her brow and ran her hand
slowly through her hair. 'It's a long time ago, and he expressed
himself very indirectly.' I swore to myself and thought, trust

100

Carter to be bloody devious: double negatives right down the line if I knew my man. 'He said something like, "It was convenient, wasn't it, that car that ran over your husband? I think you would be surprised if –" '

'Yes?'

' "– if you understood how deliberate some accidents are. Fate is very kind sometimes." I remember that bit perfectly. "Fate is very kind sometimes." Those were his very words, Mr Wellington, and he obviously meant them to have great significance, because his eyes –'

'Is that all? The words you've just quoted and Carter's bloody eyes?'

'Isn't that enough?'

'No, it's not bloody well enough, Mrs Wiseman.' I got angrily to my feet and started pacing up and down. 'I may not be the world's most eminent journalist, Mrs Wiseman. I may work for the crappiest paper in Fleet Street and have a joke nickname and write a load of drivel which everyone takes with two kilos of salt. But I do still have a passing interest in facts, you know, and with this sort of story the facts are everything. You said a little while ago that Carter told you he was driving the car which ran over your husband. *Now* you tell me that he just produced some philosophical balls about fate and that you thought this must be significant because of something in his eyes. It's a bit bloody much, you know.' I was so incensed that I would have stormed out of the room in protest, which would have been plain crazy, if she hadn't interrupted.

'Have you ever slept with a man, Mr Wellington?'

What was I supposed to say? The question was so absurd that, by the time I'd worked out she wasn't interested whether I was gay, I was shocked into listening. She saw the blank horror in my face and realised she had expressed herself clumsily, because she corrected the error as she continued.

'If you have slept with someone, you will know that you can always tell what they mean from their eyes. Isn't that so? I *know* what John was trying to say to me, Mr Wellington. Please don't treat me like a child.'

'I know you know,' I said bitterly. 'But it would help if I knew too. Didn't you ask him to be more explicit?'

'There was no need. I knew exactly what he meant, and I was too upset to go into details. I just ran away, as I told you.'

'And this evening? Didn't you discuss it again this evening?'

'There wasn't time. Our meeting was too short, and we had more important things to discuss.'

'Like sex?'

'Like *love*, Mr Wellington. Or, to be precise, the impossibility of love.'

There was a painful finality in the words and she looked me earnestly in the face, appealing to my better nature. I'd almost forgotten I had one, but her eyes were eloquent and she got through to it.

'Trust me, Mr Wellington. *Please*. I do know what I'm talking about.'

And I did trust her. Not absolutely, you understand, and not because I shared her faith in sleeping with people as a means of interpreting their eye-signals, but because I had no choice. For all its woolliness, her story had stood up well to my questioning. There were more inquiries to be made and the chances still were that Carter was clean, but I couldn't just drop the whole thing. I was a journalist, so I had to assume my man was guilty until he had been proved innocent. My professional duty lay in pursuing the matter and, if my inquiries bore fruit, in gratifying the public's right to know. I believe every cliché in the book when I'm hot on a trail.

Mrs Wiseman was already falling asleep. All the soul-baring had exhausted her and, although there were still questions I wanted to ask, there was no point in continuing. I took down her address and telephone number in Maidenhead and promised to contact her in the next few days. Then we parted. I began to shake hands, but she suddenly flung her arms round my neck and kissed me impulsively on the cheek, whispering 'You're magnificent, Mr Wellington' in a husky voice. She meant it as a compliment but, if you're not used to women's blandishments, you distrust them, and I'm afraid I treated the

102

incident as fresh evidence of La Wiseman's emotional instability. After taking my leave of her, I wiped the lipstick carefully off my cheek in the mirror next to the lift.

Downstairs, George was waiting for me, crouching behind an aspidistra in the corner of the foyer, like an overgrown leprechaun. He sprang out of his hiding place when he saw me and tiptoed over.

'Well, Mr Parnassos? A successful interview with the Countess?'

'Very successful, thank you, George.' I paused for melodramatic effect and lowered my voice to a whisper. 'You will be pleased to learn that the jewels are now in safe custody and that a scandal that would have brought shame on the whole Government has been averted.'

'Congratulations, sir, warmest congratulations.' He seized my hand and started shaking it manically. 'A great triumph for you and very well deserved. Will it be in the papers tomorrow?'

'No, George, I'm sorry.' I felt the biggest shit in Wopsley as his face plummeted. 'The matter will be settled privately. Goodnight then.'

'Goodnight, sir.'

I struggled through the revolving door and out into the street. The rain had stopped and it was not much after eleven, so I walked the mile and a half back to my hotel at my leisure.

10

At Westminster, it's known as Wellington's Law. I formulated it one evening in the Press Bar, after a woman had stripped off in the Public Gallery while I was away drinking in another part of the House. It states that the likelihood of news being made is in inverse proportion to the likelihood of Beef Wellington being there to cover it; or, more succinctly, the shit always hits the fan when I'm out of the room. I knew that Wellington's Law had operated with a vengeance when I got back to my hotel room and turned on the radio to catch the midnight news bulletin.

The headlines were unremarkable: more bad economic news, some diplomatic activity in the Middle East, a bomb in Londonderry, wounding two. Then the newsreader's voice changed tone slightly and I bent my head to listen.

'On the eve of the Wopsley by-election, a local opinion poll to be published in the *Wopsley Echo* tomorrow morning shows the Government's lead in the constituency narrowing. According to the poll, Charles Denver, the Government candidate, is only ten points ahead of his nearest rival, compared with a lead of nearly 30 per cent a week ago. If translated into votes, this could mean a Government majority reduced from 32,000 to about 13,000.' The newsreader coughed and paused before continuing. I could imagine him sipping some water, if not something stronger, and I felt like something stronger myself when I heard the next item. 'Also in Wopsley tonight, a campaign speech by Government Minister John Carter has fuelled speculation about differences of opinion in the Cabinet. In a carefully worded passage, Mr Carter said that it would be wrong for people to assume that the Government was setting its face against alternative economic policies. This appeared to conflict with the words used by the Prime Minister in the Commons yesterday, when he said that no alternative policies were feasible in the present economic climate. Here's our political correspondent, Clive Masters.'

I switched off in disgust and pulled on my shoes. There was no time to listen to Masters' little analysis, and I could imagine it all anyway. 'Grave misgivings about present policies . . . worries about electoral effect of Prime Minister's apparent intransigence . . . high cost of manifesto commitments now being recognised . . . Carter not a lone dissenter . . . keeping the flag of moderate opinion flying . . . full-scale rebellion possible at the Party conference . . . some discreet counting of heads . . . high Government sources . . . backbench opinion . . . West-minster . . . Wopsley . . . Whitehall . . . tension . . . speculation . . . tension . . . Whitehall . . . Wopsley . . . Westminster . . .' Masters was a smarmy bugger, widely loathed in the Press Gallery, and I didn't feel like listening to the clichés rolling off his tongue as he told a story I should have been telling myself. I had telephoned some copy through that afternoon and said I would only report again if anything exciting came up in Carter's speech; now I had cocked it up totally. I would get a well deserved bollocking when I got back to London unless I could prove I'd deserted my post to follow a better story. An hour ago I thought I had, but the head-cooling walk back from the Crown had made me sceptical about Anna Wiseman's allegations. She was Dutch and sexually frustrated, I thought, and had learnt her English from Mills and Boon. Why should I believe a word she told me?

I stumbled downstairs to the pay-telephone in the hall and rang the night desk on the paper. The first edition would have gone out but I could eat humble pie in the second if necessary. I was put through to Larry Dooley, the senior sub-editor on duty, who laughed raucously when he heard my voice.

'Jesus, Beef!' Larry has a thin, squeaky voice and refers to the Deity more than any atheist I know. 'We've been waiting for you to call, you bastard. I've got a message somewhere here from the Chief. Hold on a second. Here it is.' He was always completely out of his tree by this time of night, and he slurred his words drunkenly as he read from the bit of paper in front of him. ' "Ask Beef Wellington where the fuck he's been all evening." Well, that sounds pretty clear. "Ask – Beef – Wellington – where – the –" '

'OK, Larry, I got it the first time. Listen, have you got a copy of the first edition in front of you?'

'Sure, Beef, sure.'

'Is there anything about Carter's speech?'

'Dunno. Who the hell's Carter?'

'Cut the crap, Larry.' The biggest pisshead on the paper, I thought grimly, and he's the one I have to get through to. I was seething with the intolerance the drunk always feel for the very drunk, but I gritted my teeth. 'He's a Cabinet Minister. There might be something about it on page two.'

'Oh *yes*. So there might.' There was a long wait as he ponderously turned over the first page. 'Let's see. "Bishop Blasts Video Nasties": that's not it. "Customs Swoop: Police Quiz Three": *that* can't be it. Ah, here we are. "Minister Challenges PM's Life." Jesus! What a bloody silly thing to do! Oh, it's *line*. "Minister Challenges PM's Line. Dissension surfaced in Government ranks last night when Cabinet Minister John Carter –" '

'That's enough, Larry.' I wiped my brow. The London staff had obviously got the story off the tapes and saved my bacon. I like people who save my bacon. 'Now turn to page five.'

'Page five, page five.' More protracted fumbling. 'Here it is. Page *five*. Jesus Christ!'

'What is it, Larry?'

'There's a piece here by someone called Beef Wellington. Is that you, Beef?'

'You know bloody well it's me, Larry. Now stop farting about for Christ's sake, and concentrate. Could you read out what I've put in the last sentence?'

'I am now reading out the last sentence. Ready? "I will be

106

amazed if the Government doesn't hold this seat by about 20,000 votes." Somebody, it seems, Beef, is going to be amazed if the Government –'

'Yes, Larry, I know. It was me.' I swore under my breath and stopped to think. I had filed my copy in the usual mad rush, so I couldn't remember the size of majority I had predicted. 20,000 sounded too high now, but it was too late to change and, if the result made me look a fool, it wouldn't be the first time. Carter's speech had been picked up, which was the main thing; even on a tabloid, it's more important to get the news stories right than the horoscopes. I thanked Larry, suggested he put his head under a cold tap and was about to hang up when he stopped me.

'By the way, Beef.'

'What is it, Larry?'

'You haven't answered the question.'

'What question?'

'Where the fuck have you been all evening?'

'Oh, that question. I'd forgotten.' I hesitated. If I was going to confide my adventures in anybody, it wasn't going to be Larry, but a bit of tail-twisting could no harm. 'Tell the Chief I was with a Dutch woman called Anna. She's a really classy bitch and she's very accomplished in bed.'

'No sweat, Beef?'

'No sweat, Larry.' Why are half-truths so much more fun than lies, I wondered as I hung up. That story would be round the paper twice before I got back to London.

I went upstairs to bed, but my brain was still so awake that I needed three more whiskies before falling asleep. I then had a colourful dream set in Amsterdam, in which I ate a lot of blackcurrant cheesecake and met Anna Wiseman in a funeral parlour. She was wearing a low-cut turquoise dress, but I don't remember any of the rest.

Mad Maggie woke me at half past eight. Maggie lived near the hotel and liked to harangue people in the street for worshipping Sex and Mammon rather than her own God, who was a good fellow, no doubt, but a little humourless. 'Re-*pent!*' she would scream. 'Re-*pent!* Yield to the flesh and die! Yield to the flesh and die!' She was in good voice that morning, so I looked out of the window to see who her audience was, and was surprised to see a trickle of people going into the municipal library on the other side of the street. This was Wopsley not Wittenberg, and I couldn't recall anyone using the facility before, so I was puzzled. Then I remembered it was polling day and this must be the local polling station. I gulped a quick Alka-seltzer and watched the spectacle for the next ten minutes.

Maggie was having a field day. I hadn't made a study of sexual practices in Wopsley, but the town's devotion to a pedestrian kind of Mammonism was obvious and Maggie's stinging rebukes brought a tinge of guilty red to the burghers' faces as they filed past. They were well wrapped up, in prosperous navy overcoats or brown donkey-jackets with mufflers, and their breath formed thick clouds in front of them in the morning air. It was too cold to loiter and they moved briskly, although without any urgency. Don't ask me how or why, but you can always tell voters who are merely dutiful from voters of the heart, driven to the ballot-box by raging indignation or enthusiasm. The latter have a purposefulness not shown by any of the people I watched trouping glumly into the library and glumly out again. They were discharging their civic responsibilities seriously but would be grateful, thank you very much, when all the excitement was over and they could go back to sleep.

'Do not vote for the fornicatress! Do *not* vote for the fornicatress!'

Maggie's wispy voice rose clearly above the rumble of traffic on the main road. Strange I thought, how eclectic some people's vocabularies are. To listen to her, you would think she was semi-illiterate, but she pronounced this word as meticulously as any television announcer. The fornicatress was Jill Appleby, I assumed, the candidate with the doubtful past who might or might not have had two concurrent affairs in Ibiza in 1980. I couldn't see her losing votes because of Maggie, but it

108

was nice to hear the important issues being debated right to the end. Apathy is the great enemy of democracy.

I pulled on my clothes, did a token shave and went down to breakfast. I can usually last through to lunch on a coffee and a few doughnuts, but I eat more when I'm stimulated or, for that matter, depressed, and this was one of those mornings – the stimulating ones, that is. I had to do some concentrated thinking, so I pinched the morning papers from the hotel lounge, ordered a cooked breakfast and set up shop at the table by the window. The sausages were cooked to perfection and I didn't stint on them.

Wopsley Decides, Wopsley Goes to the Polls, Wopsley Gives its Verdict. The papers all plugged the town's moment of glory in their own styles, but coverage was sparse and everyone uniformly predicted victory for Denver with a reduced majority. You could almost hear the correspondents yawning as they filed their copy. Carter's speech was mentioned only briefly, as these were the first editions and the heavyweight political analysts hadn't had time to decode his words and see if they amounted to anything. I flicked impatiently through the rest of the news, but read only about the pound doing badly on the foreign exchanges and a man with three ears making medical history in Belgium. West Ham had beaten Liverpool 3–0, with two goals in the last ten minutes, and a plumber in Ilford had predicted that the world would end in 2002 AD. That took me past retirement age, so I didn't finish the article but started planning my day.

In the words of those pompous police spokesmen on television, I had a murder inquiry on my hands. The unreal solemnity of the phrase accorded with my own sense of unreality ever since I had brushed Anna Wiseman's lipstick off my face ten hours before. I now wished I'd left it there, if only to prove that the evening had passed as I remembered and hadn't just been a hallucinatory trip by a drunken hack out of sorts with the world. Was there really a link between a dead man in Maidenhead and one of Her Majesty's Ministers and, if so, how could it be traced with any certainty nearly a year later? To get

109

to the bottom of it, I would have to establish motives and alibis, visit the scene of the crime with a magnifying-glass, hold slow, methodical conversations with slow, methodical policemen. It sounded hideously like hard work, with a sex-crazed emotional neurotic as my only accomplice, and I wouldn't have gambled on the off-chance of its being true if the stakes hadn't been so high. My wishful thinking was ludicrous and brought out the same naïveté in me as I found repugnant in Christopher, but one's own naïveté is more exhilarating than other people's and I indulged mine shamelessly.

A second interview with Mrs Wiseman seemed a good idea, so I rang the Crown only to find she had checked out. There was no way to contact her till she got back to Maidenhead, so I was forced back on my initiative. Then I remembered her little tease about Oxford, the suggestion of a skeleton rattling away at the back of Carter's cupboard which a clever journalist might unearth. She had trailed the story mysteriously, in that maddeningly offhand way of hers that hinted at a goldmine and so far seemed to lead to a potato-patch, but it could cost nothing to spend the day nosing around in Oxford. I could come back in the evening for the count, or go straight on to London if it didn't look like being worthwhile. At least it would get me out of Wopsley, which would be a thrill. I wolfed the rest of my breakfast with gusto, then checked out of the hotel.

'You'll have to push the seat right back,' said the man in the garage where I went to hire a car. 'No, *right* back. That's better.' He looked at me doubtfully, wedged tightly into the driving seat with the steering-wheel pressed against my stomach. 'Are you sure you wouldn't rather take a train, sir?'

'Quite sure, thank you. I'm used to driving a car not much bigger than this.'

I smiled jocularly, but didn't convince him. He was plainly a compassionate man, more concerned for my well-being than for the safety of his car. He ran through the hire costs in merciless detail, hoping to find something in them to deter me.

'Mileage is extra, of course.'

'That's quite all right.'

'And there's a deposit of £50 to pay.'

'Fine.'

'And an insurance surcharge.'

'Fine.'

'With VAT on almost everything, I'm afraid, sir.'

'That's fine.' It would have been a kindness to tell him I was on expenses, but the thought came too late and I was enjoying his manoeuvres too much. From my air of financial nonchalance, he must have thought I had money to throw away and eccentric habits to go with it. I could see him giving me a final once-over in the mirror as he shut the door gingerly after me and handed me the keys through the window.

'Drive carefully, sir.' I imagine he said it to every customer, but he invested the line with very special feeling. 'There'll be ice on the road, and you may run into some fog later in the day.'

'Thank you. I'll look out for it.'

I waved him goodbye and drove off slowly to reassure him. Then my sense of humour got the better of me and I stepped hard on the accelerator. I could see him holding his head in horror as I shot round the corner, and I grinned in the mirror as I slowed to a pace more conducive to digesting eggs, bacon, tomato, fried bread and sausages.

On the outskirts of the town, I passed another polling station, in a primary school. I'm an idle bugger but not quite as idle as I seem, because somewhere under the idleness is a conscientious attitude to work which sometimes horrifies me with its insistence. I'd had this by-election up to the gills, but I couldn't drive away without saying goodbye, so I stopped the car and did a final *vox pop* exercise. Of the three voters I talked to, one was for Denver, another for Jill Appleby, and a third for someone called Jameson. I couldn't think who this was, then remembered he was the pro-dogshit candidate and felt strangely reassured. He must have appealed to a rebellious element in Wopsley's character which wasn't normally visible, because the woman who had voted for him didn't seem at all one of nature's anarchists.

'I wouldn't have done it if I'd thought it was going to be close,' she confided in me. 'But people have to take a stand sometimes, don't they?'

'They certainly do.'

'There's far too much of it about, is what I say. If people don't stand up and be counted, where's it all going to stop?'

'Where indeed?'

'Dogs one week, people the next. And all because a few busybodies can't let other people get on with their lives in peace. Did you know that a man *kicked* a dog in Wopsley the other day? In Queen Mary Street, next to the Odeon. With hob-nailed boots and on a Sunday. It's worse than the Nazis.' She broke off and smiled, mistaking my easy journalist's sympathy for the real thing. 'You must be a dog-owner yourself. You look the doggy sort.'

'I'm afraid not, actually.'

'Ah.' She ran her eyes over me sorrowingly. 'I suppose it's the walking you find inconvenient?'

'Just a little.'

'You probably have a cat instead. *Such* beautiful animals.'

'I'm afraid –'

'You do surprise me. I thought you had to be a pet-owner from your eyes. Such gentle eyes you have. Has anyone ever told you?'

No, I would have had to say, nobody had told me, but she didn't wait for my answer. A bob of her head, a twirl of her umbrella, a 'Come on, Horace!' and she was gone, lumbering down the street with a reluctant cocker spaniel behind her. I watched her stride into a butcher's, then got back into the car and looked at my eyes in the driving-mirror. They were so far from gentle that I drove out of Wopsley wondering why it had kept its best joke till last.

11

From the other side of the mahogany desk, a wise old face confronted me.

'Were you an undergraduate at this university, Mr Wellington?'

'No, sir.'

'Or at any university?'

'No, sir. I'm a late developer.'

'A *very* late developer, Mr Wellington.'

'I know, sir, but one's never too old –'

'Oh please, Mr Wellington. Not that tiresome old cliché, I beg you. In my experience, people become too old to learn when they're about twenty-five. After that, the barriers of dogmatism are impervious to the most *elemental* forces of change.'

He smiled languidly, pleased with the polished aphorism with which he had sent my intellectual long-hop scurrying to the boundary, and adjusted his spectacles on his nose. He looked as if his own closest experience of the elements had been getting caught in the rain in Eights Week without an umbrella, but he mouthed the word lovingly, with the affection which the intellectual reserves for the primitive. His whole world was quite alien to me, but I was beginning to like the man.

Ask Dr Trumper, they had said at the lodge when I had tracked down Carter's old Oxford college and pretended I was doing a profile of him for a Sunday colour supplement. Ask Dr Trumper, because he was the senior history fellow and had been around since the year dot and would have taught Carter

113

history if that had been his subject, as I had assured them it had. Ask Dr Trumper but don't say you're a journalist, added the spotty undergraduate who had shown me to Trumper's rooms; say you're writing a book about the Middle Ages, and he'll talk to you for hours. So I was back to bluffing, and finding it uphill work. Dr Trumper's study was like a musty greenhouse and his air of condescension so demoralising that it froze the bluff smile from my face. His gimlet eyes bored right through me, and he addressed most of his remarks to some imaginary spot on the furthest wall.

'For a man who hasn't been able to benefit from higher education, it strikes me you are attempting something too ambitious, Mr Wellington. Wouldn't it be prudent to lower your sights a little? Some aspects of the Middle Ages have already been very thoroughly documented, while others are practically virgin territory, crying out for examination by a scholar of energy and imagination. A couple of years studying Paduan society in the 1150s would benefit you far more than a general prospectus. Have you read Mattock on Padua?'

'No, sir.'

'Intellectually jejune, I am afraid, but thorough, Mr Wellington, very thorough. Julian liked it, of course.'

'Of course.'

'He goes quite overboard about thorough books which don't require him to think. His enthusiasm suggests an obsession with facts for their own sake which is almost fetishistic. Don't you agree?'

'Absolutely.'

'Have you met Julian's sister, by the way? She has the misfortune to live in Gosport, and I fancy that Julian is rather ashamed of her, although he invited her to a garden party in Wadham last summer. A remarkably unsympathetic person, with large teeth and very small children. They seem to be permanently out of control.'

'The children?'

'No, the teeth. Will you take tea with me, Mr Wellington? There is a kettle on the table over there and some tea-bags in

114

that blue tin. You will find it a primitive brew, but I have never mastered the intricacies of a teapot.'

I had done it. An earnest manner, a few judicious sirs and an affected familiarity with someone called Julian, and I had been accepted without demur into the academic world. Like those in other worlds – the theatre, the clergy, the aristocracy – who find it easier to act out the popular caricature of themselves than escape it, Dr Trumper was everything I might have expected and more. The affectation of otherworldiness, the professional bitchiness, the intellectual certainty and hauteur, the trick of delivering perfectly formed sentences in a lazy, almost slangy manner, the slight veneer of camp; it was all there, just as tradition had prescribed, and I was grateful. It made my role-playing more excusable to be acting opposite a master of the university stage, and I almost relished the prospect of stalking him through the Middle Ages in search of Carter. I didn't realise how much I was outclassed.

'What will be the title of your *oeuvre*, Mr Wellington? Have you given the matter any thought?'

'I'm still trying to decide, sir. My publishers –'

'Publishers? You have publishers and you have not yet begun writing? A considerable piece of salemanship, if I may say so, Mr Wellington, but hadn't you better be careful? Suppose the publishers don't like what you've written when you've finished it?'

'They'll have to like it. They've given me an advance.'

'An advance too. Dear, dear.' His voice coarsened in timbre as he permitted himself a vulgarism. 'How much?'

'Two thousand pounds.'

'Two *thousand* pounds? How very –'

'They said they expect to sell 6,000 copies in hardback in the first six months.'

'Ah,' he said sniffily. 'A popular work. I was beginning to fear as much. They are paying you to make the Middle Ages accessible – no doubt that is the word they used – to a wider audience than we humble scholars can command. How very generous of them, and how very obliging of you.'

He looked at me disdainfully or, rather, he looked over my left shoulder disdainfully, and I thought I had blown it completely by my instinctive foray into the bottom end of the market. One look around the room should have warned me of the cultural chasm I was opening up, for none of the thousands of books on his shelves was brightly coloured or had its title blazoned on the cover in the big print of the block-buster. His dry, wizened face was suddenly as inaccessible as his dusty old books, and he sipped bleakly at his tea, all the animation of scholarship fled from his features. I could see that my lowering of the tone had made any discussion of the Middle Ages impossible, so I was grateful when he said, 'I suppose you're a journalist or something,' and I was able to confess my crime.

'We don't get many of those around here,' he said sadly. 'Of course, I should have guessed from your shirt.'

'My shirt?'

'No man of scholarship would wear a shirt that colour. Don't ask me why not. I suppose it's something to do with the reticence which comes with a lifetime's devotion to books. Is it tailor-made?'

'No.'

'You surprise me. I would have thought a man of your generous proportions would have had difficulty –' He tailed off, not fearing to give offence, but because his interest in the subject of my shirt was exhausted. Then he eased back into his chair and continued morosely sipping his tea. I had thought he was only sixty, but now realised he was much older. The lines on his face were very deep indeed and only his sharp, beady eyes had much mobility; the rest was tired, ossified, monumental. They talk of the serenity of old age, but you could see that this man had suffered and wasn't yet at peace. I wondered whether Julian had got some professorship he had wanted, or whether his wife nagged him about the gardening and didn't leave him in peace in his beloved Middle Ages.

'You must have taught hundreds of undergraduates in your time,' I said blandly, making the first cautious move in my inquiries. 'Do you ever wonder what becomes of them all?'

116

'One keeps in touch, Mr Wellington, one keeps in touch.' He strummed nervously on the table with his fingers. 'The world of historiography is a more closely knit community than you would imagine. John Caswell at Oriel was one of my first pupils, for example. Then there's Bellinger at Magdalen and McGovern at St Peter's. Bellinger has turned out a rather better historian than I expected and McGovern a rather worse one. His wife drinks, I believe, although I haven't seen her. Bellinger and I dine together on alternate Wednesdays during term. We have a common interest in early Flemish architecture, so it helps to exchange notes on a regular basis. One really does keep in touch, Mr Wellington. It's not just sentiment.'

'And the others?'

'Other universities? I have a most brilliant pupil at Cambridge at this very moment. He's studying medieval abattoirs.'

'No, I meant other professions. What happens to all the ones you teach who don't go on to become academics?'

'They make money mostly.' He snuffled again. 'A few come up in Eights Week with expensive-looking wives and wave at me from the quad. Then they shoot off back to London in fast cars. It's all a bit transitory.'

'Do any go into politics?'

'One or two. I discourage them, of course, but they still delude themselves they're doing something useful in the real world.'

'Do they do well in politics?'

'I've no idea, Mr Wellington. Today isn't my period.' He squirmed comfortably in his chair at his little joke. 'I'm far too busy to keep myself informed about all the absurd happenings in that rabbit-warren next to Westminster Bridge. Don't you find it all rather jejune? Is there still someone very important called the Lord Privy Seal?'

'I believe so.'

'And the – what is it? – Chancellor of the Duchy of Lancaster?'

'Yes.'

'How quaint. I do adore this country sometimes.' He chuckled long and deep, like a rusty carburettor, and I chuckled with him in a minor key as a good interviewer should. He noted my chuckles and nodded approvingly, so I chanced my arm with a direct question.

'Did you ever teach a man called John Carter?'

'John Carter? I may have done. It's quite a common name, I fear.'

'He had a friend called Peter Wiseman. I believe they both read history here in the late fifties.'

'Did they now?' I could see his mind travelling effortlessly back in time. What was twenty-five years to a medieval historian? To my excitement, a definite shadow of disapproval passed across his face when he reached the 1950s. 'Yes, I remember them. Carter got a first and Wiseman a good second. He did a very weak paper on the English Constitution and got all his dates in the fourteenth century muddled. They gave him a viva, but he had drunk an excess of fortified wine the night before and was frankly incoherent. I remember it well because I was one of the examiners that year. Whatever became of him, I wonder.'

'He died.'

'I'm so sorry. Drink?'

'No, a car accident.'

'You don't surprise me. It was probably a very fast car with an open roof. He always went through life in too much of a hurry. And Carter?'

'He's in the Cabinet.'

'Is he now? I suppose I must have read that somewhere and forgotten it. Politicians' names and faces have a way of thrusting themselves upon you, however much you try to shut them out. Does he still steal?'

'I'm sorry?'

'I said, does Mr Carter still steal?'

He blinked and looked at me quizzically, quite unaware of the thrill his words had caused me. At the lowest ebb of my expectations, when his ramblings had begun to irritate me and

118

I was sure my afternoon would be wasted, he had suddenly delivered. Not perhaps as spectacularly as Mrs Wiseman, but a hundred times more convincingly. The allegation of theft rang much truer than the story of a hit-and-run raid in a car, and I didn't find it incredible that a now respectable figure should have taken short cuts in his youth. I leant forward eagerly, waiting for Trumper to elaborate, when my chair suddenly collapsed underneath me. It had been creaking from the first and now disintegrated with pitiful finality. All four of its spindly wooden legs were fractured and the padded seat was completely pulverised, as if a steam-roller had been over it. I struggled to my feet and apologised, reaching into my wallet to make some payment in lieu of damages, but Trumper would have none of it.

'Please don't wave your money at me, Mr Wellington. I shall have my scout order a new chair from the Bursar, and that will be that. To make a man liable for his physical disabilities would be contrary to civilised practice, unless, of course, one accepted that there had been contributory negligence in your case.' He chuckled mischievously, enjoying my discomfiture hugely. 'Did I offer you a biscuit, by the way?'

'No, I don't believe you did.'

'Help yourself. They're in that tin next to the Gibbon. You may find that the ones with the chocolate coating are a little past their best. I've tried to finish them, but the palate is strangely resistent. Where were we? Oh, yes. The Middle Ages. The Middle *Ages*.'

'Weren't we talking –'

'The first thing you will have to decide, Mr Wellington, is when the Middle Ages actually started. A number of different dates have traditionally been given, but none of them seems to me entirely satisfactory because they isolate events of political significance from that much more important phenomenon, the emergence of the medieval *mind*. No doubt, even in your little pot-boiler, you will be devoting at least a chapter to this.'

'I –'

'The important thing to remember about medieval man is

119

his respect for a hierarchical notion of existence in which, rather like a pyramid – I apologise for the fusty simile, but your less gifted readers may find it a convenient point of reference – rather, as I say, like a pyramid –'

He was off. Before I could interrupt, it had become impossible to do so. To have burst in with a trivial question about a Cabinet Minister's criminal past would have been like farting during a performance of the *Ring* at Bayreuth. I wanted to do it badly, but the solemnity of time and place stifled my ambition and all I could do was listen. Trumper was in majestic form and I could have learnt more history in the next ten minutes than the rest of my life if I'd been able to concentrate, which I wasn't. My mind was racing with historical speculations of its own, and I had to think desperately how to get him back on my wave length. He was still discussing something that happened seven hundred years before the period I was interested in, when a rare brainwave found its way into my head. With a sweeping movement of my right arm, I knocked my teacup on to the floor.

There was a brief period of mayhem. Trumper scowled at me, implying that a chair *and* a teacup made excessive demands of his tolerance, then panicked as he saw a thin stream of tea trickling across the carpet towards a dusty old manuscript by the fireplace. By the time tragedy had been averted and the tea mopped up, his hands were trembling uncontrollably and he stuffed them into his jacket pocket out of harm's way. When he finally calmed down and said 'Where were we?' again, I leapt on my cue like a tiger.

'Carter. John Carter, the Cabinet Minister. A former pupil of yours. You said something interesting about him stealing.'

'Did I? How mystifying.' He didn't sound remotely mystified and, as his face creased in thought, I had a sinking feeling he was back in Chartres in 1239. But I had underestimated him.

'It was a strange business,' he said. 'Nobody ever found out the whole story. Carter was the ringleader, I remember that, and this man Wiseman was his main accomplice. He later died in a car accident. Did you know that?'

'I think someone may have told me.'

'There were two others involved, but I don't remember their names. One of them had red hair and took a third in Greats. The other was a rowing blue. Or was it cricket? I can't honestly remember.'

'What happened exactly?'

'One of the oldest rackets in Oxford, I'm afraid, Mr Wellington. You won't find a college where it hasn't happened, although this was one of the worst examples. Provost Wilberforce never got over it. He started drinking port heavily before lunch and was passed over for the vice-Chancellorship, which was a minor tragedy for the university. Dawson wasn't a man of the same calibre at all. He was a gifted administrator – everyone acknowledged that – but he didn't have Wilberforce's almost reverent attitude to scholarship. Did you know that in 1964, when I was Dean of Degrees –'

'Tell me exactly what happened with Carter,' I said firmly, sensing that this might be my last chance to pin him down. 'From the beginning.'

He sighed sacrificially at having to abandon a favourite anecdote, and muttered 'Very well' into his tea. Then, to my surprise, he did tell me the story from the beginning, without embellishment or digression. I could imagine his history books being filled with passages like this, quick canters through the facts before the more leisurely business of analysis and interpretation, and his lucidity impressed me after the earlier discursiveness.

'1959 was a very important year for the college,' he began. 'It was our quincentenary and major celebrations were planned, including a Commemoration Ball. Carter, Wiseman and the others formed a Ball Committee, on which I sat as Senior Member. I wasn't able to attend many of the meetings, unfortunately, as I was finishing my *Medieval Monasticism*, but I had the impression that everything was being competently administered. Carter was Chairman and Wiseman was Treasurer. The other two knew a lot about wines and spent a great deal of time trying to lure the best bands up from London.

121

The arrangements all seemed satisfactory and the Ball itself was a triumph. The weather was almost indecently perfect and everyone agreed that it was the best organised Ball the college had ever had. Then the bills started coming in. Do you have any knowledge of accountancy, Mr Wellington?'

'I'm afraid not.'

'Neither do I. That was my undoing. I should have insisted on a much more rigorous system of auditing from the beginning, but I was too trusting. The Bursar was really shocked when he was called in later to examine the books. He couldn't believe that the whole thing had been handled in such a slipshod way, and it was he who first suspected that a serious act of theft had taken place. There is a charming euphemism people use to describe such practices.'

'Embezzlement?'

'That's right, Mr Wellington. Embezzlement. Money had been embezzled and the college, in the vulgar modern parlance, "ripped off".' He took out a handkerchief and dabbed his forehead. Was it the crime against the college which made him sweat, I wondered, or the crime against the language? 'It was cunningly done, of course, but the Bursar was quite convinced of his case. He got very excited, I remember, about something called a double book entry. A lot of the evidence was purely circumstantial, because there had been many cash transactions of which no receipts were kept, but there was one small slip down in black and white which the Bursar regarded as prima facie incriminating. He said as much in his report to the Provost.'

'What did the Provost do?'

'What could he do? The Bursar's evidence, though generally convincing, was by no means watertight. A scholar as renowned for his intellectual rigour as Wilberforce couldn't possibly accept it as *proof*. He was also in a difficult position personally, because Wiseman's father had been a friend of his at Cambridge. It was extremely delicate, so he handled the matter in the most discreet way possible. He summoned the members of the Ball Committee into his study on a Sunday

122

morning and laid his case before them. He said that the manner in which the Ball's accounts had been handled had been most unsatisfactory, and that the Bursar had been asked to look into the matter and make a confidential report to him. He repeated the Bursar's conclusion that the college had been cheated of an estimated £800 – a lot of money in those days – and that the principal suspects were the members of the Ball Committee. In view of the lack of sufficient proof, the Provost said he wasn't in a position to take disciplinary action, but that he regarded it as morally incumbent on the undergraduates concerned to make reparation to the college, if indeed they were guilty of what they had been accused. What do you think happened?'

'If he simply appealed to their moral decency, nothing.'

'Right, Mr Wellington, right. Your cynicism about human nature is warranted. Or is it?' His eyes twinkled with pleasure as he teased me, and I could see that he had warmed to his story utterly. It was hard to believe that I had had such trouble coaxing it out of him, or that it had lain buried in his memory for so long, whole strata below those other stories about an earlier and better age.

'The Ball episode passed off with mercifully little publicity from the college's point of view, although it left an extremely bad aftertaste, as you can imagine. Poor Wilberforce started hitting the bottle only six months later. Then, in 1968, the college launched an Appeal for its new library. People gave rather sparingly at first, but then there were some larger donations, one of the most generous of all coming from Mr Carter himself, who gave £470. Does anything about the sum strike you as unusual?'

'It's not very round. He might have stretched it to £500 or left it at £450.'

'Exactly. I was Chairman of the Appeal Committee, and the same point struck me. I remembered the Ball episode, of course, so I did a few small calculations of my own. I took £800, the sum, you remember, which the Bursar claimed had been embezzled in 1959, and I divided it by four because there had been four members of the Ball Committee under suspicion.

That gave me £200. I then calculated what £200 in 1959 would have been worth in 1968, using the annual rates of inflation reported in the financial press. And what do you think the answer was?'

'£470?'

'Not quite, Mr Wellington. That would have been too much to expect. The exact answer was £468. If Mr Carter had used the same calculations as me, he must have rounded the sum up, which was kind of him. It's a good story, don't you think?'

'Extremely.'

'You were wrong to be cynical about human nature, Mr Wellington. Provost Wilberforce's appeals to moral decency didn't fall on completely deaf ears. It was ironic, however, that by his very act of reparation Mr Carter should have given me conclusive proof of his guilt. The figures were much too close to be coincidental.'

He stopped and sank an inch deeper into his armchair, satisfied with a good story well told. For the last five minutes, he had kept me riveted to my seat and I was breathing heavily with excitement. I hadn't a clue how to exploit the story and wasn't convinced that Carter emerged from it in disgrace, but journalists' blood-pressure always rockets when they discover that politicians are fallible, however unsurprising the discovery ought to be.

'Did you tell anyone about this?' I asked quickly.

'Certainly not. It was a private matter.'

'So nobody else knows the complete story?'

'Nobody. Except you now, of course.' He looked at me suspiciously. 'I do hope you're not one of *those* journalists, Mr Wellington.'

'What do you mean?'

'The sort of journalist who thinks he's doing everyone a service by washing dirty linen in public. I don't read the newspapers myself, but my friends tell me that kind of journalism has reached epidemic proportions in this country. It's an American import, no doubt, like sex.'

I smiled at the joke, but didn't confirm or deny that I was one

124

of those journalists. His contempt would have been withering if I'd admitted the fact, while I was reluctant to lie to him after the rich pickings he had given me. His story carried complete conviction, particularly in the light of one further fact of which he was unaware. 1968 was the year in which Carter had entered Parliament. What better moment than the beginning of your public career to assuage any awkward ghosts from the past?

'I've enjoyed our little chat about the Middle Ages,' Dr Trumper said when we parted five minutes later and the story of the Centenary Ball Committee had disappeared back into the basement of his memory. 'You must send me your manuscript before you submit it to the publisher's and I'll be happy to run an eye over it. Accuracy obviously isn't as crucial in a popular work as in a work of scholarship, but it would sadden my declining years to see some of the wilder misconceptions which have arisen about the Middle Ages being spoon-fed to the public at large. Take my advice and try to look at the spiritual life of the period before examining the architecture. Approaching it the other way round can be fatal. Carey tried it, but we know all about *his* book, don't we?'

'Absolutely. Barking up quite the wrong tree.'

'Oh, I don't think *barking*, Mr Wellington. Whimpering would be a better word, I think. *Whimpering* up the wrong tree. Don't you agree?'

'Absolutely.'

'Jolly good.'

He patted me on the back, then, just as I was opening the door to leave, ran his spidery fingers along the top bookshelf and pulled down a large, crumbling tome. He brushed a thin layer of dust off the top and handed it to me.

'*Medieval Monasticism*, Mr Wellington. The first edition. I'd like you to have it as a small memento of our meeting. You might find its conclusions a bit extravagant, but all the evidence is there and you can reach your own judgments.'

I stammered my thanks, feeling the emaciated man inside me shrivel up with embarrassment, and was turning to leave when Dr Trumper snuffled again and I knew he was thinking

125

about money.

'They gave me a £20 advance and printed 500 copies,' he said wistfully, before adding with a fierce gleam in his eyes: 'It's the definitive work on the subject.'

12

Outside in the quadrangle, everything was quiet. Darkness had descended while I had been talking to Dr Trumper, and the curtains of the ground floor windows had been pulled shut. A few undergraduates bustled past and shouted greetings to each other, but it was too cold to dawdle and they soon disappeared up their staircases to their rooms, from where fragments of precocious conversation drifted through the college and reverberated gently off the grey stone walls. It didn't seem like a community where secrets could survive for long, but you realised instinctively that those walls did hold their secrets, and murkier secrets than Carter's. The sense of profane history – of countless centuries of dirty work at the crossroads, of whole generations of men and women taking short cuts to get what they wanted, of lying and cheating and killing since the dawn of time – was briefly so sobering that I didn't feel as elated at my afternoon's detective-work as I might have done. Yes, I thought, I had got my man; but will anyone read about it in seven hundred years' time, as Dr Trumper reads about those fallible old monks in the thirteenth century?

I say the quad was quiet, but a sudden spurt of activity did catch my eye. As I made my way round the right angle of the quad, I noticed someone darting hurriedly up the next staircase to avoid me. Fat people encounter cold shoulders daily, but this seemed an extreme reaction and made me suspicious. I squinted up the staircase as I passed but couldn't see anyone, so I walked slowly along to the next staircase and hid in the doorway, waiting to see if I would be followed. About ten

127

seconds passed, then I heard stealthy footsteps approaching from the direction in which I had just come. When they got closer, I stepped out to confront my pursuer and was flabbergasted to find it was Christopher. He reacted as guiltily as a shop-lifter caught stuffing Mars bars into his pocket, and his attempt to sound casual was farcical.

'You,' he said simply, his cheeks assuming an almost ghostly pallor. 'What a fantastic coincidence!'

'Fantastic.'

'I'm just in Oxford for the day visiting an old friend.'

'How agreeable.'

'Called Smith.' Come on, Chris, I thought, pitying his ineptness, you can do better than that. 'John Smith. He's a philosophy don here. How about you?'

'Oh, I'm just pursuing some private researches,' I said airily. 'One misses the academic world in London, don't you find? I've developed a passionate interest in the early Cistercians and I've just been checking some footnotes for an article in the *History Quarterly.*'

'Come off it, John,' he snapped, irritated by my sarcasm and guessing that I had seen through his own lies. I could have put him out of his grief straight away but, when you hold all the cards, it's tempting to play them in the most humiliating way, so I calmly produced my copy of *Medieval Monasticism* and watched with glee as his mouth fell open in amazement. He stared at me in awe, half hoping my absurd fabrication might be true and half terrified that I was just playing some ruthless game, the professional liar outclassing the amateur by his judicious use of props.

'Come off it yourself, Christopher,' I said softly, when I saw he was out for the count. 'You've been following me, you sly bastard, and I want to hear all about it. Have you had tea?'

'No.'

'Then let's go get some.'

We made our way out of the college into the street, pausing only while I humiliated Christopher more by questioning the porter. ('John Smith? No, sir, you must be mistaken. The

128

philosophy tutor is called Grumbleweed. A logical positivist? I wouldn't know, sir. Related to Percy Grumbleweed at Wadham? Not that I'm aware, sir.') Then we looked for somewhere to sit down and talk. The best we could find was a student dive near the High Street, but we squeezed through a bubbling throng of undergraduates to a table. They stared wonderingly at my unusual physique and I heard one girl whisper '*He* can't be a first year!' to her companion, a lugubrious youth in black who looked eighteen going on eighty himself. I growled quietly, but had no idea how to fade into such a background; my only refuge was to cling on to *Medieval Monasticism* and seek acceptance as an eccentric don. Christopher was even less at ease than me. He stirred his tea miserably for nearly a minute, and refused to join me in a Black Forest cherry cake, looking enviously at mine instead.

'How did Carter know I was coming to Oxford?' I asked. There was no point in wasting time. I was ninety-nine per cent sure Christopher was following me because Carter had asked him to and, if I pretended I knew more than I did, it might prompt him into indiscretions.

'He didn't,' he replied. 'He didn't know where you were going. I've been following you since first thing this morning.'

'Are you being serious?'

'Perfectly.' He had the grace to blush, but there was a definite relish in the accuracy of his report, which made me suspect he had spotted trains as a boy. It would explain half his problems if it was true. 'You left your hotel at a quarter to ten and walked to a garage near the station, where you hired a car. I nearly lost you, you drove off so quickly. Then you stopped at a polling-station on the road out of Wopsley. Then you –'

'OK, Chris, I believe you.' I stopped him in mid-sentence and tried to get a grip on the situation. He couldn't possibly have made all this up, but my sense of unreality mounted the more corroborative evidence he produced. Members of Parliament, you see, are perfectly normal people. Sometimes they're so normal it's worrying, and at other times their normality transmutes itself into common sense of exhilarating

129

sanity. Now Christopher, of course, wasn't normal in quite the same way, and I had quickly stumbled on that crazy obsession with Carter which seemed to distort all his perceptions about everything. I had always assumed, though, that the obsession would be governed by prescribed limits of behaviour, that, if you like, it was a normal obsession. If Christopher had reached the stage where he was prepared to tail me clandestinely across the country because his political master told him to, then my assumption was wrong. I was dealing with a certifiable lunatic, so I pleaded with him in the rough-gentle way which laymen use to handle insanity.

'Doesn't it strike you as rather ridiculous spending your day like this, Christopher? You're a Member of Parliament, not a plain-clothes policeman. Just because you're Carter's PPS, it doesn't mean you have to do everything he tells you, however ludicrous. Did he explain *why* he wanted you to follow me?'

'Not exactly. It all came up quite suddenly last night. After his speech in the Town Hall, he stopped off to have a drink with the Wopsley party chairman in a hotel near the centre. Is anything wrong?'

I suppressed my smile with difficulty. 'No, carry on.'

'As we were driving away from the hotel, he suddenly looked in the mirror and said, "That's funny!" He had seen you coming out of the hotel after him, I think. Did you do that?'

'Yes,' I growled, wishing I had been more circumspect. 'And after that he put two and two together and told you to find out what I was up to – right?'

'Yes.'

'Did he tell you why he was getting his knickers in a twist about me?'

'Not in so many words. He said –'

'Yes?'

'He said you were dangerous and were trying to destroy him.'

'Come on, Chris, do I *look* dangerous?'

He studied me closely, taking my question at its most literal value. 'I don't know,' he said at last. 'You're not dangerous in

130

the sense of being violent, but you may be dangerous in other ways. You're a journalist and you see things differently from us.'

'Isn't that the way it should be?'

'Yes and no.' He paused while the young couple at the next able got up and squeezed past us. Then he launched a timid little counter-attack. 'You destroy people's reputations sometimes for no good reason, just for the sake of a good story or a boost in circulation. I'm not saying it's deliberate, but the media can be very irresponsible sometimes. Everyone knows that.'

'I quite agree, Chris. I know it too.' His smug sermonising was repulsive, but I couldn't be bothered to take issue. 'And you think I'm being irresponsible now?'

'I just don't know,' he said in a small voice. 'I'm completely in the dark, aren't I?'

'I suppose you are. It's rather unfair of Carter to leave you there, don't you think?'

'Well, I –'

'If he's going to have you panting round the West Midlands like an oversexed bloodhound, he might at least take you into his confidence.'

'He's a very busy man.'

'Balls. He could tell you in five minutes.'

'And he's got to be discreet.' He looked at me appealingly, like a schoolboy trying to coax the more arcane facts of life out of his older brother. 'I don't suppose that you, John –'

'No, I couldn't,' I snapped. 'You'll have to find out for yourself.'

We were deadlocked, so we scuttled back into our corners and sat there in silence, as ill at ease with each other as with our environment. Around us, the timeless drama of student life was playing itself earnestly out, a comedy masquerading as a tragedy. At the next table, a boy with a loud voice was telling a boy with a less loud voice why his argument was hopelessly flawed, and beyond them I could see, without hearing a word, a boy telling a girl he would kill himself if they didn't sleep

131

together and the girl saying she would kill herself if they did. French films were being eulogised, American ones disparaged. A girl of nineteen was telling a friend how old she felt, and a boy with red hair announced that he found party politics ersatz. The whirl of buzz-words and hyped-up emotion hardly impinged on my own sour thoughts, but I couldn't help reflecting that Christopher must have been a student himself less than ten years before. It was easy to imagine him chattering half-baked nonsense with this sort of crowd; but by what miracle of insularity had he passed through his student phase and ended up more adolescent than he started?

'Just listen, Chris,' I said bitterly. 'You've made a bloody fool of yourself today and you'll go on making a bloody fool of yourself until you've got rid of this obsessive notion that Carter's the Messiah. I'm not going to tell you what this is all about. You'll have to find out for yourself or ask Carter. He won't tell you, of course, because he's like that, but you should get a reaction out of him if you simply tell him what you know. Just say that you've talked to me, that I've had an instructive afternoon with Dr Trumper and that I'm going on to Maidenhead this evening. If that doesn't bring a flicker of interest to his shifty little face, then nothing else will. Now piss off. I want to be alone.'

They were the most brutal words we had ever exchanged, and they had the desired effect. I could see angry retorts forming on Christopher's lips, but he wisely left them unsaid and stumbled out of the room like a jilted lover. That must have been the impression given to the world at large because the girl with the suicidal boyfriend, who had just told him to piss off as well, winked at me sympathetically across the room. I winked back and had a fleeting impulse to buy her a piece of chocolate cake, listen to her problems and give her some cynical advice for nothing. But time was running short, so I paid up and left. When you've made a threat, it's occasionally worth carrying it out, so I returned to my car, tore up the parking ticket on the windscreen and set off for Maidenhead.

132

13

'Wopsley' (crackle) 'low turn out' (crackle) 'possible upset' (crackle). The car radio performed badly and left me guessing what had happened in that town of all the talents. From the prominence given to the bulletin, my estimate of a 20,000 majority for Denver was absurdly high, but I was past caring. I had the smell of dirt in my nostrils and nothing makes a journalist happier. I whistled as I drove and made faces at the other drivers, like a teenager on his first unsupervised drive after passing his test.

My visit to Oxford had gone well, amazingly well. Dr Trumper's rambling memory had come to rest in the right spot for just long enough and not even Christopher's comi-tragic appearance could take the gilt off my gingerbread. It left a nasty taste in the mouth, as encounters with mixed-up adolescents always do, but it also proved that Carter was running scared. Why else should a Cabinet Minister send his PPS haring round the country like a demented husband chasing his wife's lover? I was winning and winning big and could take my winnings to the bank before the year was out. The paperback rights alone would be worth hundreds of thousands and, if I could devise a decent final reel, the film would be a sensation. Dirk Bogarde could play Carter and someone just out of drama school Christopher. If Central Casting was stuck, I could play the hero myself. It was fun just thinking about it.

I stopped in Henley for an early evening snack and made a call from a telephone box. The line was poor, but I recognised

Anna Wiseman's slight Dutch accent before she identified herself. She wasn't too thrilled to hear from me again so soon, but I blundered in confidently. 'Can I come round and see you this evening?'

'If you insist, Mr Wellington. I'll be out till nine o'clock, but –'

'I'll come at half past. I've been in Oxford all day.'

'Oxford? Why Oxford?'

'Don't you remember? You told me there was a skeleton in the cupboard there, and I found it.'

'What are you talking about, Mr Wellington?' There was a pause while she tried to remember what significance Oxford could have. It was she who had given me the lead, but she obviously regarded the incident as too trivial to get excited about. 'Oh, *that* skeleton. I'm with you. How clever to find it so quickly. It's amusing, isn't it?'

'That's one way of putting it.'

'Like two naughty schoolboys stealing apples and getting away with it. Peter always laughed about it later when he and John were together, but John was a bit more nervous. He can be very shifty sometimes, like all politicians. His eyes –'

'Exactly. By the way, did the Maidenhead police make any inquiries about your husband's death?'

'Of course. There was a lot of concern about it locally.'

'Who was in charge of the investigations? Do you remember?'

'Yes, I remember him well. He had a sad face, with a little moustache, and he wasn't very energetic. His name was Inspector Popplewell, I think. There was something very feminine about his hands, because he never –'

'Thank you, Mrs Wiseman. I'll see you at nine-thirty.'

I hung up, glad to have kept the conversation to essentials, and returned to the car. I was at Maidenhead police station before seven and caught Popplewell just as he was leaving.

'You might have come earlier,' he said glumly, showing me into his cramped, functional office. 'We got a bollocking from the Chief last week for our public relations, so we've got to make

134

ourselves available to you chaps night and day. Wednesdays I don't mind, but Thursdays is steak and Beryl fusses.'

'I won't keep you long, Mr Popplewell.'

'Keep me as long as you bloody well like.' He shrugged his shoulders with a martyr's abandon. 'If the Chief wants better PR, it's not for the likes of me to argue the toss. Do you mind if I make a quick call? Beryl fusses.' He dialled a number with his pencil, fumbled over the last digit and had to start again. I tried to be unobtrusive by staring out of the window at the drab row of shops on the other side of the street, but I heard Beryl fussing as promised and Popplewell trying to pacify her by referring to me as 'a gentleman from the national Press'. The pomposity worked, because the tone of the conversation suddenly softened and Popplewell put the receiver down with the satisfied grunt of a husband who has put his wife in her place.

'Now, Mr Wellington. What can I do for you?'

'It's the Wiseman case.'

'I thought it might be.' He took out a cigarette-packet and offered me one, but I refused. 'You chaps never seem interested in our successes. All you want to hear about is the failures. Isn't that right?'

'Maybe, Inspector, maybe. Success we take for granted, but the failures can be very disturbing. It's the public as well, of course.'

'Of course.'

'It's our job to make sure they're given all the relevant facts.'

'Of course. I wasn't being personal, you understand.'

'Quite so.' I took a breath and plunged in. How easily the jargon of one's trade drops off the tongue after thirty years! Now that I had staked out a respectable philosophical position, clothing myself in the unlikely garb of citizens' friend, I could trade in particulars without causing suspicion. 'Peter Wiseman died on 8 May last year. Is that correct?'

'Correct. It was a Wednesday.'

'He was knocked over by a car while out walking his dog.'

'Yes, sir.'

'But the driver of the car never came forward?'

'No, sir.'

'Did that strike you as suspicious at all?'

'Unusual certainly, but not suspicious.' He shrugged and covered a yawn with the end of his pencil. 'If the man had been drunk, after all, he'd have been up on a manslaughter charge, so it wouldn't necessarily have been in his interests to come forward. I'm afraid it happens quite often.'

'Is that the official explanation, then? That a drunk was responsible?'

'No indeed, sir. You mustn't quote me as saying that.' He ran his pencil nervously through his moustache. 'There is no official explanation as such. We still have an open mind on the case although, for practical reasons, we have more or less had to abandon it.'

'The practical reasons being what?'

'Resources, sir. And lack of evidence. The usual story. The road surface was wet, so there were no tyre-marks or anything like that, and no eye-witnesses came forward. It's a quiet stretch of road, with no houses in the vicinity, and although we traced one or two cars that passed there at the right sort of time, there were no suspicious circumstances.'

'I see.'

'The reason we inclined to the view that a drunken driver must have been involved was the position of the body. Mr Wiseman had been walking facing the oncoming traffic, as the Highway Code recommends where there is no pavement, but the forensic evidence showed that he had been knocked down by a car coming from behind him.'

'So the driver must have swerved right across the road?'

'Exactly, sir. And, although the road was wet, it seemed to us that an excess of alcohol in the driver's bloodstream –'

'Or deliberate intent.'

'I'm sorry, sir?'

'I said "or deliberate intent". Mr Wiseman might have been murdered.'

'It's possible, sir.' His face grew greyer but more relaxed, as if he had already guessed where my questions were leading and

136

was relieved that the crisis-point had been reached. 'I rather thought you would use that word sooner or later. You gentlemen from the national Press don't usually come this far out of town if it's only a case of manslaughter. So be it, Mr Wellington, so be it. But let me assure you straight off that the possibility of murder was immediately recognised by us and the appropriate inquiries made.'

'Well?'

'Nothing, sir. Absolutely nothing. Apart from the fact that it would appear to be a very chancy way of killing somebody, there simply wasn't a motive we could lay our hands on. We did a routine check on his wife, but she had a reasonable alibi and nobody else seemed a plausible suspect. He was said to be a very pleasant gentleman, was Mr Wiseman, with no real enemies and some well-connected friends, as it happens. There were more than 150 at his funeral, including some whose faces one recognised without quite being able to put names to them. You know the sort of people I mean.'

'Yes indeed, Inspector.' I couldn't have described Carter better myself. No doubt he had been there in the crowd, grieving in the restrained way which English public figures tend to adopt and concealing, maybe, his own guilt. Popplewell hadn't yet convinced me one way or the other. A drunken driver might well be the explanation but, equally, someone who knew Wiseman's walking habits and wanted to murder him in a way that would look like an accident couldn't have done a neater job. If anything, the big swerve across the road pointed to murder rather than drunken driving, because a murderer would have deliberately approached his victim from behind, while a drunk who lurched yards off course probably couldn't have finished his journey safely. I put this point to the Inspector and he chewed it over for a minute or two, more out of politeness than any faith in my reasoning.

'You can never tell with drinkers,' he said pensively, pleased at the chance to throw in some professional know-how. 'We did a man on the M4 once who'd driven 65 miles with 480 milligrams of the stuff inside him. That's six times the limit. We thought we'd made a mistake with the equipment, but the blood-tests confirmed it.'

'Very interesting, Inspector. But was that man lurching from one side of the road to the other?'

'No, he was speeding. That's why we stopped him.'

'Well then.'

'Well what?'

'Well everything. The question isn't whether a drunken man can control his car, but whether a drunk who obviously *can't* control his car because he's driving all over the shop can drive very much further after doing a swerve like that.'

'I dare say you're right, Mr Wellington,' he said in a mechanical voice, rejecting my argument as too complicated to follow. The vigour of my questioning was disconcerting him and he countered it with flat-footed defence, searching lethargically for means of tempering my excitement. He stifled a second yawn and made an alternative suggestion. 'Man may have just nodded off at the wheel, of course. Happens all the time.'

'It's possible.'

'If he'd been feeling tired and loosened his grip on the wheel, the car could have shot across the road in no time in that rain.'

'It's possible.'

'Well there you are.' He pounced on my concession gratefully, as if it meant I accepted his whole argument, and offered me another cigarette, forgetting I had refused the first one. Then his face worked itself up into a smile and, afraid of seeming graceless or uncooperative, he attempted geniality. 'Do you mind my asking what your interest in all this is, Mr Wellington? The case has been stone cold at this end for six months now. What brings a gentleman like yourself down from Fleet Street to nose about, if you'll forgive the expression?'

'I was asked to make a few inquiries by a friend of Mr Wiseman's,' I said slowly. I can usually make up extravagant stories without difficulty, but this wasn't the place to go overboard, with police cells in the vicinity and a pair of handcuffs sitting snugly in Inspector Popplewell's top drawer, if the television series were to be believed. I didn't want to bother him with the whole truth, because he was a busy man and had his wife to get home to, but I stuck carefully to the truth. 'He – she was never convinced by this hypothetical drunken driver and suspects foul play.'

Popplewell raised his eyebrows. I would like to say they shot up, but he was not an energetic man, as Mrs Wiseman had warned me, and he used the moving parts of his face sparingly. 'Of whom does she suspect it, Mr Wellington? It would be helpful if the police were told these things.'

'I dare say it would, Inspector.' I hesitated. 'The lady's suspicions are only vague ones, unfortunately. It would be quite improper for me to pass them on gratuitously without her permission.'

'Can't see why,' said Popplewell gloomily. 'We are capable of respecting confidences in the Force, you know. That's what Joe Public doesn't always understand, Mr Wellington, and I'm afraid the media must take some of the blame for that, without wanting to be personal. People won't come forward with vital evidence any more because they don't trust the police to handle it with sensitivity and discretion. I'm not saying we're any better human beings than other people, because we're not, believe me, but don't you feel that we deserve a fair crack of the whip sometimes?'

I nodded cautiously, wondering why such a gentle man should use such an ungentle metaphor, and had to listen to more sad reflections on the diminished prestige of the police in society. He seemed to forget that I was a member of an untrustworthy profession and appealed to me as a fellow has-been, someone who had seen better days and was bound to agree that the world was going to the dogs. He wasn't entirely right – my own view is that the world went to the dogs some time ago – but I was glad the conversation had drifted into generalities, as I now stood to lose more from his questions than I could gain from my own. Five minutes later, we parted amicably.

'It's been nice talking to you, Mr Wellington,' he said as we shook hands. 'I don't care too much for some members of your profession, but you seem more sympathetic than the general run, if I may say so. It's satisfying to get a bit of PR under one's belt before going home at night. Beryl will understand. She's a social worker.'

It was a strange exit-line, but he had driven off in his Ford Cortina before its strangeness struck me.

14

Anna Wiseman looked puzzled. 'Why did he say his wife was a social worker?'

'I've no idea. Probably because they're good at handling people's problems. From his point of view, journalists are one hell of a problem. We're like drug-pushers: people get hooked on what we sell them, but they hate us for ignoring moral values. And they're right. We don't really have moral values; we just strut about and throw nuts at people like baboons.'

'Poor Mr Wellington. You're in the wrong profession. You should be a dentist.'

'Why a dentist, for Christ's sake?'

'I don't know. Something about your face. Have some more wine.'

She stretched her long slender arm across the table and replenished my glass with the solicitous air of a nurse dispensing Lucozade. Half the time she was just exasperating, but when she was good, she was very, very good and she was at her best right then. She had welcomed me more like an old friend than an ageing hack with whom she had once gossiped about murder in a provincial hotel bedroom, and had fed me royally, a large steak followed by Dutch apple tart, with raisins and whipped cream. I like women like that.

Over coffee, as I had feared, she did become a bit less good and started talking about love. She tried – God, she tried – to interest me in the distinction between loving and being in love, and between falling in love by accident and falling in love deliberately. She described how sex altered love and how love altered sex and recounted, in great physiological and psychological detail, something strange she had once experienced in an aeroplane over the Pacific. Her amorous *tour d'horizon* took in Paris and Vienna, Nassau and New York, and if my eyes stayed open it was only because of the mesmerising gleam that issued from hers as she talked. I wished I was still in Trumper's or Popplewell's cut-and-dried world and could have said 'It's not my subject, Mrs Wiseman; I've finished a thesis on theft and am researching in murder', but I listened politely and waited until Carter entered the conversation, as I was certain he would, before interposing questions. As she talked, my eyes wandered round the room and I realised that her husband hadn't just been rich, but seriously rich, with expensive tastes to go with it. Like the faces Inspector Popplewell had seen at Peter Wiseman's funeral, the paintings on the walls were by artists one recognised without remembering their names, and the furniture oozed affluence at every mahogany pore. If I broke one of these chairs I'd need to take out an overdraft to replace it. I sat on the sofa instead.

'There was something about him in the news today,' she said suddenly, not bothering to say who 'he' was. She had just been saying how love made her eat less and I had been thinking how ludicrous of her to get things so out of perspective, so the connection wasn't obvious, if there was one. 'He said something indiscreet in his speech last night, I think. Did you know that? They said he might be forced to resign: can that be true?'

I shook my head. 'No way. They always say it might happen, but it never does.'

'Why not?'

'It would look bad for the Government.'

'Then why do they say it will happen?'

'Because they want the Government to look bad.'

'You're teasing me, Mr Wellington.'

'No, I'm not.' It was a lie because I was teasing her, partly to snap her out of her romantic groove, partly to get her to think politically for a change. ' "They" are two different sets of people, you see: the Government and the media, hacks like me.

142

Their interests are totally different. It's what we call a them-and-us situation, like football.'

'And John is the ball in this little game, I suppose?'

'Right,' I said with a grin. 'I couldn't have put it better myself.'

'How bloody silly!' Her tone was really bitter, less a snort than a savage snort, the kind an angry rhinoceros might produce if its mate started sleeping around. It suddenly struck me that, if she found the political scene as banal as I found her romantic dream-world, there must indeed be something infuriating in the way Carter had relegated her to second place. She could have understood sharing him with another woman, but sharing him with red despatch-boxes and Cabinet sub-committees and Parliamentary Questions must have been cruel beyond description. Somewhere inside Beef Wellington the tough guy and Beef Wellington the jovial alcoholic is a much softer soul and, as I felt something stirring in this marshmallow centre and realised it couldn't just be the wine, I reached across and took her hand in mine. She was startled but didn't retract it.

'Poor Anna,' I said, using her Christian name for the first time. 'Poor Anna. Life must be very tough at the moment. I know just how you feel.'

'How?' She had seemed sulky and withdrawn, but she fell on my little lie like a leopard. 'How? How can you possibly know?'

'I just know,' I said firmly, and then again, drawing strength from repetition: 'I just *know.*'

'Yes, I think you do know.' Her eyes met mine in sympathy and I thought, please don't ask me to tell you all about it, Mrs Wiseman, and she said: 'Tell me all about it, John.'

It was the 'John' that did it. If she'd said 'Mr Wellington' as usual, I would have spun some story of frustrated love, waited till she was about to cry and said, 'And *that's* how I know.' But I couldn't bring myself. I had pulled up too many buckets from that well of deceit lately, so I thought, keep it simple this time, Beef, and nobody will get hurt, and I said: 'It's a very long story, Anna, and I don't think I've come to terms with it

143

enough to talk about it.' How pleased I felt at remembering that feeble cliché from a bad novel I'd once read on holiday! 'Let's just say I *know*.'

'All right, John. I understand. Would you like some more coffee?'

We had made it. A few minutes' dialogue of shattering banality, and we had crossed some invisible Rubicon of which the Johns and the Annas were only the outward signs. I hadn't the faintest idea what it was I knew that I'd said I knew, but I could see that Anna believed that I did know it and that this shared body of knowledge would transform our relationship. I was a true ally now, because I knew something that Carter would never know, and if I could assist her in destroying him for his ignorance of that better world, *our* world, then she would adore me for ever. That, anyway, was the impression she gave as we chattered idly over our second cup of coffee and, when I introduced a more businesslike note into the discussion, she was more responsive than I had dared to hope. She walked me the few hundred yards from the house to the spot where her husband had been knocked down, and pointed out various landmarks with a torch.

'That's where his body was lying. Just this side of that tree. And that's where they found his hat. He always wore a hat when he went walking. And that's where Roly –'

'Roly?'

'The dog.'

'Oh yes, I'd forgotten. What happened to him by the way?'

'I gave him to a friend. He was Peter's dog really, not mine, and he just pined afterwards. I hated having something so miserable around, so I got rid of him in the summer.'

'What sort of dog was it?'

'A black-haired retriever. Why?'

'Just curious. Every little detail, you know.' I took a long look up and down the road. It was perfectly straight for four hundred yards in each direction and, apart from the odd tree, there was nothing to impair visibility. Even in the rain, the cat's eyes would have beckoned drivers along an undeviating course,

144

and this hypothetical inebriate of Popplewell's, swerving off course but proceeding home safely, made less and less sense. I'm familiar with paralytic drunkenness from both sides of the footlights, but this was an imaginative leap I just couldn't manage; if Popplewell could manage it, it probably meant he was a teetotaller, unschooled in the ways of the bottle. I'd kept an open mind up to now, but the visit to the scene of the death had removed all my doubts. I could even see a tiny lay-by back on the road into Maidenhead where the murderer – Carter, whoever – could have waited for Wiseman to emerge on to the road and timed his attack to perfection. There were no other houses in the vicinity and traffic was light; only one car had passed in the five minutes we'd been standing there. It was all so obvious that I *knew* – far more than I knew what I'd told Anna I knew – that a murder had taken place.

'Very interesting,' I murmured when we were back in the house. 'Tell me: did Peter always walk his dog at the same time?'

'Between ten and ten-thirty, every night the same. He was a very methodical man.'

'And always along this road?'

'Yes. It's the only place you can go at night.'

'And who actually knew all this? About his routine for walking the dog.'

'I did, of course. A few close friends too, I suppose. John *certainly* knew.' It was almost a hiss.

'Are you sure?'

'Of course I'm sure. We were lovers, you remember. Knowing a husband's routines is how you survive; it's essential.'

I nodded, trusting her automatically on her specialised subject. From the look on her face, I thought she was about to launch into another comparison between Peter's cold, mocking eyes and John's stronger but more tender ones, so I forestalled her. 'What about you, Anna? When did you get home that night?'

'About half past eleven. The police had already arrived and

145

taken Peter's body into the house. It was hideous.'

'Where had you been?'

'At the cinema.'

'What was the film?'

'Does it matter?'

'No, I'm sorry.' I bit my lip and didn't ask what I wanted to ask next, which was who she'd gone to the film with. If there'd been anyone, she would ask if it mattered and I would have to say no again, and if there'd been nobody she might take offence at my assumptions about her social life. I asked her instead about Carter, some sharp, precise questions which needed answering before I could proceed with confidence.

'There's one major gap in this story, Anna.' Back in the drawing-room, we had settled down with whiskies on either side of the fireplace, like any old husband and wife. 'I can believe now that your husband's death wasn't an accident, and I don't find it incredible any more that Carter was responsible. But there has to be a reason, and a very compelling reason at that. Carter's a public figure and a very ambitious politician. He wouldn't put all that at risk unless he thought the risks were justified by what he stood to gain by killing your husband. So what did he stand to gain? It wasn't you because you've said so.'

'No, it wasn't me.' Her face assumed its wistful, far-away look, and I waited respectfully for her to come down to earth. It frightened me to think that, if Carter had murdered Wiseman for her sake, she wouldn't have been telling the tale to a clapped-out hack, but living happily with her glamorous new husband, without fear or regret. But I hadn't come here to moralise. That goes in the editorials, after the reporters have grubbed around for the facts, and I knew my paper would make a thorough job of it, as moral vigilance is the house style.

'So what was it then?' I asked, when she was back in the land of the living. 'Do you have any idea, Anna? The police will just laugh at us if we can't produce a convincing motive.'

'Will they? Yes, I suppose they will.' She was as naïve about the criminal law as Christopher was about politics, which was

146

quite an achievement, I thought blackly. 'They really hated each other a lot, I know that.'

'I thought they were friends.'

'Not by the end. Not for the last couple of years.'

'Because of you?'

'Maybe.' A look of proud defiance flickered across her face as she reappeared in the story. 'Peter never found out about John and me, but he must have guessed. That wasn't the main reason, though.'

'What was the main reason?'

'Money, I think. Some quarrel long ago when they were business partners which surfaced again later.' She rubbed her hand sleepily in her eye. 'Does it matter?'

I clenched my fist behind my back. 'Yes, it *does* matter, Anna. This time it matters a lot. It's absolutely bloody crucial; can't you see that?'

'Yes, I suppose you're right.' She yawned again; I just couldn't believe her indifference. 'Peter was probably going to put the details in his book, but it's too late now, isn't it?'

She said the words nonchalantly, so it must have puzzled her when I started gibbering like a baboon given double rations of bananas. '*Book!* What book, Anna? You didn't say Peter was writing a book. It could be incredibly significant. What sort of book was it? What was it about? Was it an autobiography?'

'No, I don't think so. It was mainly about the City. I read part of the manuscript once. It seemed to be mainly about economics, very boring. Peter didn't have much imagination, you see.'

'Where is the manuscript? Could I see it? This could be terribly important, Anna. Please try to treat it seriously.'

She looked at me suspiciously, the way one looks at Buddhist fanatics in Oxford Street. 'I can't show you the manuscript, I'm afraid. It disappeared.'

'It *what?*'

'It disappeared. Shortly after Peter's death. What's the matter?'

I was pacing furiously up and down the room and, if I looked

147

as excited as I felt, she might well have been alarmed. The thoughts I was having began to spurt out of my mouth in wild confusion. 'A book, she says. Very *boring*, about economics. Just another boring book about the City which nobody's going to read. Then the man writing the book is killed and the manuscript disappears. *Disappears!* Anna Wiseman, Anna Wiseman, are you as stupid as you pretend or is this just a game?'

'I –'

'A *funeral*. That's it. You must have had a funeral. Peter was dead, so he had to be buried. Or was he cremated? All right, all right, it doesn't *matter*. I'm sorry I asked. So he was cremated. Then you had some friends back here for a drink. Everyone in black looking miserable, including Carter. Yes?'

'Yes, but –'

'Including Carter. The guests stay for an hour or two. They wander round the house a little and, magic, Peter's precious manuscript *disappears*. Somebody didn't like that book, Anna. It may have been boring to you, but to him it was very exciting. It told little stories he didn't want told, *murderous* little stories. It probably –'

I stopped, finding it very hard to talk, and noticed with horror that I was foaming at the mouth. A steady flow of salvia was streaming down my chin and neck, and something in the system had overheated badly. Not even five-star French restaurants have this effect on me, so I was terrified. I tore open my shirt-front and collapsed panting on the sofa, breathing heavily and unevenly and sweating like a fully clothed pig in a sauna. Anna stationed herself anxiously beside me and dabbed my face ineffectually with her handkerchief, sighing 'Poor John!' over and over again, but my condition only stabilised when she produced a brandy. I knocked it back in one, shut my eyes beatifically for about a minute, then opened them again. The ceiling was no longer circling above my head and my breathing was more normal. I sat up weakly on the sofa and looked around me.

'What happened? Did I faint?'

148

'No, John, it's all right. You just got excited.' She started gently slapping the back of my hand to quieten me down. 'You thought you'd solved the whole mystery and, do you know something?'

'What?'

'I think you're *right*.' She stressed the word too heavily, the way one would to a doubting child, and I looked at her hard to see if I'd really convinced her. I needn't have worried, because she glided out of the room and returned holding a letter.

'Look at this, John. I didn't really understand it at the time but, after what you've said, I think it makes a lot of sense.'

She started to read it aloud, but her measured delivery irritated me and I snatched it from her hand before she had finished the first sentence. My eyes were still focusing badly, but I managed to get the gist of it and I could feel my heart beginning to pound again.

It was from one of the racier London publishing houses and was dated 8 July, two months after Peter Wiseman's death. It began ordinarily enough, extending commiserations with the brisk efficiency of literary folk, then went into details about the book. 'Quite inappropriate to publish in the circumstances . . . manuscript only half finished . . . naturally no question of the advance against royalties having to be returned . . .' The sentences were strung effortlessly together, tidying up the whole enterprise economically and without fuss, and only one passage caught my eye. I read it and reread it and finally, with a vulgar cry of 'Eureka!', read it aloud to Anna.

' "There were anyway, as we intimated to your late husband, several legal difficulties" – *legal*, Anna, have you got that? – "posed by the manuscript. Our latest advice was that we could not have published chapter four in its present form without exposing ourselves to retaliatory legal action on grounds of libel." '

Anna looked at me and I looked at her and the penny which had dropped for me some time before dropped for her too. I knew and she knew and nothing could take that knowledge from us. I gave a final gurgle of pleasure and fell back on the sofa in a deep sleep.

15

'Wake up! Wake up! There he is.'

It was only a whisper, but the voice forced itself remorse-lessly through the oblivion. At first I was only conscious of a splitting headache and some sadist trying to yank my arm out of its socket, then I opened my eyes and blinked. Mrs Wiseman – no, Anna, I remembered that at once – was kneeling on the floor next to me and pointing at something. I turned to look and saw John Carter's familiar face about six feet away. He was talking and smiling quietly, and I heard the words 'wait and see' rounding off a typically convoluted sentence. Then he reached into his pocket. It was a gun, I thought, it had to be a gun, and it was going to be pointed at me. I felt too sluggish to move, so I shielded my face with my arm in a forlorn gesture and waited for him to pull the trigger. Nothing happened for a few seconds, then I heard Anna laughing gently and asking if I was drunk. I snapped at her not to be so bloody silly, but the objects in the room were swaying gently in front of me, as if reflected in water, so I privately conceded she had a point. It was only when I eased the protective arm away from my face and realised I was watching a television set that I recovered my bearings. I sat up very slowly indeed and shook myself like a wet dog to clear my head.

'I'm sorry,' I said lamely, impoverished for once of a colourful excuse. 'I must have dropped off for a second or two. Long day. Sorry.'

'It's quite all right, John.' She smiled and squeezed my hand, and I remembered dimly that there was something strange and

150

important we both knew which allowed her to be so intimate. 'Now watch.'

I looked obediently at the television. Carter was still holding forth, making a pumping gesture with his right hand to emphasise a point. I heard an interviewer off-camera try to interrupt him, but he swept on relentlessly, crushing the other man with his fluency and developing his argument in a single cathedral-like sentence, buttressed by subordinate clauses of effortless construction. It was impressive stuff, whatever he was talking about, and I was trying to think of a delicate way of saying to my hostess that I found it quite understandable that a woman should want to go to bed with a man who used the English language as well as that, when the focus of attention shifted. The camera swung away from Carter before his great sentence was complete, an excited presenter said something about a count and we were suddenly swept across the country to Wopsley Town Hall. The name of the town meant nothing for a second, so totally had the day's events supplanted the by-election in my mind, then everything tumbled into place. I said 'Shit!' a couple of times, mindful that your correspondent wasn't being paid to watch all this on television, and waited anxiously for the result to be announced.

'I, Albert Saul Throstleton, the undersigned, being the returning officer . . .' Get on with it, you arsehole, I screamed to myself; nobody's listening to you. But I was wasting my time. He looked sternly at the camera, as if he had heard my heckling, and continued at an even more funereal pace. '. . . hereby give notice . . . votes cast for the respective candidates . . .' He droned on imperviously, then kept everyone waiting longer by blowing his nose in a red check handkerchief. Democracy, democracy, I thought, and wanted to yell obscenities at the set.

'Appleby, Gillian Anne Camille . . .'

'Democrat,' whispered the commentator.

'Fornicatress,' I muttered for Anna's benefit.

'. . . eleven thousand, three hundred and seventy-eight.'

There were loud cheers from the back of the hall and Jill was beaming, so I assumed she'd got second place despite the smear

151

campaign against her. Wopsley had proved a less straight-laced electorate than expected.

'Bavin, Antony Edwin . . .'

'SF.'

'Raving loony.'

'. . . eight thousand, nine hundred and seventeen. Beeston, John . . .'

'Reform Party.'

'Cretin.'

'. . . ten thousand, six hundred and two. Campbell, Rolf Andrew . . .'

'Action on Public Health.'

'Anti-dogshit.'

'. . . seven hundred and thirty-six. Denver, Charles Humphrey . . .'

'Government candidate.'

'Biggest shit of the lot.'

'. . . *two* thousand . . .' The returning officer spoke slowly, so there was no chance of mishearing. '. . . one hundred and seven.'

'Jesus Christ!'

'What is it?' Anna looked at me in amazement. I was stunned by the figures and started gibbering for the second time in the evening.

'He was supposed to win by a landslide, ten thousand votes at least. I said twenty thousand yesterday afternoon, then there was an opinion poll and I – he's been *murdered*! He must have lost his bloody deposit . . . serves the bastard right, he wanted deposits put up to £2,000 . . . victory for democracy . . . incredible, bloody incredible . . .'

I yammered on, scarcely listening while the returning officer read out all the other cranks' results, then another familiar name penetrated the haze of my disbelief.

'Jameson, George Roy Arkwright . . .'

'Libertarian Humanist Animal Rights Protection.'

'Pro-dogshit.'

'. . . two thousand, one hundred and eight. Langoustine,

Sandra . . .'

I wasn't listening any more; I was panting, dehydrated by emotions much too various to comprehend. I was ecstatic at the sheer scale of Denver's humiliation – when was a Government candidate last beaten by a proponent of dogshit? – but my elation was already being overtaken by sterner feelings. A sensational story had happened under my very nose and I had totally missed it. How could I ever show my face in the Press Gallery again? What would my editor think? He'd sent me up to Wopsley on the off-chance of an upset and he'd been totally vindicated. This wasn't just an upset; it was the biggest democratic tidal wave for years, a political bombshell which must have been ticking away all along in that sleepy, clapped out town, but which I hadn't even heard. Now it was exploding in everyone's face and I was a hundred miles away, three-quarters pissed and watching it on television with a million other people. You don't have to be conscientious to be embarrassed about that sort of cock-up. The most hard-bitten, gin-soused hack in Fleet Street would have bowed his head in shame at such a catastrophe. It was the sort of gross professional negligence which got people like doctors, people doing serious jobs, thrown into prison for twenty years. It was contemptible, disgraceful, derisory, every blush-word in the hack's handbook – like being on the Titanic and not filing a story because your pencil was wet. As the prospect of everyone's derision loomed, I knew there was only one escape. I had to get this Carter story sewn up pretty damned quickly or there'd be a vacancy for a lobby correspondent posted in the office. 'Applicants must be able to remain in the general vicinity of where their editor has sent them.' Someone with a sense of humour could have a field day with the job description.

In the television studio, a psephologist was going completely beserk. I thought I had overheated once or twice, but this character was a closet epileptic and someone had opened the door of the closet. 'Never in living memory . . . probably not since 1832 Reform Act . . . Orpington . . . Crosby . . . Bermondsey . . . storms in teacups in comparison . . . *unprece-*

dented swing . . . computer prediction of effect of same swing at a General Election . . . *ooh*, look at that . . . *unparalleled* swing . . . redrawing of political map . . . PM couldn't survive any more dead backbenchers, ha ha . . . *unexampled* swing . . . opinion polls totally misleading . . . voting patterns of a lifetime . . . don't-knows must have known all along, ha ha . . . *unfathomably* extraordinary swing . . .' His glasses had steamed up completely, and the hair on the top of his head was beginning to defy gravity and stand upright of its own accord, when the producer put him out of his misery. A quick change of camera and we were back on the other side of the studio with Carter, flanked by senior politicians of other parties.

'Let me begin with you, Secretary of State.' The eminent interviewer was wetting himself. His normally intimidating glasses were almost falling off the end of his nose, they were shaking so much, and it was only by monumental self-control that he finished his question at all. 'Would you say this was a *good* result for the Government?'

'No, of course I wouldn't.' The camera cut to Carter in profile and you could see how still he was holding himself. Everyone else in the studio was hopping around like fury, but he was almost chillingly calm. When he had made the interviewer's question sound infantile by the measured acerbity with which he dealt with it, he produced a quick flurry of excuses. The Government had lost the by-election but won the arguments, it was the next General Election that mattered, public opinion was volatile, a week, nay a day, was a long time in politics . . . One after another, he trundled them out, those shrivelled fig-leaves that the defeated politician always gropes for, and I thought, if I were in this man's party, I would take off my hat and cheer. There are moments in politics when there is no scope left for originality and only clichés remain and, at those moments, only one thing matters: the style with which the clichés are delivered. Carter delivered them *superbly*. You could tell he knew they were clichés, which lesser men wouldn't have realised, but he still conveyed the impression that a dangerous and original mind lay behind them. That was his real genius.

154

When I also reflected, remembering my conversation with Christopher, that a double bluff was involved and that Carter had wanted Denver to do badly, in order to boost his own political position, his sublime insouciance under fire was breath-taking. Even my armour-plated cynicism began to melt into admiration. This rare bird didn't deserve to have his wings clipped, I thought; he should be soaring freely above the whole flock, not locked up in a cage for murdering somebody.

A gentle tugging at my sleeve interrupted my reverie. I was so absorbed in the television that I had forgotten Anna.

'Don't you see what I mean about his eyes?' she whispered. 'Aren't they magnificent? Like a young lion's.'

I nodded mechanically. It wasn't the comparison I would have made myself, but you can't argue with a fanatic. She was back in her dream-world and her face had the shiny brittleness of an adolescent in love. I had seen exactly the same expression on Christopher's face when he had talked about Carter's concrete vision of the future, and I thought, which was worse – to be ravished by a man's eyes or by his political philosophy?

'Some people will say, Secretary of State . . .' The interviewer had regained his habitual sang-froid. 'Some people will say that it was your injudicious speech in Wopsley last night which tipped the balance against your candidate. They may *even* say that, if the Prime Minister is looking for a scapegoat, then you are the obvious candidate. What do you have to say to that?'

It was a neat piece of tail twisting, but Carter just flicked his tail and the danger passed. Perhaps Anna was right about the lion, I thought admiringly, as he made the suggestion that his own future was in jeopardy look ridiculous, a little joke on the interviewer's part. With that air of infinite patience with which the clever politician defends the indefensible – the less clever one gets impatient – he explained why the passage in his speech which *elements* in the media (how sinister he made them sound!) had interpreted as contradicting the Prime Minister's views had actually been *supporting* those views. It was patent nonsense, of course, and I knew he was just papering over

155

cracks in the Cabinet which the by-election defeat would accentuate. But it was cleverly done all the same. He might be the Prime Minister's most dangerous rival now – but how could someone who could gloss over differences with such panache be given the sack at a time like this?

'He's good,' I said, when he had had his say and the other politicians in the studio were being given their chance to gloat over him. 'He's very good, much better than I used to think. All this talk of sacking him's nonsense. He's there to stay, Anna.'

'What a pity.' She loved him because he was powerful, I thought, but hated him for holding power. How painful the paradox must be. I put my hand on her arm and offered her a few more precious crumbs of my sympathy.

'You'd rather he was on the backbenches, wouldn't you, Anna? He would have more time for the important things in life, what you think are the important things in life. Ministers have less time, less freedom. They have to be circumspect. Is that why he left you?'

'What do you mean?'

'Did he leave you because he saw the Election was coming up and knew you were a liability? When you're a prospective Cabinet Minister, it's a bonus to be happily married, isn't it?'

'Ah, Mr Wellington'. She looked mournfully at my stomach at the point where it spilled over the top of my trousers. 'He's so much cleverer than you it's pathetic. That marriage of his has really fooled you, hasn't it? You look at Sophie and him together and you think, what a contented pair! He may have had this "thing" with the Dutch woman, and she's probably had "things" of her own, but it's all over now. Can't you see what a sham it is?'

'Now look, Anna, just because you –'

'It's not just me, you poor fool! Do you think I'm the only lover John's had? There have been others, you know.'

'Really?' I nodded sagely, masking my underlying excitement. From a tabloid point of view, this latest disclosure was distinctly promising. Embezzler, murderer and philanderer: the charge-sheet was getting longer and longer. Politicians with colourful sex lives are usually known about at Westminster, but the odd discreet operator escapes notice and Carter was certainly an expert at adjusting his visibility to suit his political ends. It was quite possible he had conducted a few low-key affairs, although it was equally possible that they were just figments of Anna's fetid imagination.

'Did he have someone at the time of the murder?' I asked casually. 'It could be important. She might know something.'

'That's true.' She winced, and some invisibly burning knife seemed to twist in her. 'I think I can guess who it was. She was very mousy, I remember that. So plain I couldn't imagine what he saw in her.'

'What was her name?'

'Names, names, names! Why do you keep asking these stupid questions?' She sighed in exasperation, then raised an apologetic hand, acknowledging she was at fault. 'I don't remember, I'm afraid. I could probably find out. I have some very indiscreet friends in London who tell me all the gossip. Isn't gossip fun sometimes?'

'Definitely.'

'Especially where sex is concerned. Don't you agree?'

She looked at me across the arm of the sofa and smiled. I wasn't conscious of anything out of the ordinary, then something indefinable about her expression made me nervous. The smiling lasted much too long, for one thing. At about the point when normal smiles die, having expressed the feelings of joy or affection that inspired them, it seemed to take on new life and be animated by a powerful inner energy. Her lips pouted rhythmically and her eyebrows began leaping up and down like extrovert MPs on points of order. I realised, to my consternation, that it was a sultry smile and that its sultriness was beamed at me. I must have weighed less than 15 stone when a pair of female eyes had last been focused on me so intensely, and I'm afraid I panicked. Handling women just isn't my speciality and, if the emotional temperature was rising, then I was getting out fast. I stood up and made the exploratory

157

arm-gesture customary in other people's houses, when you want the loo but aren't sure of the local euphemism, but it was too late. She glided across the room and thrust herself in front of me, with her face only centimetres from mine. It was quite agreeable for a second, as the expensive whisky on our breaths blended into a virile bouquet, but then she suddenly kissed me gently on the lips and said, 'I think you're a lovely, lovely person; did you know that?' What was I meant to say? She had that menacing, come-up-and-see-me-some-time look in her eyes, so it was no time for ambiguity. I was about to clap my hand to my forehead and say I'd just remembered my sister in Blackpool was seriously ill, when the telephone rang in the hall and, with a gesture of irritation, she went to answer it. I took out a handkerchief and wiped the sweat off my face. However would I cope when she got back?

Don't get me wrong about this episode. It isn't puritanism or middle-class morality that makes me sexually defensive, but a simple sense of the ridiculous, the knowledge that some kinds of self-indulgence make other kinds impracticable. Anna Wiseman had her faults, but they hadn't made me dislike her and, if she'd offered me a cocoa while she got the guest bedroom ready, then tucked me up in bed with a little peck on the cheek, I'd have been flattered. There's not much love in a lobby correspondent's life, so he has to make each scrap of love go a long way. But love is one thing, sex-starved Amazons another. Anna's sudden kiss had totally demoralised me and I was determined to stop her repeating it. I was debating whether to tiptoe quietly out of the house when she returned, looking mercifully subdued. The look of abandon in her face was gone, and she addressed me as coolly as my bank manager.

'It was him.'

'What did he want?' I was surprised, but knew who 'he' was immediately.

'Me, of course.' A serene smile settled on her face. 'He was quite, quite charming. Apologised for being so rude last night and asked me to lunch next week. What about that?'

'Splendid, splendid.' I soft-pedalled, but my mind was

158

working furiously. Carter must have rung to try to mollify Anna and stop her talking to me. The first part had worked, but he was too late for the second. 'Did he ask about me?'

'Yes he did, as a matter of fact.'

'Did you tell him that you told me all about the murder?'

'Yes, of course. He asked about that.'

I banged my head with my hands and swore. 'Why the hell did you tell him? Couldn't you have kept quiet about it? Now he'll be on his guard.'

'I might want him to be on his guard.' She smiled at me teasingly, and I knew I had lost her as an ally. Five minutes ago, she would have done anything to destroy Carter's political career, but now she was right back under his spell. Even if I got her into the witness-box, defending counsel would chew her into little pieces and spit her out. It was too bloody infuriating for words, and my fists were clenched tight behind my back as she wandered round the room switching off the lights. She was day-dreaming again, and she addressed her next remark as much to herself as to me.

'He said something very interesting. He said –'

'What?'

'He said he might have some good news in the next few days which would please me. Isn't that exciting?'

'Thrilling.' Another bloody riddle, I thought bitterly, too tired to puzzle this one out. Why couldn't I take three steps forward for a change, instead of two forward and one back? At this rate, Carter would be in the House of Lords before I nailed him. I looked at Anna and watched the love flickering again on her face and wanted to strangle her. She really was the most impossible woman I had ever met, and the only blessing was that her interest in me was stone dead. Without referring to the pass she had made earlier, she tucked me up in bed in the spare bedroom with a mug of cocoa and kissed me goodnight.

16

'You should have let her seduce you,' said Jenny with a smile, as my fevered narrative got to its climax. 'It would have been a scream.'

'No way. She was a lunatic. I was lucky to get out alive.'

I was home at last and home had never seemed sweeter. One of Jenny's qualities which I don't always appreciate is that she is in no way highly strung. Talking to her after Anna was like a tranquilliser. She had been a little cool at first, remarking that I must have put on twenty pounds in Wopsley, but that was behind us. I had kept her enthralled with my story, which I spun out over my second breakfast of the day, and she greeted each new revelation about Carter's private life with un-restrained glee. With his polished, smoother-than-smooth manner, he had long been a pet hate of hers and, when I had finished, she announced with shameless hindsight that she had always known there was something wrong with him.

'What are you going to do next?' she asked. 'Shouldn't you tell the police?'

'What's the point? I haven't got anything concrete to show them. They'd sit up and listen if this bloody woman would talk to them but, if it's now all sweetness and light between her and Carter, she just won't deliver. All I can do is make more inquiries and wait. Right now, I've got other things on my mind.'

I looked glumly down at the morning papers in front of me. Every single one led on the by-election, and the headlines vied with each other to express the enormity of the Government's humiliation. 'POLL-AXED!' was my own paper's contribution to the nation's literature and there were gleeful exclamation marks at the end of every paragraph. It was torrid stuff and the only problem was that Beef Wellington's name wasn't at the head of the article where it should have been. They must have gone beserk on the night desk waiting for me to telephone in my copy, and I didn't fancy putting in an appearance there for a month or two. A hack has to do what a hack has to do, though, so I took a taxi to Fleet Street and was standing on the Editor's carpet with a hang-dog face before half past ten.

As bollockings go, it was on the mild side. I was too senior to get the full treatment and Brian sounded more exasperated than outraged, although he rattled off a fairly impressive list of charges: gross lack of professionalism, disgraceful deriliction of duty, irresponsible behaviour in a crisis, failure to meet minimum journalistic standards, etc. Strange, I thought as he talked, that the editor of such a crappy publication should expect his staff to accept the disciplines of a monastery. If I'd trusted him, I would have felt obliged to tell him the whole story and explain that I'd deserted my post for the best of journalistic reasons, the hope of getting some dirt on a public figure. As it was, I only hinted at the true facts and said I *hoped* to have a story soon which would make the by-election look pretty small beer. He nodded politely but didn't appear to take the promise seriously, assuming, I suppose, that I was just whistling in the dark to lessen my humiliation. Then he suddenly interrupted me.

'How old are you, Beef?'

'Fifty-three. Nearly fifty-four. Why, Chief?'

'Just wondered.' He chewed gently on a pencil and looked out of the window towards St Paul's. I thought I know what's coming next, you bastard, and he said: 'Have you ever thought about early retirement?'

'Never seriously, Chief.'

'Well think about it now.'

It was an order, so I furrowed my brows and pretended to

161

think about it. My thoughts really were about retirement, but not the kind he envisaged. I was thinking, I bloody well will retire, you bastard, and I'll live off the royalties of *The Carter File*, and I won't let you serialise a word of it if this is how you treat me. A smile must have crept on to my face, because he said: 'Did I say something funny, Beef?'

'Not at all, Chief, not at all.' I furrowed my brows more fiercely, so they would stay furrowed,then added, in case he'd missed the point of the brow-furrowing: 'I'm still thinking about it.'

'Sure, Beef.' He leant back in his chair and continued staring out of the window. After a while, the lack of action at my end made him impatient and he took up the running himself. 'Can I think aloud for a minute, Beef?'

'Sure, Chief.'

'You're fifty-four. Right?'

'Fifty-three.'

'Fifty-three. And you've been in the House twenty-odd years.'

'Yes.'

'You're bored fartless with your work there, because you said so. I get you an assignment out of town and you make the most God Almighty cock-up of it. You leave some crazy message with the night staff that you were having it off with a Dutch woman called Anna. Is that true?'

'Only vaguely.'

'What the hell do you mean, "only vaguely"?'

'It doesn't matter, Chief.'

'Oh doesn't it?' He was about to deliver a stinging rebuke about the sexual ethics he expected from reporters on a family newspaper, when he noticed I was trying desperately not to laugh and realised he was in the vicinity of a banana skin. He sighed wearily and dismissed me with a growl, leaving my future hanging in the air, which was better than where it deserved to be. If Brian had handled his staff as ruthlessly as the circulation war, I'd have been given my marching orders straight away; but he tended to dither over personnel matters.

162

The tough news magnate who could decide in seconds whether to lead with a story about a bishop's son on drugs or one about a pop-star's rocky marriage to an alcoholic had a less sure touch with real human problems, if an ageing hack can be so described. He had made it clear I was on probation, though, so I looked forward with relish to the moment when I would come bouncing back from the dead. CABINET MINISTER ON MURDER RAP: he would have to relegate the pop-stars and bishops' sons to page two for that one, I thought, and I whistled cheerfully to myself in my taxi to the House.

Part 3
3
Westminster

17

It was hard to believe it was a Friday, there were so many people about. Scores of Members who always pushed off home to their constituencies on Thursday night and hacks who spent every Friday on the golf-course had come into the House specially, determined to enjoy the repercussions of Wopsley at first hand. An unexpected banana skin had found its way under the Prime Minister's foot and, politics being what it is, the bystanders were doubled up with laughter. They didn't show it, of course, and they wore grave faces for the outside world's benefit, but the merry twinkle in their retinas was unmistakable. It wasn't just the Opposition either. Dozens of disaffected Government backbenchers, the surly crew of paranoiacs and bad losers who are permanently in mourning for their exclusion from office, now trod the green carpets of the Commons with renewed enthusiasm, like Napoleon waiting at the Elba Hilton for the telephone call that was bound to come.

In the Chamber, a Private Member's Bill to ban under-sevens from skate-boarding was being debated. The opening speakers were worthy rather than Ciceronian, and they were interrupted by bogus points of order as Opposition Members jostled to cash in on the Government's humiliation. 'Should we be debating this minor measure, Mr Speaker, when the country's lack of confidence in Her Majesty's Government has just been so strikingly demonstrated?' 'Would it be in order, Mr Speaker, to move the adjournment of the House under Standing Order No. 10 to express our sense of the moral bankruptcy of Government policies?' 'Do the rules of the House allow you, Mr Speaker, to ask the Prime Minister on behalf of the House to make a statement here at two o'clock?' 'Further to that point of order, further to that point of order . . .' From every side, the Speaker was bombarded with irrelevancies, and his patient reiterations that Members should address their remarks to the question of skate-boarding were flagrantly ignored. When he finally snapped at one Member that he would be better advised to talk about the by-election in the Strangers' Bar, the Member produced roars of delight by retorting 'I will do, Mr Speaker', and storming out of the Chamber. Once there, he probably found only one thing being discussed. It was that sort of day. My friends the burghers would have been amazed at the feverish way the name of their town was passing from lip to lip.

Naturally I enjoyed myself hugely. The Mother of Parliaments excels at expressing many emotions, but its unbridled *schadenfreude* at times of embarrassment for the Government is very hard to match. The whole place was humming and, as a battle-scarred veteran of the Wopsley campaign, I was greeted with special interest. 'What was it like, Beef?' 'Tell us all about it, Beef.' Nobody seemed to care that I had failed to predict the result as comprehensively as anyone. I had been there, that was what mattered. I knew what sort of people these Wopsley voters were, these fiercely independent souls who had told the Government where it got off. Did they seem angry? Were they bitter about the state of the economy? Had they listened carefully to the arguments, or had they just been following their instincts? Had they been taller than average or had red hair? Questions were fired at me in every corridor and over every whisky and, with a prudent application of hindsight, I turned them to my advantage. Yes, I said knowingly, the scale of the Government's defeat had come as a shock to everyone but, strangely enough and without ever putting my finger on it, I had had a *tiny* hunch, just a very little one nestling right at the back of my mind, that something like this might, just *conceivably* . . .

'Heads will have to roll, of course,' said Jim Tyndall

lugubriously as we chatted in a corridor. 'The Party's completely demoralised. Even if it's only window-dressing, the PM will have to make a change or two at the top or people will think he doesn't care about public opinion at all.'

'Who's for the chop then, Jim?'

'Search me. It's anybody's guess. But *someone* will have to go.'

'Just for window-dressing?'

'Well, and morale, of course. If you can't sustain morale, you've lost half the battle.'

I looked at his grave young face and remembered him pontificating at Christopher's dinner party about the evil of short-term solutions and pandering to public opinion. Now he was panicking just like everyone else and dressing up his panic as political shrewdness. There's nothing like a kick in the teeth from the voters to start a stampede at Westminster and, if the herd was stampeding, Tyndall wasn't going to be left behind looking silly. For a lobby correspondent in search of backbench opinion, he was the perfect person to canvass, as his views could be relied upon to coincide with the conventional wisdom of the moment, unencumbered by original thinking.

'Tell me,' I said blandly. Don't ask me why, but Members trust my blandness. 'What are they saying in the Tea Room about Carter? Is he a candidate for the chop?'

'No way. Did you see him on the box last night?'

'I don't think –'

'Marvellous. Bloody marvellous. Made the interviewer look a complete illiterate. No, he's a survivor all right.'

'I thought his economics were meant to be unsound.'

'What?' He sounded genuinely baffled by my question. How could such trivial things be important when the survival of the tribe was at stake? 'No, that's all right. He sometimes suggests using fiscal powers in odd ways, but he shares the same broad philosophy as the rest of us. We all believe in the same objectives; the only arguments are about how to achieve them. Carter's a softly softly man, but he's not interested in the politics of lowest common denominators. Did you know –'

I probably did know, if the thought was as original as the

169

rest, but Tyndall never finished his sentence because Christopher suddenly came round the corner towards us. My first reaction was relief at being saved from asphyxiation from political cliché, but then I remembered how bitterly we had parted the previous day and averted my eyes as he approached. He greeted me with a smile, however, and, as if anxious to talk to me alone, shifted rather unsubtly from foot to foot waiting for Tyndall to go. A more sensitive man would have got the message at once, but sensitivity wasn't Tyndall's strong suit and, when the significance of Christopher's foot-shifting finally seeped through, he thought Christopher must be waiting for *me* to go and looked at me in anticipation, wondering how I could be so slow on the uptake. Then he began shifting his own feet. This would really get the point across, he thought, and he juggled his feet around with gusto until he noticed that Christopher had stopped shuffling his own feet and was looking expectantly at *him* – at which point he made one last intellectual effort and nodded his head to indicate that he had worked it out. As his feet were now in motion, while ours were stationary, it was comparatively simple for him to get them pointing in the same direction and march off down the corridor. The whole exercise had only taken about ten minutes and we had made lively small-talk about the by-election during that period, so perhaps I exaggerate Tyndall's gaucheness. He just *seems* thick; no doubt his constituents have a higher opinion of him.

'I'm sorry about yesterday, John.' When we were alone, Christopher came to the point with quite sublime directness. 'I shouldn't have followed you like that. I should have told him where to get off. I'm sorry.'

'That's all right, Chris.' I could almost love the boy, I thought, if he were like this all the time. 'I'm sorry I was so rude to you. It's the first time a Member's tried that one on me and I was a bit taken aback. Come and have a drink.'

We went down to Annie's, but it was crowded with people chattering about the Wopsley fall-out, so we went across to the Strangers', forced our way through the crush and took our drinks out on to the Terrace. It was cold and deserted, a total

170

contrast with the sea of colour and activity in the summer, but we stood beside the parapet and looked across to St Thomas's. I knew that, if secrets were to be exchanged, there was no more private place to exchange them.

'I gave him the message,' said Christopher. 'About you and Dr Trumper and about Maidenhead. He –'

'Well?'

He gave a little shiver, which was nothing to do with the cold wind from Lambeth, and dug his hands deep into his pockets. 'He was frightened, John. He didn't show it, of course, and I wouldn't have realised if I hadn't watched him very closely for the next five minutes. But his hands were trembling. I'd never seen that happen with him before, even when he speaks in the House, so I knew something was wrong. John, please tell me what this is all about.'

I nearly did. His face was so weak and his frankness so disarming that it got that close. But then I thought, you'll be just as frank with Carter, won't you, my darling boy, if you get half a chance, so I clammed up. In my job, you don't trust politicians and you don't expect them to trust you. The cynicism balances itself out and we congratulate ourselves on the healthy equilibrium we achieve.

'Wait and see, Chris,' I said, using gentler tones than I had in Oxford when he made the same requst. 'It'll all come out in the open sooner or later. I take it Carter wasn't too anxious to talk about it?'

'No. He just said it wasn't important.'

'Did you believe him?'

'Not for a minute. His hands were trembling, as I told you. It's important all right.'

'You bet it is.'

'Could you tell me just one thing?' He pouted his lips and fluttered, like a teenage girl trying to look lost and vulnerable. It was repulsive, although he meant it to be charming. Why hadn't his mother told him he was more charming when he made less effort? 'Is his future career in jeopardy?'

'It may be.'

'Yes or no?'

'Yes, I suppose. It depends.'

'On what?'

'On whether he's lucky or not.'

'And if he's unlucky?'

'If he's unlucky . . .' I stopped. I didn't want to say too much, but this cagey question and answer session was getting on my nerves. I felt like a doctor treating a cancer patient with a persistent relative breathing down my neck, asking the $64,000 question about life expectancy. I toyed with another form of words to say that the patient might live, but I knew it would only prompt another question, then another, so I took the plunge. 'If he's unlucky, then he's in shit up to his eyeballs, Chris. It's as simple as that.'

He gulped hard, as if he'd just swallowed a golf ball, and I could see those bluer-than-blue eyes moistening with disappointment. None of my lies had hurt as much as this simple truth and I regretted abandoning my normal mendacity. It was a moment pregnant with pity, if I could have felt it or he could have asked for it, but we both stared out across the Thames and the moment passed.

'I see,' he said at last. 'And what if –'

'If he's lucky? If he's lucky, he'll be Prime Minister tomorrow and start building his concrete vision of the future. There'll be zero inflation and zero unemployment and free opera and free football and sex on the National Health and you'll be a Cabinet Minister, with responsibility for pets. My own money's on the first scenario. How about yours?' I smiled smugly and wished I had a cigar in my mouth, so that I could blow smoke in his face, the way they do in black-and-white films when the good guy's up against it. I could see he wanted to ask more questions but knew he could only expect sarcastic answers and lacked the spirit to continue.

'Do you have to make a joke out of everything?' he asked forlornly, then added with greater passion: 'I'll tell you what really gets me: it's not all this bloody cloak-and-dagger stuff you and he are playing at. That's your business and, if you

172

don't want to tell me about it, I'll just have to accept that. But why does it all have to happen now? The Government's in chaos, the Party's demoralised and the public are impatient for Parliament to do something to steady the situation. If ever there was a moment for him to step forward and play a more prominent role, if ever his qualities were really needed, if ever –'

'If ever nothing.' I wasn't in the mood for rhetoric, so I stamped on it. 'You've no idea how fatuous you sound, Christopher. "Cometh the hour, cometh the man": you make it sound like the Knights of the bloody Round Table, but the reality's nothing like that. Carter *wanted* you to lose Wopsley – remember? Now he's trying to capitalise on it in the most cynical way imaginable. He may have more brains than the rest of the Cabinet put together, but there's nothing noble or heroic about the way he's behaved. Can't you see that?'

'Yes, of course I can.' He made a gesture of frustration, irritated by the cold force of my argument, then checked himself. 'I'm sorry, John. I got a bit carried away. I just admire that man so much, I forget he has feet of clay sometimes. But you must see the point I'm making. When the Government's up against it, Ministers of his calibre are like gold-dust.'

'If you say so.'

'They can restore stability and confidence in a way that lesser politicians can't.'

'That's true.'

'So let's just hope he is lucky. Right?'

I shook my head, unwilling to be swept along any further on his tide of optimism. 'You hope what you like, Chris. I'm a journalist, I have to take a different view.'

He looked at me contemptuously, seeing through my principled platitude more easily than I would have wished. 'I suppose you hope he lands in the shit? You would.'

'I didn't say that, Chris.' He was right, damn him, but I was too proud to admit it. I didn't mind him finding my conversation cynical, but I didn't want him to see the cynicism of my behaviour too, so I made a statesmanlike cop-out. 'Do you want to know what I hope? I hope he gets the luck he deserves.'

'That's fair enough.' He smiled, ready to grasp at the flimsiest evidence that I was an honourable man, and we left the Terrace together in good humour. On our way to the Central Lobby, we passed the PA telex machine and stopped to look at the latest news flashes. Christopher's eyes were sharper than mine, because he let out an uncharacteristic expletive and pointed in horror at the last item on the tapes. I looked to see what had caught his eyes and read: '12.15 URGENT. POUND DOWN NINE CENTS, REPEAT NINE CENTS.'

'Bad business,' I said calmly, although I found the news quite as dramatic as he did. 'Bank of England bungled again. I'd better get on the line to my stockbroker and have some investments transferred to my Swiss portfolio. I wonder –'

It was no good. He had gone, without bothering to get exasperated by my flippancy. I went immediately up to the Press Gallery and looked into the House to see if there was any early reaction to the news. Half a dozen Members were still conducting an impassioned debate about skate-boarding, but I knew it wouldn't last as soon as I saw a self-important Yorkshire Member called Houghley bustling into the Chamber. Houghley's love affair with his own voice was one of the most enduring of parliamentary romances, and I couldn't imagine him failing to consummate his love at such a moment. Sure enough, he bobbed to his feet almost as soon as he had sat down.

'On a point of order, Mr Deputy Speaker. It may be of interest to the House –'

'Order, order.' The Deputy Speaker rose smartly to his feet to quell the intervention. 'Many things may be of interest to the House, but the Honourable Gentleman should not bring them to the House's attention by means of a point of order. If he is trying to say something about recent events in Wopsley, I should warn him –'

'No, Mr Deputy Speaker. It's a different point of order.'

'Very well.'

'Would it be in order then, Mr Deputy Speaker . . .'

174

Houghley trod his way more carefully. '. . . for me to ask the Leader of the House, through you –'

'Order. Will the Honourable Gentleman kindly get to the point?'

'I am doing so, Mr Deputy Speaker. To ask the Leader of the House to make an immediate statement about the calamitous performance of the pound on the foreign exchanges today –'

'Order. This is not a genuine point of order.'

'– where it has already fallen nine cents against the dollar.'

Houghley sat down smugly, having slipped his announcement through just in time under heavy flak from the Chair. The Deputy Speaker rebuked him for wasting the House's time, but the other Members were too electrified by the news to care. Two or three tried to raise non-points of order of their own and one Member let out a strangulated cry and fled in panic towards the City, where he had extensive financial interests. I savoured the mounting pandemonium, then left the Gallery at one o'clock. Falling pound or no falling pound, there are things a working man had to do at lunchtime which command all his attention.

18

Back numbers of Hansard aren't everyone's idea of a good read. Without the BBC's farmyard sound effects in the background, even the liveliest debates can seem stodgy on the printed page, and the Written Answers to Questions which punctuate the daily records of debates are the literary equivalent of crushed glass. 'The numbers of men and women employed by the Property Services Agency for each three-month period in the last two years, including both skilled and unskilled workers, with the figures for temporary employees distinguished by asterisks, were respectively as follows.' When I began my researches after lunch, I flicked impatiently through the pages of mandarinese to the only thing I was interested in: the division-lists for the night Peter Wiseman had died.

The House had been debating the committee stage of the Finance Bill and there had been divisions at 7.00, 7.15, 10.15, 11.30, 1.00 and 1.45 – quite a heavy schedule, although the Whips had engineered the dinner-break with customary efficiency. Carter had voted at 7.00 and 7.15 but not at 10.15, I noted with excitement, and not at 11.30. At 1.00 and again at 1.45, his name was back on the list, which was very interesting indeed. Although Members with engagements elsewhere are often 'paired' with their opposite numbers and don't vote after an agreed time in the evening, for a Member to be paired for just two divisions and then start voting again in the early hours of the morning is unusual. The scope for cock-ups with such an arrangement would be enormous; and Whips aren't noted for

176

their fondness of cock-ups. The rat I'd been smelling had started to stink again, for it looked as if Carter might have gone AWOL from the House at exactly the time of the murder.

At 2.30, I telephoned some copy through to the paper. As it was just after lunch, there was a fair chance of talking to another pisshead, but luckily I got Wendy, the best and soberest copy-taker on the paper, and could concentrate on getting the article right. With the pound tumbling and the Government still concussed after Wopsley, there was an outside chance the Editor might put a bit of politics on the front page, even if it was only tucked into a corner. It would be page five as usual if an actress had got divorced in the course of the day, or a dog had barked at a burglar, or a member of the royal family had got a headache, but I was confident of three paragraphs, maybe even four, whatever page I was on, so who was I to complain? Give Beef Wellington the chance to go over the top, and he seizes it with alacrity. My economic know-how is no profounder than my knowledge of ballet, and didn't extend to an appreciation of the short- and medium-term consequences of a falling pound, so I just said it was bad news for home-owners, council tenants, motorists, pensioners, holiday-makers and owners of video-machines and hoped that would send a nasty chill down the backs of my entire readership. Panic was raging through the Palace of Westminster like a forest fire, I went on, in case the first chill hadn't been nasty enough, and there had been an ominous procession of Government backbenchers to the gents' next to the Library.

'You can't say that, Beef.'

'Of course I can. It's a metaphor to create the right atmosphere. Figuratively speaking, they are all shitting themselves, so it's true on one level. Then I suppose we'd better say something about this being the most important weekend in British politics since the war. We haven't had that for a couple of months. How about: "Not since Hitler's bombers flew their deadly missions over London have the British people looked more anxiously towards their leaders for inspiration and guidance."? That should do the trick.'

'It's a bit flowery isn't it? There are more than fifteen words.'

'It's a flowery article. The Chief may stretch the limit to eighteen for this edition, you never know. Can we have something now about the Prime Minister's blood-pressure? We had something on that when he fell off his horse, so people may still be interested. "In Downing Street, as the rain lashed down outside . . ." No. Wait.' An idea with a capital 'I' had suddenly struggled to the surface of my brain. It was infantile rather than coruscating, but it had a certain foolish logic and, in the first flush of invention, I was convinced it would work. I squinted out of my telephone booth in the Press Gallery to check there was nobody about, and spoke softly into the receiver.

' "One Minister to watch in the present crisis is John Carter." '

'Is the rain still lashing down?'

'What?' I gagged. 'No, sorry, Wendy. Scrap the last bit. This is a new paragraph.'

'But people will want to read about the Prime Minister's blood-pressure.'

'Bugger that. This is far more important. ". . . John Carter." Have you got that far?'

'Yes, but are you sure people will be interested, Beef?'

'They will by the time I've finished. Just stop arguing, love, and take this down. ". . . John Carter." '

'I've got that.'

' "He angered the Prime Minister on Wednesday by stepping out of line in a speech on the eve of the Wopsley poll. But now that a full-scale crisis has erupted, he is far too important a figure to be sacked." New paragraph. "Carter's ministerial career began quietly. Friends say he was privately shaken by the death of his close friend Peter Wiseman just before the General Election. But he has now established himself as one of the most brilliant and forceful members of the Cabinet." New paragraph. "Meanwhile, in Downing Street, as the rain . . ." '

I could hear Wendy's sigh of relief that my irrelevant digression was over. There was a fair chance the sub-editors would take the same view and cut the vital paragraphs, so, when I had

178

finished, I said: 'I can't explain why, Wendy, but the bit about Carter is the most important part of the whole piece. Ask the news desk to see that it gets slotted in somewhere. It doesn't have to be in the main story, but it mustn't just be spiked. OK?'

I hung up and had a celebratory gin before the bar closed, pleased with the low animal cunning of my plan. If I couldn't nail the bugger down, I was going to have to smoke him out and this little bonfire would help. Ministers read the tabloids with a paranoid curiosity, trusting us to be close to the pulse of public opinion and knowing that a bad popular Press can cost more votes than the most stinging leader in *The Times*. Carter wouldn't have my paper delivered at his home, but his press officer would alert him to the article and he would have an uncomfortable half-hour over his cornflakes the next morning. Or over his muesli, more likely; I imagined he would find cornflakes too noisy a cereal for a man of his importance.

'See you Monday, Beef,' said Gerry Bennett, a fellow scribe, as I was leaving the House. 'Things should have really hotted up by then.'

'There'll be bloody chaos, Gerry.'

'Great.' He grinned. Is there a hack who doesn't love it when governments get custard-pie in the face? Gerry and I have a similar outlook on life and share a lot of laughs during accident-prone administrations, when Ministers' trousers are falling down at the despatch-box. I find Gerry's unashamed glee a far more honest response than the sober tut-tutting of the Press Gallery 'heavies', and I like his company a lot, although what he said next froze the smile on my face.

'There's a story going around that Carter's about to resign, Beef. Have you got anything on that?'

'Resign? Carter?'

'Yes. I heard it from someone who'd been talking to a friend of a friend. Nothing definite, just a rumour.'

'I don't buy it, Gerry, I really don't.'

'Why not? Somebody's going to have to get the concrete boots treatment.'

'Yes, I know, Gerry. But I think Carter's all right. He must be all right.'

'Why must he?'

'I can't explain, Gerry. I've just got a hunch he's a survivor.'
I put my hand on my forehead and noticed I was sweating
heavily. Ninety-nine per cent of the unsubstantiated rumours
at Westminster fizzle out quickly, but it would be catastrophic
if this one were true. Scandals involving ex-Ministers pay half
as much as scandals involving Ministers, and I didn't want my
precious fox shot by the Prime Minister in a Cabinet reshuffle. I
couldn't explain that to Gerry, of course, so I gave him a
reassuring pat on the shoulder and told him there were half a
dozen heads likely to roll before Carter's. When he asked whose
and I couldn't think of any smart answers, he looked at me
suspiciously.

'What is this, Beef? You really want Carter to stay in there,
don't you? He's a creep, for Christ's sake. What's he done to
make you feel so sympathetic?'

I shuffled and looked coy. It was time for creative fiction and
the Muse didn't fail me. 'He's a dog-lover, if you must know,
Gerry.'

'You're joking, Beef.'

'No, I'm not. He takes in stray dogs from the street and looks
after them. We're doing a feature on it next week, so it would be
a pity if he was out of office. The man's a real St Francis in his
constituency, apparently. People bring their pets to him and he
heals them by homeopathy. He once cured a sick Dalmatian by
putting a plastic bag over its head and telling it about the mixed
economy. Then there was a horse with a migraine –'

Gerry clapped his hands together with delight. 'So you *were*
joking, Beef!'

'Of course I was, Gerry. See you Monday.'

We parted chuckling. It's bad form for a lobby correspondent to be thought to be an apologist for a particular Government Minister, and I hadn't wanted Gerry to misinterpret my
anxiety about Carter's future. Total secrecy would be essential
as I began pulling the final threads together, and there was no
point in becoming the subject of gossip myself. I'd tell Gerry the

180

whole story one day and I knew he'd understand, for he muck-raked as enthusiastically as anyone and would enjoy Carter's demise hugely. He worked for a rival tabloid, so he knew real news when he saw it.

Parliament Square was clogged up with traffic, so I walked up Whitehall to Trafalgar Square to get a taxi. The lights in the Treasury and the Foreign Office were burning fiercely, and you could imagine the frantic minutes buzzing between the two. 'Foreign exchange problems aren't our pigeon. Of course they're your pigeon. No, they're *your* pigeon. Do something for Christ's sake. Do something for Christ's sake . . .' The panic was even more evident in Downing Street, where a crowd of more than two hundred ghouls had gathered on the pavement. Their impassive exteriors masked a ravenous appetite for calamity, and they seemed determined to stay there until the corpse of a Cabinet Minister had been carried past in a coffin. It was no joke disturbing their concentration, as their eyes were glued to the door of Number 10 as if to a television screen, but I sidled up to a middle-aged man with his coat pulled up over his chin and asked him what was happening. He turned and scowled at me, as if I was a popcorn-scruncher in the back row of a cinema, then whispered in a hoarse voice 'Emergency Cabinet meeting at 3.30. To discuss the state of the pound.' This was succinct, if colourless, so I nodded and thanked him for his pains, at which he growled and resumed his vigil in silence. I was a bit stuck for polite chit-chat and, failing further inspiration, was about to ask him why one of his ears was thirty per cent bigger than the other when I realised he mightn't appreciate the question, being plainly a shy man with a limited interest in his own physiognomy. At this point, the crowd suddenly surged forward, as if expecting a shot at goal, and I saw a man leaving Number 10 looking like a deranged buffalo. I didn't recognise him at first, then remembered he was the Governor of the Bank of England. He snapped something unprintable at the TV reporters, then lurched towards his car, where one hoped a stiff brandy was waiting for him. The Prime Minister was legendary for his ingenuity in finding scapegoats for his own cock-ups and, if the pound had shed nine cents in a day, the Governor of the Bank would do nicely for starters. I could imagine the wildly unfair bollocking he had just had, and felt a twinge of sympathy as his car limped back to Thread-needle Street.

'Who was that?' asked a disembodied voice in the crowd.

'Undertaker,' shouted a wag.

'Brain-specialist,' said another.

'It was the Chief of the Defence Staff,' said a man with polished teeth and an umbrella. He sounded so like a scout-master from a minor public school that nobody challenged him. 'There'll be implications for the Forces.'

'What sort of implications?' asked the woman next to him.

'Security implications, of course,' whispered the man irrit-ably. Didn't she realise that, if the pound had lost nine cents, our boys had to go in there and get them back?

'Oh I *see*,' said the woman. 'Clever that.'

The crowd fell silent again, looking alternately at the door of Number 10, in case someone else was flung out into the street, and at Whitehall for any new arrivals. At 3.25, Cabinet Ministers started arriving in their Princesses. The Foreign Secretary was moving with the enthusiasm of a dead aardvark, and the Lord Privy Seal limped heavily in a bid for sympathy. Carter was one of the last to arrive. His car glided down Downing Street in the unobtrusive way which was his own hallmark, and he covered the short distance from the car to Number 10 in stately, unhurried fashion. He reminded me of the sort of actor who gets rave reviews in simple-looking roles, because the roles aren't quite as simple as they seem and he makes damned sure the critics realise it. How much longer would he be giving this quietly understated performance, I wondered, and how ready was his understudy to take over?

Three-thirty arrived and, inside Number 10, a ferocious post-mortem began. It would last several hours, I knew, because the Cabinet would have to appear to be doing something about the pound, even if they were only holding hands in the dark and whistling 'Auld Lang Syne'. But still

182

none of the crowd left. They craned forward eagerly in the hope that a voice would be raised in anger and a word or two, expletives preferably, penetrate to the outside world. If a whole sentence had been audible, it would have embarrassed them because they sincerely believed that Her Majesty's Ministers should be able to hold private counsel in such a crisis and make statesmanlike provision for the national good. A word or two would have been nice, though, if only to tell people back home about, so they waited vainly to hear one. I left them to their vigil and took a taxi to an address in Soho.

.

19

'I know your name well, of course, Mr Wellington. My wife is a great fan of yours. Please come this way.'

The man was corruptible. I knew it as soon as I shook hands with him and followed him into his spacious, brashly furnished office. His little eyes darted nervously about him, as if he imagined faces staring at him from the orange floral patterns on the wallpaper, and the stripes on his suit were too widely spaced for a publisher. I didn't know his price, but I was sure he had one, so I dug myself in for the siege.

The publishing house of which he was chairman (a medium-sized outfit, with its heart in obscure Scottish fiction and its head in coffee-table books about the royal family) was tucked away in a side street off Soho Square, flanked by a massage parlour and a delicatessen. That placed it half-way between hell and heaven on the Beef Wellington scale, so I privately nicknamed the man Purgatory. His real name was longer and Greek, I think, although he insisted that I call him Harry. That was another reason I knew he was corruptible. A man of professional rectitude would never have been so intimate with a visitor asking such unprofessional favours.

At first, he did give the answers an honest man would have given. No, he couldn't discuss the contents of Mr Wiseman's manuscript with me. No, he couldn't say if it had contained material about Mr Carter. No, he wasn't in a position to disclose any legal advice he might or might not have received. But then he wavered, offered me a drink when he should have showed me the door, and asked in a casual-sounding voice, as phoney as Christopher's, what lay behind my questions.

'Money,' I said firmly, going straight for the jugular. Purgatory's eyes weren't so small that I couldn't see the proverbial cash registers in them, and he smiled when he heard me speak his language. The part of a seedy vulgarian was suiting me so well that no acting was needed. 'I'm working on a big story, Harry, a really big story, and I need to get all the details right. Every extra twist to the story adds another nought to the final pay-off. I'm sure you understand.'

'Of course, of course.' Above his head, a thought-bubble the size of a hydrogen balloon said: WHO WILL PUBLISH YOUR STORY, MR WELLINGTON? But he didn't ask the question aloud, not yet. With a smoothness that would have passed for sophistication if his twitching eyes hadn't betrayed him, he asked, 'Does the late Mr Wiseman's manuscript have a bearing on this story?'

'It may do.'

'You don't seem certain.'

'How can I be? I haven't read the damned thing.'

'And if you had read it?'

'Then I'd know if it was important.'

'I see.'

'And how much jam it added to the sandwich.'

'I see.'

He offered me a cigarette, which I refused, and we looked at each other warily, not knowing which of us would show his hand first. Then we talked on a bit more, hedging round what really interested us, approaching it at tangents but never confronting it head on. It was apt that we were in Soho, the home of striptease; no professional artiste ever teased an audience more subtly, hinted at hidden treasures more artfully, peeled off layer after layer with more tantalising slowness. Purgatory was the first to crack. He looked studiously at his Japanese watch, as if only a pressing engagement in half an hour's time made him resort to such vulgar directness, and coughed. It was only a very little cough, but little coughs often mean more than big coughs, as every hack knows.

185

'Have you given any thought, John, to the actual process of, er, marketing this story?'

'How do you mean, Harry?'

'Well, presumably your newspaper will want to run it first.'

'Yes, presumably. Or one of the big Sundays.'

'But then you'll want to recycle it to a less ephemeral audience, very possibly a *larger* audience.'

'I don't quite understand, Harry.'

'A good story can be sold in more than one market, John.'

'I'm sorry?'

'People don't only read newspapers, they read . . .'

'. . . Books! Yes, of course, *books*! I wasn't with you for a minute there, Harry. How silly of me!' I slapped my forehead with my hand in mock penance for my stupidity, but he scowled suspiciously and I had to pinch my leg hard to stop myself smiling. One of the problems with pathological liars is our megalomania. As soon as you identify someone as gullible, there's an urge to sell him the really big lie, tell him bigger whoppers than you need to, make a mockery of his inferior grasp of the difference between fact and fiction. It's exhilarating but, if you assess your opponent's IQ at zero, it can backfire. I could see Purgatory hadn't been fooled by my affected ignorance of the existence of books and was twitching all over with distrust, so, as soon as I had got my smirking under control, I made good my mistake. I went on bullshitting, but used greater guile.

'I appreciate, of course, Harry, that finding a book publisher will be very important once the newspaper rights have been settled. A story of this importance should do equally well in hardback or paperback. Serious readers will be interested in the political implications and, unless the man in the street's tastes have changed in the last five hundred years, ha ha –'

'Ha ha.' His answering laugh was forced and hollow, and I think he was salivating.

'– then he'll want to read about the sex angle.'

'Sex angle?'

'And there's the South African connection, of course.'

186

I nearly added, 'And the inclusion of a black-coated retriever pining since his master's death will open up the children's market', but I bit my tongue just in time. I had already done enough, more than enough. The reference to South Africa had added lustre to an already glittering package, and the poor man had well and truly bought it. He summoned his secretary and, in a crude effort to raise the status of our discussion, asked her to make some coffee. When she asked how we took it, he said 'Sugar, John?' in the most neutral tones possible, terrified of giving offence by appearing to expect the answer yes. He could see bloody well I took sugar, but wasn't going to risk upsetting me. His cravenness was pitiful, and I swear his bald little head was prostrating itself further and further in deference the longer we talked. When the secretary had produced the coffee, I moved in strongly and confidently for the kill.

'Now that I've set out my stall, Harry, and given you a few insights into this project of mine, I wonder if I could ask you a favour in return.'

'Surely.'

'I quite take on board what you were saying earlier about the importance of someone in your position, a man of discretion in business matters –'

'Surely, surely.'

'– having to treat manuscripts submitted to you in strict confidence. That was exactly the line I expected you to take and, between ourselves, I very much hoped you *would* take it, because of the reliance I might one day wish to place on your discretion myself.'

'Surely, surely, surely.'

The surelys were beginning to fall out of his mouth like lemmings over a cliff. As well as the hint that I might ask him to publish my book, I had now dispelled any impression that I was a grubby old hack, ferreting round for confidential information. Conversations with long Byzantine sentences are exhausting for a man of my girth, but this one was worth it. I took a deep breath and entered the final lap.

'I'm not asking, of course, to see a copy of the text of Mr

187

Wiseman's manuscript. That would be quite improper, Harry, and we both understand that. But I would be grateful if you could tell me one thing.'

'Surely.'

'The book was to be a general study of how the City works. Right?'

'Right.'

'But there was at least one chapter which contained material damaging to a certain public figure's reputation. You know the man I'm referring to.'

'Certainly.'

'As you will have gathered, my own book deals with the same man and contains several very damning revelations.'

'I guessed that.'

'I knew you were a shrewd operator, Harry. Now all I want to know is this. It has a direct bearing on the way I arrange the material in my book and will partly determine the form in which it hits the bookshops.'

'I understand.'

'Did Peter Wiseman accuse John Carter of improper financial dealings?'

'Yes.'

'Illegal financial dealings?'

'Yes.'

'Giving chapter and verse?'

'Yes.'

'Thank you, Harry. I'm obliged.'

I sat back in my chair and sipped smugly at my coffee. My direct, hard-edged questions had been perfectly timed, emerging so starkly from the fog of long-winded flannel that they took their prey without a struggle. Purgatory blinked back at me nervously. The thought was slowly penetrating that he had given me what I wanted and got nothing in return, just a nod and a wink which I could disclaim whenever it suited me. He had ransomed his professional integrity for a slice of cake he might never taste, a blockbuster he might never publish, a dream he might never experience. As his pride began to ache at

188

the ineptness of his bargaining, the steely control evaporated and he came back at me hard, asking me what I knew about Carter which had me so excited and pressing for details of the sex angle and the South African connection. I stonewalled doggedly and, the more I stonewalled, the angrier he got. He paced the room with the menace of an indignant wart-hog and made abusive references to my figure, which I ignored. As he got more desperate, he even tried to retract his earlier statements, saying he had meant to answer 'maybe', not 'yes', to my questions about Carter, and he went absolutely bananas when I produced a tape-recorder from my pocket to discredit him. I suppose he had a point, in that I hadn't mentioned I was taping our conversation, but it was rather pedantic and he should have known that the words 'off the record' aren't recognised by my sort of journalist. To be honest, I don't like arguing with people who don't know the meaning of humour, so, as soon as I had finished the chocolate biscuits which had come with the coffee, I got up and left. I could feel Purgatory's daggers burning into my back, but I was grinning all over my face. I had won.

Or had I? Half an hour later, my victory had lost its shine and I felt slightly ashamed. The more observant passengers on my bus home probably saw a few flecks of red in my sallow cheeks as I reviewed my triumph over Purgatory. Did that poor man really deserve my contempt, just because of his floral wallpaper and his loud suit and his nose for a lucrative deal? And what had I actually achieved? Self-satisfaction? A little. But what else?

The brutal truth is that a bad journalist will make a bad detective or a bad anything else. My wham-bam-thank-you-Sam style was bringing success, but only superficial success of the kind it's hard to consolidate. I was always asking the wrong questions in the wrong order, or finding some baroque way of blowing my chances. All right, so I now knew what I had suspected, that Carter had been involved in crooked dealings in the City; but what use were those three yesses on my tape

189

without the corroborative details? I had got my foot in the door, but how was I going to find out what was on the other side? I wouldn't get another squeak out of Purgatory, that was certain, and I didn't have a clue how to set about investigations in the City. The man I really wanted to interview was unavailable for comment, in an urn in the Maidenhead crematorium. It was galling to admit, by my afternoon's triumph was just another balls-up. Why is it only thin journalists who can get their facts right?

20

Back at home, Jenny was quietly reading a novel, unruffled by the drama of the collapsing pound. We ate a compromise meal consisting of a low-calorie first course and high-calorie dessert, and only over coffee, when I was still digesting the second helping of dessert which I had wolfed while she was in the kitchen, did she ask about my day. The main point of discussion was not the pound, but Christopher. When I described our conversation on the Terrace, her face turned to total disbelief.

'I just don't understand. How can he still feel the same about Carter after the way that man's treated him? Making him follow you like that and not giving any reason. It's so crazy. He must realise by now that Carter's a fake. It's just common sense.'

'He hasn't got common sense. That's the whole point. He's obsessed.'

'He must be mad.'

'He is. Oedipus complex, Electra complex, schizophrenia, tunnel vision: you name it, he's got it.'

We smiled, snug in our own sanity, but a certain gravity had interposed itself. The Christopher I had first described to Jenny – the gawky, naïve, well-meaning puppy who had mooned on to the Terrace the summer before and rhapsodised about Carter – had imperceptibly darkened in the intervening months. The man himself hadn't changed, but his very lack of change was a symptom of his psychological problems and his circumstances had changed dramatically. A comic *ingénu*, whom Jenny and I could laugh at unreservedly in the privacy of our home, was fast turning into the sort of luckless incompetent who becomes the second corpse out of seven in a Jacobean tragedy. I'm hard-bitten and I bite back hard, but Jenny is made of softer and better stuff and I could see traces of maternal anxiety stealing into her face.

'Wouldn't it be better in the long run if you told him everything?' she asked. She sincerely believes, I should explain, that the truth never does anyone any harm. 'He'd be upset, and he'd get mad with you for bursting his balloon, but he'd probably get over it eventually. Don't you think?'

I shook my head. 'He'd probably throw himself into the Thames, and I don't want to be responsible for that. Anyway, if I told him everything, he'd just go blabbing to Carter and demand an explanation and put Carter on his guard. It's too big a risk to take.'

She nodded agreement, but only half-heartedly. That poor mad boy was starting to worry her, touching deeper chords of sympathy than he'd ever struck in me. We're a classic example of the truism that men marry better women than they deserve: our respective humanity is inversely proportionate to our respective weights, as the case of Christopher proved. They say fat people are more generous than thin people, but they hadn't met me when they said it. Was it only professional detachment which kept me at arm's length from Christopher, I wondered? A lifetime spent handling politicians with asbestos gloves? Or had his awkward attempts at friendship exposed a deeper lack of feeling within me?

At nine o'clock, we watched a specially extended edition of the news. 'The pound has fallen nine cents against the dollar,' intoned the newscaster, in the same beyond-the-grave voice as she would have said, 'The world will end at midnight tonight.' She had got her job because of her sincere blue eyes, and because she was expected to give a bit of zap to stories about South America and lung transplants, but economic catastrophes weren't her forte and she escorted us ponderously through the day's events. There were pictures of the Chancellor of the Exchequer walking his poodle before breakfast, of young men with loud ties stampeding across the floor of the Stock Exchange, then of Ministers arriving for the afternoon Cabinet.

'Look!' said Jenny. 'There's a man there who looks exactly like you.'

'It is me.'

'Two of your shirt-buttons are undone. You look awful.'

'I had a good lunch. How did I know I was going to be on television?'

On the screen, Ministers were leaving Number 10 like survivors of the *Titanic* who wished they had gone down with the ship. Journalists rushed forward to shove microphones down their throats, but were brutally cold-shouldered. Too early to comment, announcements in due course, situation under control, wait and see, no need to panic: everyone made their own excuses and was whisked off into the night in cars. There was no sign of Carter, but his absence could mean everything or nothing. Boys do sometimes stay behind with the headmaster to receive some special punishment or reward but, for all I knew, Carter might just be attending a reception for the visiting Venezuelan Prime Minister. Either that, or he'd got lost on his way out. I once went to a reception for lobby correspondents at Number 10, took a wrong turning on the way to the gents' and ended up in the Prime Minister's bathroom with my trousers covered with toothpaste. It can happen to anyone.

After the scenes in Downing Street, an economic correspondent explained why the pound's sharp depreciation against the dollar was such an undesirable thing to happen on a Friday in February. It didn't mean the Americans had worked any harder than us recently, or were financial wizards or even spoke proper English, but it did suggest that some very rich people in New York and Washington didn't think we were a smart buy at the moment. It was now up to HM's Government to sock it to them hard, prove there was life in the old dog yet and generally make it clear that we weren't going to be ripped off by a country which wasn't even in business when Shakespeare wrote *The*

193

Merry Wives of Windsor. All right, those weren't his exact words, which were a mite too technical for me, but I've paraphrased the tone pretty fairly. I certainly saw Jenny's back stiffen as the reporter's voice cracked with emotion and, as the bulletin continued its Cook's tour of places in the news – the Bank of England, the Treasury, even Wopsley, yesterday's town, where farmers in one of the outlying pubs debated whether they had voted for the right candidate – she became more and more engrossed. After her admirable calmness earlier, her decline into sentimentality was lamentably rapid. By 9.40, when the bulletin ended, I felt like the only person in England not totally hooked on the drama of the ailing pound. My own thoughts had turned to the lonely road in Maidenhead where Peter Wiseman had died, and I wondered how long it would be before a very different national drama drew the ghouls to Downing Street again, and before my own face filled the television screen relating a funny thing that happened on the way to the by-election. I debated whether to demand £200,000 or £250,000 for the serialisation rights and, deciding on the higher sum, went to bed happy. With that sort of money, nine cents is pretty small beer.

194

21

Weekends are like weekdays: they don't see me at my most energetic. Without the discipline of work, levering myself out of bed can be a Herculean task, more manageable after midday than before. Jenny calls this sloth, but she often compounds my felony by bringing me cooked breakfasts in bed which take an hour to settle. I get up for lunch, as no serious meal can be consumed horizontally, but that's usually my first physical activity after getting dressed.

That Saturday was different. I had just begun burrowing through the bundle of morning papers when the telephone rang. It was Christopher, sounding as if he'd been stung on the inside of the nose by a large wasp. I didn't think there were wasps in Pimlico in mid-February, so I was curious to know what had given his voice its strangely anguished timbre. I didn't have to wait long to find out, as he plunged into his catalogue of woes like a jilted lover in a call-box with only 10p in his hand.

'You can't do this, John.' (Snuffle.) 'You really can't.' (Snuffle.) 'I just find it incredible that a responsible journalist' (snuffle) 'should write such a thing when the pound's in such trouble.' (Loud snuffle.)

So that was it, I thought, gesticulating at Jenny to turn off the hair-dryer with which she was wandering around the room. I had forgotten my sly insertion about Carter in the newpaper. If it upset the organ-grinder as much as his monkey, then I was motoring.

'I'm not quite sure what you're talking about, Chris,' I said

195

stiffly, stalling for time as I opened the paper to remind myself what I'd written. It was tucked innocuously into a corner on page five, but the bit about Peter Wiseman's death was there in black and white like a police charge-sheet. I'm not much of a romantic, as you may have noticed, but I'm a sucker for the romance of the printed word and I grinned like a schoolboy at the sight of my deathless prose staring mischievously up at me. Christopher punctured my moment of sentiment as ruthlessly as I had punctured some of his.

'Of course you know what I'm talking about, John. Stop bloody pretending.' The wasp up his nose seemed to have made its way to the other nostril and stung him a second time. He was fast becoming inaudible. 'How can you write an article like that after what you told me yesterday. It's just pure hypocrisy.'

'Why's it hypocrisy?'

'You know perfectly well why it's hypocrisy. Pretending someone's got a great future ahead of him, when you really think he's about to land in the shit. I think it's despicable. Downright despicable.'

What is it about being called despicable – and it's happened many times – that always makes me want to laugh? It's an important-sounding word, with four syllables and an impeccable Latin root, and, if a man is vulnerable to moral criticism, it ought to get home to him, especially if 'downright' is added. But, in my case, it never does. I find the word anodyne, appropriate in a spinsterish schoolmistress but much too genteel for the rough-and-tumble of politics. Coming from Christopher, it had the impact of a subsonic ping-pong ball and made me feel so sorry for him that I hoped he would dream up something ruder, if only for his own self-confidence. Needless to say, he didn't. Indeed, as soon as he'd used what he thought was his heavy artillery, he quietened down and apologised for sounding 'huffy'. I said that was quite all right, some of my best friends were huffy and I knew how he felt, and that placated him. If he'd known me better, he would have realised that huffiness is as common among my friends as anorexia, but the point escaped him. He stopped snuffling and took a deep breath; I could almost hear the wasp extricate itself from his nose and fly out of the window, allowing the tone of the conversation to normalise.

'Who is this Peter Wiseman, John?'

'He used to be a friend of your lord and master. He died last year in a car accident. I'm surprised you haven't heard of him if you know Carter so well. They were close friends.'

'The name does ring a bell. I think they were business associates too, now you mention it. But I still don't see why you –'

'Just padding, Chris, just padding. They asked me to produce 600 words and I was a few short. Just padding, I promise.'

'Come off it.'

'It's true.'

'Is it? Are you sure?'

'Of course I'm sure.'

I could hear him breathing heavily as he came up against a 22-stone brick wall, but he was learning a thing or two about me and he didn't waste any effort banging his head on it. Instead he tried to woo my confidence by tossing me a meaty little bone.

'You're right about one thing, though.'

'What?'

'About Carter being too valuable a Minister for the PM to sack. He offered to resign yesterday, but was asked to stay.'

'I know,' I said, controlling myself well. I didn't know, of course, and my eyebrows shot ceiling-wards at the news, but I wasn't going to put myself in Christopher's debt by admitting it. He sounded a little chagrined.

'How did you know?'

'Just Press Gallery gossip. And common sense, of course.'

'What do you mean?'

'If you think you might get the sack, you offer your resignation when your boss isn't ready to accept it. It's the oldest trick in the book. The last Chancellor but one offered to resign seven times, but he never did because he timed his offers

197

just right. Remember that when you're a Minister, Chris. You'll go a long way. It's not whether you make cock-ups that matters in politics: it's when and how you *admit* that you've made them. If you get it wrong, you get pissed on from a very great height, so you must avoid that at all costs.'

'Thanks a lot.'

'It's like playing the piano. All that really matters is the timing and keeping your fingers clean.'

'Yes, I'm sure.'

His tone was ironic and irritable, but the strange thing was he meant his thanks half seriously. My sour brand of *Realpolitik* had a horrible fascination for him, which explained why he still looked on me as a friend. I was the darker side of that shining world of hopes and ideals into which he had wandered, and he seemed to realise that he couldn't scale the peaks of that world without first coming to terms with people like me. That may make him sound uncharacteristically sensible and pragmatic, but it left me feeling uneasy about this aspect of our relationship when he rang off a few minutes later. Why had he bothered to ring me at all? He couldn't seriously have expected me to spill the beans about Carter, and he must have known that anything rude he said about the ethics of my article would fall on the deafest ears in Fleet Street. So why telephone? I half-suspected that his motives weren't so much practical as emotional: the cold-shower syndrome, a featherweight's perverse pleasure in sparring with a heavyweight. His ingenuousness might feed my exasperation, but my exasperated sarcasm seemed to give him something in return which I couldn't put my finger on. No doubt if I got him to that psychiatrist, there would be a perfectly simple explanation involving toilet-training and a suppressed childhood, but for the moment I was baffled. Jenny was advancing a complicated theory of her own when the telephone rang again.

'It's for you,' she said, and faded discreetly into the background. I can gauge the likely seriousness of a call from the way she hands me the receiver, and she handed me it so gingerly this time, as if it was a priceless Chinese vase of the

198

T'ang dynasty, that I adopted my most formal telephone manner.

'John Wellington speaking.'

'Good morning, John. It's me.'

With such an introduction, the voice at the other end should have been instantly recognisable, but wasn't. Only when I remembered how often people referred to Carter as 'he' did I guess who 'me' was. After the monkey the organ-ginder, I thought, and I sat very still in my chair, having little experience of telephone conversations with murderers and not wanting to get the formalities wrong.

'How are you?' I said guardedly. Social politeness seemed to call for condolencies about the state of the pound, but I couldn't think of anything that wasn't flippant and I didn't want to risk flippancy yet.

'Very well, thank you,' came the reply, smooth as a good whisky on a bad night. 'I've just been reading my morning papers.'

'Have you indeed?'

'I'm flattered you think I have such a brilliant future ahead of me.'

'It's only an intelligent guess.'

'Let's hope it turns out like that.'

'Indeed so.'

'Time will tell.'

'Of course.'

We would have sounded like two old golfing friends relaxing in the club-house, if it hadn't been for the taut little pauses which punctuated this exchange. I'm usually ice-cool in these wars of nerves, but Carter's determined *bonhomie* had me rattled. Get on with it, you skunk, I thought, twisting the flex of the telephone anxiously round my hand. You know I've been talking to Mrs Wiseman and you know she's told me about the murder. Why can't you do something human for a change, like panicking?

'Interesting your mentioning Peter Wiseman, by the way.' Far from panicking, he was almost insolently casual. 'His death was certainly distressing, very distressing. I believe you talked to his wife yesterday.'

'That's right. And the day before too.'

'Interesting woman, don't you think? Capable of great charm, but totally enslaved by her emotions. Did you find that?'

I hesitated. Women who make passes at men like me are passion's slaves all right, but I wasn't going to tell Carter that bit of the story in case he tried to use it against me. It was time for some tail-tweaking, so I said: 'No, I didn't really find that, as a matter of fact. She was certainly volatile, but she could talk with remarkable lucidity about some things.'

'Such as?'

'Oh, things that happened in the past. You know what women are like. Ancient history, some people would say, but extremely compelling to listen to.'

'I see.' For the first time, his voice seemed to crack. 'See' is a one-syllable word, but he dragged it out to two, he pronounced it so nervously. His conversation with Anna on Thursday night must have warned him he was cornered, but his worst fears were now being confirmed. He hesitated a long time, but then recovered well.

'I'm having lunch with her on Wednesday as a matter of fact. It will be interesting to see how our impressions of her compare.'

'It certainly will.'

My retort was calm, but I said a four-letter word under my breath which made Jenny look up from her paper. Carter's line of counter-attack was predictable, but the confidence with which he made it alarmed me. In a world of injunctions and libel writs, my position was one of near impotence without Anna's cooperation, and he knew it. Having successfully captured my queen, he started moving his pawns boldly forward.

'We must talk frankly about this, John.'

'Of course we must,' I replied, conscious of the irony. What chance was there of frankness from either of us, let alone both?

200

'I know why you went to Maidenhead on Thursday, and I don't blame you for going. You're a journalist; you have to investigate any promising leads you come across. But you're making a big mistake. A *very* big mistake. I want to tell you that.'

'Thank you. Would you mind telling me what this mistake is and why it's a very big mistake as opposed to a big mistake?'

There was a silence at the other end. Two straight questions on a Saturday morning was too much for a politician to handle, and I knew better than to expect candour. He was a devious bugger at the best of times, and he wasn't going to incriminate himself by plain talking.

'I can't go into details now,' he said eventually, with the lofty air of a Treasury Minister who's been asked for economic statistics he should know but doesn't. 'Let's just say I'm confident you are making a mistake, John, and I advise you to proceed with caution. There would be no point in distressing people we both knew by acting in a way prejudicial to the interests of all the parties concerned or by doing anything which was contrary to good legal practice. Do I make myself clear?'

No, of course you don't make yourself clear, I thought angrily. You never make yourself clear. I told him he had, though, just to keep him guessing, then it was my turn to counter-attack.

'Will your blood-hound be following me again today?'

'What do you mean?'

'Chris Jackson. Or is he your poodle?'

I winked at Jenny as I asked the question. There are times on the telephone when you ache to see the other person's face, and this was one. I imagine Carter turning the colour of an overripe peach, and I wondered whether he would try another bluster or be shrewd enough to apologise. I should have guessed the answer: like all clever politicians, he knew exactly when he could get away with a lie and when he couldn't.

'I'm sorry about that, John,' he said breezily. 'I got a bit carried away.'

'Aren't MI5 or MI6 meant to handle that sort of thing?'

'Somebody like that. I shouldn't have asked Chris to do it. I just got very worried that you –'

'That I was about to make a big mistake?'

'Yes.'

'How thoughtful of you. You should have just sent a chauffeur-driven car round to my hotel to take me straight back to London. It would have saved everyone trouble. Why did you offer to resign yesterday, by the way?'

'I didn't. How –'

'I'm watching you, baby, I'm watching you.'

With this puerile exit-line, delivered in my best Hollywood gangster style, I hung up abruptly, leaving him in the dark about what I knew. As with Christopher, I was puzzled by his motives for calling me. Had he really thought he could put me off the scent by saying two or three times in his Secretary of State voice that I was making a big mistake? If so, it was either a classic case of the corruption of power or a measure of his complete desperation. Jenny was in no doubt when I summarised our conversation.

'He's scared fartless,' she announced. The uncharacteristic vulgarism reflected her excitement at the situation, and she stamped her size 4 foot indignantly on the floor. 'What a nerve ringing you up like that! Was he just trying to frighten you?'

'I can't see how. He said something cryptic about not wanting to distress people we both knew.'

'What did he mean by that?'

'I don't know. Perhaps he's going to try to run somebody else over.'

'How childish! He should never have been elected.' Jenny takes democracy more seriously than me, I might say; she wants a Parliament composed entirely of adults. 'What sort of car does he drive?'

'I've no idea. That's a very good point. Wait, I think I can find out.'

I kicked myself for missing this trick earlier, picked up the receiver again and dialled Carter's home number. His wife

Sophie answered and I treated her to my widely admired impression of a policeman with laryngitis.

'Police Sergeant Tupper here, ma'am.' The secret of impersonating policemen on the telephone, incidentally, is to keep your head right back and dilate your lower lip as you talk. 'We're trying to trace the owner of an illegally parked vehicle. It's a red Ford Cortina, registration number –'

'I think you have the wrong person, officer. We drive a Volvo.'

'A red Volvo, madam?'

'No, it's grey.'

'Were you in possession of this vehicle on 8 May last year, madam?'

'Yes, we were as a matter of fact. We've had it two years. Why –'

'We need all the information we can get in cases like this, madam. I'm sorry to have troubled you. Good morning.'

I put down the receiver and smiled. Sophie Carter was too nice a woman to lie to on a regular basis, and she was also too intelligent to be taken in by my inventions. Half my questions had been irrelevant to tracing the owner of an illegally parked vehicle and, the more she thought about our conversation, the odder she would find it. If she reported it to her husband, it would be even better. He would either realise it was me and I was drawing my net closer, or think that the police themselves had him under suspicion. Either way, it would put him right off his spam and lettuce or whatever appetising fare he had for lunch on Saturday. I giggled sadistically at the prospect and ate a mountainous lunch myself, after which Jenny and I took a short walk in the High Street. We kept meticulously to the pavement and gave all grey Volvos a wide berth.

22

As it was Saturday, there was no way of telling if the pound was recovering or still sick. Was it gung-ho and waiting to bounce back on Monday morning, or would it get worse before it got better? Would those who priced such things still think it a good buy, or would we be valued at the going rate for off-shore banana republics? These worries probably gave a few people in SW1 and the City a sleepless weekend, and they even made an unconscious impression on the man in the street, judging by the number of faces which looked mildly anxious for no discernible reason. But Friday's feverish panic had passed. Like a football team which goes two goals down in the first five minutes, attacks desperately for the next ten, then realises it has time on its side and can afford to be more patient, the country had got a grip on itself. The announcement of the Chancellor's resignation therefore came as a surprise.

I was dummy at the time – we were playing bridge with some friends of Jenny's – and had only sneaked a look at the TV news headlines out of casual curiosity. If Carter had run anyone else over or Christopher had joined a monastery, I wanted to know about it. As it was, neither of my *bêtes noires* had been misbehaving, and the picture accompanying the news' jaunty signature tune showed the Chancellor of the Exchequer crying. At least, he appeared to be crying. It may just have been a blinking fit caused by the battery of television lights which surrounded him as he read out a statement on the steps of Number 11. At first I assumed he was announcing emergency measures to halt the run on the pound – seizure of American assets, 20 per cent surtax on petrol, meat rationing, anything to make the Government seem in control of the situation – but then I realised he was reading the text of a letter. 'I have given deep thought to my position,' he sniffed, 'and I have concluded, as a result of deliberations with colleagues and without any personal pressure being put on me, that it would be in the national interest for me to renounce the Chancellorship.' As an old stager, I could tell straight away he'd been sacked; Ministers who really have resigned don't make such a pantomime out of it.

'Jenny!' I shouted, but was told to shut up before I could continue. She was playing a Four Hearts contract with the trumps split four-nil against her, and wasn't in the mood for interruptions. She has the bridge bug badly, I should explain, and feels about the game the way I feel about lobster thermidor; I sometimes think that if the Bomb fell when she was playing, she would still find time to ask for the bidding again before choosing a lead. I left her to get on with it and turned back to the news.

A series of stills photos flashed on to the screen, a *Who's Who* of middle-ranking Cabinet Ministers. These were the *papabili* or those whom the BBC's political correspondent regarded as the *papabili* and, judging by the number of faces, he had spread his bets generously. Six or seven Ministers were mentioned, including Carter, and there was even a panic scenario in which the Governor of the Bank of England would become Chancellor in the Lords, presumably as Lord Threadneedle. The idea was so farcical that I squirmed uncomfortably in my chair. It's embarrassing to see a fellow lobby correspondent getting hysterics in public, as we're supposed to earn our living from politicians getting hysterics, not the other way round. But this poor man had so obviously flipped his lid that, if he'd started canvassing my name as the next director of Oxfam, nobody would have blinked. It was pathetic. My own feet were more firmly on the ground. With complete clarity, I saw there was only one candidate and that Carter's assumption of the Chancellorship was not just likely, but inevitable. Only when the full hand has been played does a clever card-player's skill become apparent, and so with Carter. He had distanced himself from the main thrust of Government policy at just the right time and, having apparently put his head on the block, had actually made himself indispensable to the Prime Minister. Politics is like a hall of mirrors. Doctrinal heresies which are punished when the going is smooth become positive assets in a crisis, as the captain desperately tries to ballast the ship and stop the exodus of rats. With the mud now flying around his ears, the Prime Minister would be looking to broaden the foundations of his Government, to stop it toppling over altogether, and would turn to Carter because he had no choice in the matter. It was obvious, and so was my own response. Patriotic duty might be gently nagging me to ring Number 10 and warn them against entrusting the nation's finances to an embezzler and murderer, but I put such temptations behind me. My book would now be worth £500,000 at least; it wasn't the moment for heroics.

'I made it,' said Jenny, coming over from the card-table.

'Made what?'

'Four Hearts. I squeezed Henry in the black suits and threw Mary in with a trump.'

'Well done, darling. Sorry I wasn't there to watch. The Chancellor's just resigned. Actually, he was sacked. You could tell.'

'Who's been put in his place?'

'It hasn't been announced, but I can guess. Carter.'

'*Carter?* But he *can't.*'

'Why not?'

'You know why not, dear.' She lowered her voice to a whisper so that the others wouldn't hear us, and hissed, 'He's going to be *arrested* any day now.'

'Exactly. But the Prime Minister doesn't know that, does he? As far as he's concerned, Carter's Mr Clean, just the sort of man who'll be immensely reassuring to the old grannies in Sussex who're worried about their savings. Only we know better, don't we?'

'You bet.' She giggled guiltily, sharing my pleasure at the line of banana-skins stretching out to the horizon, but plainly troubled by more responsible misgivings. Our little game of cat-and-mouse with Carter was fast getting out of hand. It now overlapped with the whole soap-opera of the pound, which had so engrossed Jenny the night before and which she wanted to end happily, with the pound rehabilitated. My clumsy sleuthing now looked as if it would put the skids under more than a single politician's career, a thought which first restrained Jenny's giggling, then snuffed it out altogether. When we rejoined the others, she reported the Chancellor's resignation as solemnly as if the man had died of dysentery. Henry said 'Gosh!', which was very much his style, and Mary said 'Wow!', which was hers, then we started playing again.

For the next three hours, my mind grappled with take-out doubles, forcing raises and deep finesses – or it should have done. I'm normally a reasonable player, not a tiger like Jenny, but not a rabbit either – a golden retriever might best convey my unspectacular competence – but that night I just couldn't concentrate. Nothing aggravates a lobby correspondent more than a big story breaking on a Saturday; it's like a friendly leg-spinner coming on to bowl when you're back in the pavilion with your pads off. You can telephone Members, of course, swop gossip with fellow hacks, take soundings, plug into the whole network of Chinese whispers that functions whether the House is sitting or not. But it's not the same as watching the show live from the Press Gallery. Take away that inimitable baying for blood from the Opposition benches, and the hunt seems remote and the fox an abstraction: you don't really care if he's torn to pieces by the hounds or rescued by saboteurs from the Whips' Office putting aniseed on the trail. I was aching to be in the thick of things, buffeted by the rumours and counter-rumours which always course through the House in advance of a new appointment (Would it be X? Had Y's hour finally come? Could it somehow be Z?), not playing bridge for 5p a hundred in Finchley. Although all my instincts told me Carter would get the job, without the confirmation of others reaching the same

207

conclusion I was riddled by doubts. Had I completely misread the situation? Would Carter soon be resigning as well? Was it just wishful thinking, the glint of publisher's royalties in my eye, which made me want to propel him further up the ladder? How could I be *sure*?

Jenny saw I was chafing and knew why, so she treated my lapses of concentration at the bridge-table with good humour. When I revoked for the second time in half an hour – a serious bridge crime, which would normally have made her look daggers at me and cut off my supply of whisky for the evening – she simply said 'Having no spades, partner?' in a sweet voice, and smiled at my confusion. Henry and Mary were keen to go on playing after midnight, but she shooed them politely away, then made me some Ovaltine. You could say a loving wife would have brought a brandy, but Jenny's love doesn't always run along conventional lines and, although I would have preferred a brandy, I drank the Ovaltine uncomplainingly, confident there was some loving wifely reason for her producing it.

'Do you really think he'll get it?' she asked. The 'he' and the 'it' were self-explanatory, so well did she understand my obsessions.

'Yes, I do. I've been thinking about it hard, and there are no other serious candidates.'

'Well then.'

'Well what?'

'Well, there you are.'

'What do you mean?'

'I mean, there's nothing you can do about it. It's not your fault if he's made Chancellor, and you'd be mad to give up on your story now. Nothing's changed at all. Just keep on at that man until you've nailed him properly. It's simple.'

Her voice had a confident ring, as though she believed it really was simple, but I knew the confidence was only cosmetic, an attempt to whistle away some of my anxieties. She was right to insist that I carry on, but wrong when she said nothing had changed. The situation was changing the whole time, in small

208

but complicated ways which were hard to assimilate. I should have been staring with my mind's eye at a jigsaw puzzle with a few missing pieces, but all I saw was a kaleidoscope in which there was no fixed point. Drink normally makes me a heavy sleeper, with the full range of sound effects, but that night I hardly slept at all. Long after Jenny had finished replaying all the slams in her head, making different opening bids and trying different finesses and giving satisfied grunts as hindsight gave her all the answers, I lay on my back with my eyes open and tried to get my bearings. I was totally, totally lost.

23

By three in the morning, all I knew was that I was a shit. These flashes of self-disgust come to me from time to time, generally after a good meal washed down by a good wine, but they don't often last. Low self-esteem is one of the natural conditions of both fat people and tabloid hacks and would make each miserable if they hadn't developed sophisticated counter-measures. Fat people's answer is to convert the universally disliked quality of obesity into the universally liked quality of exorbitance. They eat two hamburgers when others would eat one, then play up to their role as amiable eccentrics by eating a third which they don't really want. Hacks are much the same. Instead of wearying of their dreadful prose and fake emotions, they camp up their writing style and develop a professional callousness which enables them to put their name to anything. I should know. Thirty years' solid hacking and putting on weight have given me an elephant's hide commensurate in size and texture with the animal inside. My greatest strength – or shortcoming, depending how you look at it – is that I rarely let my shortcomings depress me.

But that night I did. I was comparing myself in an idle way with the two politicians – the ambitious Cabinet Minister and the young backbencher – whose lives had intersected with mine and whose destinies I now partly controlled. It wasn't at first a serious appraisal, more an exercise in do-it-yourself one-upmanship, the sort of game you might play with yourself at a pedestrian dinner party, looking round the table and thinking, well, I'm wittier than him, I go to a better tailor than him, my wife's cleverer than his, but do I, being frank, have such finely chiselled cheekbones as him? This kind of riddle passed endlessly through my head as I thought about Carter and his pathetic young sidekick, and the answers I came up with didn't flatter me at all.

I was a journalist and they were politicians: that seemed to damn us both equally. I hadn't read Dante, but I assumed he had consigned the schemers and scribblers of medieval Florence to adjacent circles close to the bottom of the pit: above the cut-throats and the child-molesters and the traffic wardens and the psychiatrists and the joggers and even the fornicators, just; but below the stockbrokers, the chartered surveyors, the football hooligans, the ski-instructors and the theatrical agents. Yet, even in the depths of our respective infamies, the politicians had more to redeem them than I did: not truth, for we abused it equally; and not love, for we were each in thrall to self-interest; but something certainly, some quality vibrant in them and absent in me, a quality you could loosely call hope. We're all in the gutter, but some of us are looking at the stars – as my Aunt Millie used to say when she was doing the ironing. Christopher's brand of hope might be naïve and adolescent, Carter's stale and familiar, a political 'vision' drummed out in so many up-beat after-dinner speeches that it had little melody left. But they still had the hope and I didn't, and that hurt. Even if my professional duty lay in deriding the tawdry illusions they peddled their electors, as human beings I envied them.

The strange thing was that, as I lay awake thinking about Carter and wondering what skulduggery he had got up to in the City, I almost convinced myself I was destroying a good man's career. After a bit, I stopped thinking about the murder and my inconclusive visit to Purgatory and ruminated more and more on the strange story of theft and reparation which Dr Trumper had told me. It struck me forcibly that, if I had embezzled money from an institution – and it's a big if because, like all sizeable citizens who know they couldn't run ten yards to escape pursuit, I have a horror of even petty larceny – then

211

there's no way I would have paid the money back ten years later, with inflation taken into account. That would only have risked reviving memories of my former crime and, if spotted by an alert mind like Trumper's, of confirming my guilt. In no way could it have been an act of practical prudence. All Carter could have gained was peace of mind and, if his mind was so susceptible to pangs of guilt so long after the event, then it was probably quite a healthy mind in the first place. That a man of such natural rectitude should become Chancellor of the Exchequer was momentarily enchanting. Having raised taxes by £1 billion in his first year, would he feel morally obliged to give the money back in tax concessions in his second? It was charming to speculate. 'He makes mistakes like the next man, but he always makes amends for them: Vote Carter for Integrity.' I was almost falling in love with my own creation, the political crook with the heart of gold, when my mind went back to Peter Wiseman's murder. How would he make amends for that? By marrying the widow? I was getting sentimental, I told myself sternly, and I tried to banish this glossier image of Carter from my mind.

But I couldn't. That was the funny thing. I kept contrasting the unalloyed cynicism with which I hoped Carter would become Chancellor, simply so that my scoop would blaze the more brilliantly, with his own more complex motivations. These included vanity, delusions of grandeur, the hunger for power for its own sake and two dozen other variations on the sin of Pride, deadliest of the whole seven, deadlier even than Gluttony, I remembered with satisfaction from my schooldays. But wasn't there also something else, a sincere belief that, as a result of his efforts, the poor might become less poor, the old and sick better provided for, the payers of VAT on theatre tickets and washing-machines less heavily taxed? It might be present only vestigially under the calculations of self-interest, but I was sure it was there somewhere, if only because Christopher's Messianic view of Carter had to derive from something more substantial than his clear blue eyes and the resonance of his voice. It all came back to hope, the thing they

212

had and I didn't. I might not embezzle money, I might not filch embarrassing manuscripts during funerals, I might not run people over with my Volvo, I might not hop from bed to bed like an E-type kangaroo. But what did I do instead that made me worthy to throw stones at Carter?

I apologise for these morbid insights into the private thoughts of Beef Wellington Esq., who is normally the most jovial of company and, in the light of my physical circumstances, the least self-pitying of men. I normally shun psychology and morality with the same determination with which I avoid vegetarian restaurants. I live from day to day and, by and large, I live well. If I mention that I slept badly and ended up out of sorts with myself, it's only to explain the fact that Sunday found me in a very different mood from Saturday. Whatever adrenalin is supposed to do when you're excited, it had completely stopped doing. I felt flat and lethargic and was glad, rather than frustrated, not to be spending the day in the busy maelstrom of the House. I ate and drank little and, when it was duly announced on the lunchtime news that the Prime Minister had appointed Mr John Carter Chancellor of the Exchequer, I was unmoved. I had worked off all the excitement of that development the previous day and didn't have a hooray left in my body. Jenny got much more worked up. When they showed pictures of Carter and his wife standing proudly together in Downing Street, she hissed loudly as if he was a pantomime villain about to abduct the heroine. I couldn't blame her for feeling like that, but I lacked the energy to join in the fun.

'He's taller than I thought,' she said, glued to the screen. 'He must be nearly six foot, but he always seemed smaller than that before.'

'It's an illusion, darling. I read an article about it once. Subconsciously, people associate height with power in the same way that they associate weight with self-indulgence. It's completely irrational.'

'Well, how tall is he really?'

'I've no idea. Five eight, five nine. Does it matter?'

'No, I suppose not. Hey, look at that. He's kissing his wife.'

'Revolting.' I tried to avert my eyes in disgust, but was mesmerised by the consummate political skill of the embrace. It certainly fooled Jenny.

'They seem so very affectionate, John. Like newly-weds. You can't be completely spontaneous on the television, but I'm sure they're not faking it. Look at the way he's holding her now, for example. Look!'

'I'm looking.'

'Charming.'

'Yuk.'

'He must love her after all. I just can't believe he's the sort of man who sleeps around.'

'Because he's nearly six foot or because he's just kissed his wife on television?'

'Neither. He just looks terribly domesticated.'

'Balls!' I was getting irritated by her naïveté, although I had nursed the same prejudice about Carter myself for years, until Anna Wiseman disillusioned me. She must be watching this tender scene with mixed feelings, I thought, and I didn't have to wait long to have the thought confirmed. The telephone rang less than five minutes later, and her distinctive voice began throbbing with emotion at the other end.

'Have you heard the news? I just couldn't believe it. Why did they choose John? There must be someone more suitable. Has something been going on I don't know about?'

I took her points patiently, one by one, hoping to instil some calm. Yes, I said, I had heard the news, and she had better start believing it because it was true. No, there wasn't anyone more suitable than Carter and, yes, one or two things had been going on she might not know about. The pound had fallen nine cents in a day, which was slightly unusual, and, if she'd read her *Sunday Times* carefully, the proper bits, not the colour supplement, she might have spotted a small article tucked away on page seven which mentioned that Britain was going through its biggest financial crisis since 1929.

'Yes, I know, I know.' She quite missed my sarcasm in her

214

excitement. 'But why him? Why John? What can he do about the pound? He's not a magician, you know.'

'I never said he was. I just said he was the best man for the job.'

'Are you sure? Couldn't someone else do it just as well? I thought the civil servants took over when there was a crisis.'

'Well, they do, of course they do. But you still need a figurehead. Someone has to appear on television in a nice suit and explain what the civil servants have decided. It's an old British tradition, like Parliament.'

'Yes, I know.' Still she hadn't rumbled my irony. 'But couldn't someone else be the figurehead? Someone older? Or even someone younger? It doesn't really matter, does it?'

'Not really, I suppose. It depends. There are a lot of different factors the Prime Minister has to take into account.' I stopped to think what they were, and it was only then that the significance of this new development really impressed itself. Anna may have been weaned on the Dutch equivalent of Mills and Boon, but she'd forgotten to read the one which said that power was an aphrodisiac and coyly explained what that meant. Carter's enhanced power and prestige meant absolutely nothing to her, I realised; as far as she was concerned, it was just a further obstacle to their *grand amour flambé*. When he had telephoned her on Thursday and soft-soaped her and asked her to lunch, she must have thought she was back in business and had stolen a march on politics in the tug-of-love she imagined raging in his heart. Now she must know she had lost, that a poor second was the best she could hope for and that their romantic mid-week lunch would be at best a sandwich in the Treasury cafeteria under the beady eye of the Permanent Secretary. She must hate him, I thought, she must really hate him. I wouldn't just get her into the witness-box, I would get her to perform brilliantly for the prosecution. Carter's fate was now as good as sealed, and I kicked one of my shoes half-way across the room to celebrate, all lethargy gone. I had learnt from bitter experience that you had to take advantage of Anna's more propitious moods or you lost her, so I was thinking how to

215

exploit her anger when she helped me without prompting.

'There was something you asked me to find out. Do you remember?' I listened with amazement to the transformation in her voice. From the desperate frustration which had accompanied her earlier questions, it had become calm and mischievous, the way it had been when she had teased me about Carter's misdemeanours in Oxford. She was my co-conspirator again, the rejected woman who wanted her pound of flesh, even if it came from the Chancellor of the Exchequer's heart. I didn't remember what I'd asked her to find out, but I gripped the receiver excitedly all the same. 'It's the mouse.'

'I'm sorry?'

'I said, the mouse.'

'What mouse? You mean House, don't you?' I was baffled. If she thought of me as a fat cat, then I suppose Carter was my mouse, but I hadn't yet noticed Anglo-Saxon word-play among her accomplishments. Then it clicked. I remembered a beautiful woman curling up her lips in disdain as she discussed a less beautiful one, and knew exactly what Anna was talking about.

'You mean Carter's woman from last year?'

'That's right. The mouse.' The contempt was increasing every time she used the word. 'I've found out her name. I don't have an address, but you'll have to find that out for yourself. That will be easy, won't it?'

'I don't know. If it's Camelia Fforbes-Ponsonby-Ponsonby or Tamara Zykwartski, it will be simple. If it's Mary Smith, I might have to get back to you.'

'It's something between the two.'

'All right then. Let's have it.'

I grabbed a pencil from the table next to the telephone and was fishing in the drawer for a bit of paper when I realised I wouldn't need either. The name was so familiar it took me completely by surprise. I asked Anna to repeat it, exchanged a few platitudes about this and that, commiserated with her that her lover should waste his time playing Chancellor of the Exchequer, and hung up. Then I slumped into an armchair to

216

steady myself.

'What is it, darling?' asked Jenny, coming back from the kitchen. 'You look as if somebody's just kicked you.'

'They have,' I said. 'They really have this time. I'll tell you about it later.'

I was back on my feet and charging towards the front door like a hungry hippopotamus. Deep down, I knew it wasn't a twist in the story that I wanted, but my next visit was too pregnant with possibilities to be postponed. I was in the car and half-way out of the drive before I heard Jenny shouting at me not to forget my coat.

24

Yes, I thought as she opened the door, she is a mouse. Not the nasty brown sort you feed poisoned cheese or use for vivisection, but one of those soulful-looking white ones parents give their eight-year-olds in the hope that they'll spare daddy's blushes and give a practical demonstration of the facts of life. Her hair was smooth and silky, tempting you to stroke it, and her eyes, if not red exactly, looked out at the world with a timid alertness to any passing cats. She twitched too, although she was friendlier than when we had met before Christmas and seemed less daunted by my physical amplitude. I had thought her a naturally subdued woman, but the welcome she gave me was almost bouncy.

'Were you looking for Christopher? I'm afraid he's at the Ministry all day while this flap's on.'

'I was hoping to talk to you actually, Sandra.'

'Really? Whatever for? Profile of a new Member's wife?'

'Not exactly.'

'Don't tell me. You're writing a Parliamentary cookery book and asking people for recipes? Well, come in anyway. I'll make some tea.'

She showed me into the living-room, and I sat down and looked around while she went into the kitchen. The furniture and paintings were just as I remembered them, except that it was now daylight and the dull streaks of February sun which filtered through the lace curtains gave the walls the sober hue of a room where someone has died. The melancholy shades reminded me that this was where Geoffrey Hammond had got

218

drunk for the last time and where I'd first appreciated Carter's consummate political skills. It had been an eventful evening, more eventful than I'd realised. I'd followed the text, but a significant chunk of the sub-text had slipped past me unnoticed.

As Sandra poured the tea and sliced two very unequal portions of cherry cake, I weighed up her sexual attractions. Not with lust in my own heart, you understand – the cherry cake accounted for that – but in an effort, and it was an effort, to visualise her as Carter's mistress. I could see little there to attract a man whose conquests had included cosmopolitan beauties like Anna, and I would have been sceptical about the whole story if I hadn't learnt that Paradox was Carter's middle name. If he could be loved by Anna, who hated anything to do with politics, and by Christopher, whose child-like honesty was the exact reverse of the older man's deviousness, then why shouldn't he enjoy a temporary liaison with a mouse? If you're not in the mood for a tigress and don't mind the smell of cheese, a mouse is probably quite fun in bed, I thought, having little personal experience of either animal.

'Isn't it dramatic about the pound?' she said excitedly. It's strange how hard it is to let go of an idea once you've seized on it; I could have sworn I saw her whiskers twitching as she talked.

'It certainly is,' I said, doing my usual yes-man bit. 'The last few days have been quite extraordinary.'

'And Carter becoming Chancellor: what about that?'

'Terrific.'

'He was being so brilliant the night we all had dinner here, wasn't he?'

'He was indeed. Will Christopher stay as his PPS, or is that all up in the air?'

'It's up in the air at the moment. We should know in a day or two.'

'You can't have been seeing much of Chris lately.'

'Do I ever?' She smiled wryly and launched into a little moan about the barbarous sitting hours in the House. It was a

219

familiar theme, something I'd heard hundreds of Members' wives complain about, and it formed the basis of our small-talk for the next five minutes. I myself have no strong views on the subject: it's true that very little worth listening to is said in the House after six o'clock but, on the other hand, drinking late into the night with friends is one of the manifestations of a civilised life, so my loyalties are torn. My general policy in such discussions is to argue passionately against the other person's case, unless it's someone cleverer than me, when I agree with them. Sandra was certainly cleverer than me, or at least used long enough words to suggest she might be, so I nodded sympathetically at her complaints and did some intensive thinking at the same time. I had come to visit her on impulse, stimulated by the shock of hearing Anna identify her as the Mouse, but what the hell was I supposed to do next? Rehearsing various scripts in my head only brought home the difficulty of my position.

'Didn't you and Carter have an affair last year?' There was no way I was going to barge in with that. Even for a journalist of notorious bluntness, it was pretty bloody unsubtle and would draw a frosty response. 'Is it any of your business?' 'Not really.' 'Do you ask women that sort of question just for fun?' 'No, not at all.' 'Then what bloody business is it of yours?' 'If you must know, I'm investigating a murder.' 'Go on, pull the other one.' I could picture the whole exchange, and it was so horrific that I abandoned my usual sledge-hammer tactics in favour of a more crab-like approach.

'How long have you known John Carter, Sandra?'

'About five years. Chris used to work as his researcher before he got into the House.'

'Yes, I know. How do you find him?'

'Very capable indeed. He'll be a first-class Chancellor.' She sounded calm, but I was watching her closely and noticed that she crossed her legs at this point, as if unconsciously erecting a barrier against my questions. 'After that, he's got a real chance of being party leader. The constituency workers adore him, apparently. He seems a bit high-brow, but he communicates

220

his ideas so lucidly that –'

'Yes, I'm sure. I think what I really meant was: how do you find him as a person?'

'How do you mean?'

'I mean – what do I mean? – I mean, do you find him personally attractive?'

'As a man, you mean?'

'Yes, I suppose so.'

'He's OK. Why?' She looked at me suspiciously and, from the rigidity of her posture, wasn't going to start discussing Carter's prowess between the sheets without someone putting a gun to her head. I tried the old interviewer's ploy of injecting a long, prickly pause into the conversation, inviting indiscretions, but she outstared me easily and I had to break the silence myself. Subtlety had proved incompatible with the Beef Wellington style, so I took a deep breath and plunged in with the question I'd earlier discarded.

'Didn't you and he have an affair last year?'

'What bloody business is it of yours?'

I wriggled miserably in my chair and ate a bit of cake to cover my embarrassment. Her retort was even blunter than I'd feared and, under those non-existent eyebrows, her eyes were blazing furiously. To prevent a rout, I told her about my murder inquiry and, when she scoffed at the suggestion, filled in the details. I didn't give names, in case she blew the whole thing, but I did convince her I was serious. I saw a flurry of emotions play across her face, then watched her features form themselves into a determinedly virtuous mould, like a nervous Victorian bride lying back and thinking of England. Not for her Anna Wiseman's faith that love was all that mattered, the cracked romantic voice, the assumption that I wanted to listen to her describe her passions at gruesome length. She was a Member of Parliament's wife, someone expected to behave with decorum at all times; in this situation, that meant truth unadorned with feeling.

'Christopher was away in Washington,' she said simply. 'I got bored. It was over in three months.'

I nodded. It was nice not having to listen to details about pyjamas and hotel room numbers, but plain English isn't always as plain as it should be. Her little triptych sounded like an entry for a Japanese haiku competition in the *Spectator*, and I'm afraid my mind turned to parody. 'The pound was falling. I weigh 22 stone. He did it with a grey Volvo.' Her own haiku was a masterpiece of ambiguity, especially the expressionless way she delivered it. Did she mean that she got bored because Christopher was in Washington, or that it was over in three months because she got bored with it? The question was crucial and, if she hadn't made it so obvious that 'it' was something middle-class English mice preferred doing to talking about, I would have asked her to elucidate. Instead I tried to match her bald, factual manner.

'Do you know anything about his movements on 8 May last year?'

'No I don't. That's our wedding anniversary.' The co-incidence was cruel and brought some colour back to her cheeks. How dare I suggest that she would spend that evening with anyone but Christopher?

'So you didn't see Carter at all?'

'No.'

'It would be better for him if you did.'

'Why?'

'Because it could give him an alibi.'

'But I didn't see him.'

'Fair enough.'

I left it at that, no wiser about Carter's movements but still in business, because he didn't yet have an alibi. Sandra perched stiffly on the edge of the sofa, mortified that her sexual relationships were under discussion but obviously aching to ask questions of her own. She offered me some more cherry cake, but I refused, making a deliberate effort to unsettle her and impress her with the gravity of the situation. I knew she would remember the gusto with which I had eaten her profiteroles at the dinner party and hoped she would reflect that, if I was off my food, there must be a serious upheaval in the order of things.

222

I may be giving my machiavellian scheme too much credit, but it was certainly just after I refused the cake that she appeared to realise the dangers of a tight-lipped response to my inquiries. Suppose she just sat there and the man whose bed she might have been sharing, but hadn't, was convicted for want of an alibi? Even with a former lover, that would be a painful irony, and it made her question me more closely.

'Isn't it possible that John was in the House that evening? Have you checked?'

'Yes, I have checked. He missed divisions at 10.15 and 11.30.'

'And that was the time when –'

'Yes.'

'But he might have been anywhere, anywhere at all. Where does he say he was?'

'He doesn't. I haven't asked him.'

'Why not?'

'It would be a waste of time. He'd just cook up some story and, anyway, I don't want to put him on his guard.'

'But that's disgraceful.'

'Why?'

'You're assuming he's guilty and not giving him an opportunity to prove his innocence, if he is innocent.'

I shrugged. She was right, of course, and I was familiar with the principle of law to which she referred, even if Fleet Street's principles are different. My bovine callousness was a ploy to shock her into greater loquacity in Carter's defence, and it worked.

'It's entirely possible that you've got hold of the wrong end of the stick. Had that occurred to you?' Her tone was suddenly didactic, and I remembered Christopher telling me she lectured in law somewhere in Fulham. 'You say that a friend of John Carter was knocked over by a passing car, which *may* not have been an accident, and that John *may* have had a motive for wanting this man killed. Is that it?'

'More or less. Except that the murdered man's widow told me that Carter said something to her which implied he had killed her husband.'

'Only implied?'

'Yes, only implied. It didn't sound definite.'

'It's a bit bloody thin, isn't it?'

'That's why I'm trying to fatten it up. Could I have some more cake now, please?'

I grinned, taunting her with my cynicism, and I didn't get my cake. Just like her husband, the more outrageously I talked, the livelier her response: she was really steamed up by now, and I didn't blame her, because she was right. Calmly considered, my story was distinctly thin and, if the jury was packed with Sandra Jacksons, there was no chance of a conviction. She was clearly someone who rated common sense above imagination, and it was with a sudden burst of common sense, a confidence that there was a simple way out of the maze if you only looked for it, that she rose to her feet and went across to the telephone. I protested vigorously, but she would have none of it.

'What are you doing?'

'I'm ringing John Carter.'

'What the hell for?'

'To ask him what he was doing on 8 May.'

'You're wasting your time.'

'Why?'

'Because – because he won't be at home.'

'Are you sure?'

'He'll be in Whitehall.'

'Then I'll talk to Sophie.'

'You can't.'

'Why not?'

'Well, you know, you and her husband –'

'Does she know that?'

'I don't –'

'Of course she doesn't. She and I are the best of friends. Now will you please be quiet for a minute.' She had finished dialling and I could hear the ringing tone. In a film, I would have bounded across the room and torn the receiver from her hand, but then in a film I would have weighed 12½ stone and had

224

india-rubber legs. From the immobility of my armchair, all I could do was watch with fascination. Sandra was standing briskly to attention, the Mouse Purposeful not the Mouse Downtrodden, and she tapped the floor impatiently with her foot, waiting for Sophie to answer. The prospect of the two women's conversation was mesmerising. 'Sorry to trouble you, Sophie. I've got a journalist asking me what John was doing on 8 May last year. He wasn't in bed with me, and I just wonder if he was in bed with you. He was? I'm so glad. Goodbye.' How on earth would she handle the call? What telephone manner was in vogue with modern adulteresses? Having been alarmed, I was now on the edge of my seat.

'Sophie? It's me, Sandra. How are you? You must be over the moon about John.'

Why do middle-class English women pick up so many of their clichés from footballers? I thought wonderingly. In civilised countries, it's the other way round. There were a few over-the-moon noises from Sophie at the other end, then Sandra headed straight to the point. To my relief, she showed more awareness of the need for caution than I expected.

'Listen, Sophie, I know you must be busy, so I won't keep you. I've got a rather odd question to ask about John. I can't explain everything, but it's to do with a bet I have with a friend about how hard politicians work in the evening. Yes, I know, it's silly.' She winked at me gleefully, indicating that her story had been swallowed, and I smiled back admiringly. You don't expect mice to be expert liars, but her affair with Carter must have given her practice. 'I know this will sound odder and odder, Sophie, but do you by *any* chance remember what John was doing on the evening of 8 May last year? Just before the Election was announced, that's right.'

She put her hand over the mouthpiece and hissed at me, 'She's gone to look it up in her diary. Where did this murder take place exactly?'

'Maid-stone.' I remembered to dissimulate only half-way through the word, but it was lucky I did.

'May 8, that's right.' She was back talking to Sophie now, her body half bent over as she listened to the answer. Then she straightened and burst into a huge smile. 'Was he really? How interesting. It sounds as if I've lost my bet, but never mind. We must be in touch again soon. Bye!'

She bounded back across the room, surging with energy and confidence. The shift in her from defence to attack had taken place with shocking abruptness. If I'd been a piece of Double Gloucester, she would have pounced on me and gobbled me up, so I flinched as she sat down beside me, fearing that those sharp rodent's teeth might be put to use. However could Christopher handle her when she was in this sort of mood? He'd be slaughtered.

'What do think?' she asked, leaning forward in her chair. I gargled something inaudible, to encourage her to get on with it and not snap my head off by mistake, then she lowered her voice melodramatically and said: 'You've got the wrong man.'

'Why? How you know? Are you sure?' I didn't really care if I had got the wrong man, she was scaring me so much. I just wanted her to finish before her eyes turned into laser-beams and roasted me alive.

'Listen to this. Sophie had to look it up in her diary because it was such a long time ago, but quite by chance she remembers that evening very well.'

'Really?'

'Yes. There was the opening night of a new production of *Idomeneo* at Covent Garden.'

'And they went to that?' I couldn't conceal my chagrin. What a bloody typical smart-arsed alibi.

'No, *she* went to that. He's not musical at all.'

'So what did he do instead?'

'I'm getting to that. He took the car – she remembers she had to take a taxi to the opera – and went to call on his parliamentary agent. The Election was about to be called, so they had things to discuss. When Sophie got back from the opera at about eleven, he telephoned her from the agent's house. He can't have been pretending, because Sophie says she talked to the agent as well as John. She's a godparent to his

226

daughter or something like that. So there you are.'

'What do you mean, there I am?'

'John Carter can't have done the murder.'

'Why not?'

'Because he was too far away at the time.'

'Why? How can you be sure? You've missed out the most vital thing, for God's sake. Where does Carter's agent live?'

'Do you really want to know?'

'Of course I bloody want to know.'

'Slough.' It's an ugly word, but she mouthed it with extraordinary love, she was feeling so pleased with herself, and it was music to my own ears, though for different reasons. 'That's nowhere near Maidstone. It must be at least fifty miles away, on the opposite side of London. Maidstone's the M2, but Slough's off the M4.' She sounded like an AA route adviser.

'It's near Maidenhead, isn't it?' I asked casually, knowing the answer already.

'That's right. About five miles away. So you've got the wrong man. I'm sorry.'

'Ah well.'

'It would have been interesting if he had done it, but he didn't, so there.'

'Ah well.'

I tried to pull a sad face, but started laughing helplessly. Exhilaration is the hardest of emotions to conceal and I wasn't up to it, though I tried desperately to disguise the reasons for my mirth. I hoped Sandra would interpret the strange noise I was making as a sardonic, resigned-to-my-fate chuckle rather than a belly-laugh, but it was hard to give my voice the right bitter timbre and my belly was wobbling uncontrollably, like a jelly with Parkinson's disease. Luckily, Sandra was too cheerful to notice anything odd. She smiled serenely, a very different woman from the guilt-ridden wife who had admitted to an affair with her husband's boss or the maniac who had gone beserk at finding an alibi for her lover. She really was just a friendly household mouse, I decided, the sort people wrote children's books about. She had scared the balls off me earlier but, when I had stopped laughing and my belly had finally subsided, I approached her without trepidation.

'There's one thing that still puzzles me, Sandra. What is it about this man Carter that attracts people to him so strongly? Can you explain it?'

'I'm not sure I follow you.'

'You see, from where I'm sitting, he's just another run-of-the-mill politician. He's more talented than most, of course, so he's moving up the ladder faster, but he's no different in kind from the rest. If he can't get what he wants honestly, then he'll try to get it dishonestly: that's politics and I don't blame him for it. But where does this magic aura he seems to have come from? There's not just you and, in a quite different way, Christopher. I've met several other people, men and women' – I didn't mention Anna as it would complicate things too much – 'who have this extraordinary thing about Carter. They – well, all you can say is that they love him. It's not just his political clout, or the fact that he's clever and powerful and good with words. There's something else, but I can't put my finger on it at all. Do you have any ideas?'

She looked at me inquisitively, puzzled by the uncharacteristic earnestness in my voice. It wasn't like me to waffle on in this philosophical vein, but the questions I asked had been gnawing away at the back of my brain for weeks. Sandra seemed to be as well placed to answer them as anyone, for she had felt the heat of the flames but not been consumed by them. I could see I was probing conundrums of the heart which she had previously taken for granted and, knowing her tendency to reticence, I pressed her a little harder.

'Is it significant, for example, that he's a politician?'

'What do you mean?'

'Well, would you – would anybody – be so attracted by him if he was just a successful man in some other walk of life? Christopher obviously wouldn't, because he's really turned on by his whole political philosophy and thinks he's going to achieve significant things in the political arena. But I know someone else who reveres him *despite* the fact that he's a

228

politician and spends so much time politicking. How about you? Where do you stand?'

'In the middle, I suppose.' She nibbled at her lower lip and started fingering the cushion on the sofa beside her. 'When he makes one of his clever speeches, I clap as loudly as anyone because it's so exhilarating to listen to. But I don't actually agree with three-quarters of the things he says, and I sometimes think he doesn't agree with them himself. If you ask me, he's just acting half the time: there isn't any real sincerity or political idealism there.'

'Christopher wouldn't agree with you about that.'

'No, I suppose he wouldn't.' She scowled at me for introducing Christopher's name, but I didn't want him excluded, so I said: 'Do you ever talk about Carter, the two of you?'

'Sometimes.' She stopped fingering the cushion and looked at me slyly. 'Chris doesn't know, by the way, about John and me, so perhaps you –'

'Of course.'

'It didn't last long and he was in Washington half the time, so –'

'So, what?'

'So – well, you understand.'

'Yes,' I said, wondering what made Washington so special and not really understanding at all. 'I understand, I understand.'

It was a small lie by my standards, but it worked, just as the identical lie had worked with Anna. I'm such a clumsy performer with the opposite sex that my claim to wisdom in affairs of the heart was ludicrous. I've often found, though, that, if you pucker your eyes and try to look like a Labrador puppy, women believe you absolutely in moments of intimacy. So it proved here. Our descent into coyness had been halted, and Sandra suddenly started talking about Carter and Christopher much more freely. She didn't put Anna's romantic gloss on everything, and there wasn't the same abundance of physical description or emotional breast-beating; but I think she was franker than the other woman. There was a certain animal realism in her assumption that women of a particular age and maturity had affairs with older men which they concealed from their husbands but didn't allow to disrupt their lives as a whole. She knew that Christopher was a better human being than Carter, she said, but he was also a baby, while Carter was a man. That was basically how the whole thing had started, although it couldn't go on after Christopher had been elected because the Party took a severe view of these things and because it was the Party that mattered. She said this ironically, with the amused incomprehension which sophisticated women often feel for the tribalism of party politics, and explained that she had never voted for the Party herself, not even when Christopher had been standing. She wasn't bitter, however; whereas Anna had been outraged at having to share Carter with the Cabinet, she seemed to have yielded graciously to *force majeure*, and even admitted to enjoying at second remove the world of competitive male values to which Carter and Christopher belonged. Politicians never lost hope, she said, reminding me of my own musings the night before, and their wild flights of optimism, however unfounded, made them stimulating company. As for Carter, he might not really be more optimistic than the next man, but he had the gift of *sounding* optimistic, and forward-looking, and that might explain what I'd asked about earlier: his charisma. She apologised for using such a hackneyed word, but remarked that there wasn't really a better one, was there?

'No, I suppose not.' I fished idly round for synonyms, like Jenny doing the crossword. 'Presence? Mystique? *Je ne sais quoi?* Star quality? Magnetism? Raw sex appeal?'

'That's it.'

'What, sex appeal?'

'No, magnetism. That's exactly the word. He's someone you can observe from a distance and not look at twice. I wouldn't have dreamed of having an affair with him when I first met him. But as soon as you move within his magnetic field, he's irresistible. I don't know why, but he is. Magnetism's closer to it than charisma, because charisma suggests saintliness and he's not at all saintly. Christopher is rather saintly, I think, but he doesn't have the magnetism to go with it.'

I nodded, sharing her perceptions utterly. She was right about Carter being insignificant at a distance, but fascinating close to. She still hadn't explained exactly what it was, this strange magnetic field in him which beckoned so irresistibly across so many divides, but she had described the symptoms of Carter-philia perfectly and I could ask no more. It was inevitable that an element of enigma should remain, for how could she, who had loved him too well, or I, who had hated him too well, hope to unearth his ultimate secrets? Did I even want that privilege? I didn't know. It had been amusing just speculating, chewing away at a tough old bone, and I thanked my fellow chewer warmly when I left five minutes later.

'It's been a pleasure,' she said, letting her hand rest limply in mine where Christopher would have retracted it. 'I've enjoyed our talk, and I'm glad we've scotched that silly murder story.'

'Ah yes, I'd forgotten about that.'

'It wouldn't do to have the new Chancellor arrested outside Number 11, would it?'

'It certainly wouldn't.'

I loitered on the doorstep, ashamed to repay her frankness with mendacity but terrified of enlisting another accomplice, especially someone so close to Christopher. I thought of sounding a warning note, something to the effect that I might have got the time of the murder wrong and Carter's alibi might not be watertight, but my nerve failed me and I simply asked her not to tell Christopher about my visit. She agreed at once, almost indecently happy to deceive her husband, then made me promise not to tell Christopher about 'the other thing', which I did. I normally make few promises, and break most of those, but I had to honour this one sooner than I expected. I was just getting into my car, which, fortunately in the circumstances, was parked some way from Christopher's flat, when the man himself appeared round the corner. I thought he'd been spying on me again, but his surprise was much too genuine for so bad an actor to have faked. He did a sharp double-take and greeted me gingerly.

231

'Hullo, John. What are you doing around here?'

I returned his smile affably. 'Just making a social call.'

'On a friend?'

'Yes. How about you?'

'I've been at the Ministry, helping Carter clear his desk. He's got to start at the Treasury tomorrow.'

'Yes, of course.' I'd meant to hold off the sarcasm, but the poison seeped slowly back into my voice. 'How exciting for him. Buying sterling all day to keep the pound steady. Or does he sell sterling? I've never understood. What does he do the buying with, apart from anything else?'

It was a cheap snipe and Christopher dealt with it contemptuously. 'You're really gloating, aren't you?'

'Me? Why me? You're the one who should be gloating. Your man's only one step from the top; you should be thrilled.'

'You know bloody well why you're gloating.' He was about to give it to me with both barrels when a young couple with a baby strolled round the corner and walked past us. Their arrival robbed him of his flow and, when he finally delivered his lecture, it was laughably weak. 'You're gloating because you're going to cause even more havoc than before and because it suits you more to destroy his career, the more senior he is. You don't give a damn about the country or about the pound or even about decent standards of journalism. You're just interested in causing trouble and, if you want to know, it makes me sick.'

I didn't want to know, not particularly, but I nodded sagely as he huffed and puffed, and waited for him to stop. All the breath he was wasting formed a little cloud in front of his face and gave him a dragon-like appearance, which was absurd, because his pinpricks barely pierced my skin. His repeated attacks were merely an irritant: it was like being harassed by a small, very determined terrier which you kicked away without difficulty but which always came back for more. I thought his lecture on patriotism and the pound would mark the end of his tantrum, but he went on to launch his most vehement plea yet to be told what was going on. He wouldn't say a word to *anyone*, he said, stressing the word so fiercely that I immediately distrusted it, and he wouldn't get in the way of my investigations. What happened to Carter was outside his control: it was his own sanity and peace of mind that were at stake. He didn't say that I owed it to him as a friend, but he made that appeal implicit with every muscle in his face and it began to filter through to me. Was he a friend? I hadn't consciously thought so but, as his great emotional outburst began to reverberate off the walls of the houses opposite, I realised how far we had travelled beyond the acquaintances stage, into something more substantial. That may sound a strange piece of reasoning, considering how quickly we were also becoming enemies, but I suddenly thought, yes, I do owe it to you, Christopher, and, if I have any pity in me, I should put you out of your pain. It was crazy, but then when were pity and common sense inseparable? I said nothing immediately, but asked him to have a drink with me in the House the next day, when I would 'reveal all'. His eyes danced with excitement at that mysterious, ironic phrase and, after wishing me goodnight, he vanished into the darkness, leaving me alone with my thoughts on a pavement in Pimlico.

25

'Just start at the beginning and tell me the whole story, even if hurts.'

'If you insist, Christopher.'

'I do insist.'

We were on the Terrace again, not from choice – it was still too cold to sit outside – but because it was the only place where we could be sure of privacy. If the House had been lively on Friday, today it was electric, and I kept seeing Members I thought had died or been kicked upstairs to the House of Lords. Everyone bustled about as if in a tremendous hurry to get somewhere, but all they really wanted was more people to gossip with, more opportunities to shake their heads in disbelief and argue whether they could remember anything as dramatic as this. Around the telex-machines they stood four deep, greeting every item about the pound on the tapes with jubilation or dismay. It actually recovered one and a half cents in the course of the morning, but there were sudden dips in its fortunes which made a further decline seem perfectly possible, and people wrung their hands at each apparent setback as if a wicket had fallen while England were batting against Australia at Lord's. Shortly after 12.00, it came up on the annunciator screens that a statement about the pound would be made in the House at 3.30. Carter couldn't have had a fierier baptism as Chancellor if he had tried, and you could tell from the gleeful anticipation on Opposition faces that an almighty row would be effectively stage-managed and that roars of well simulated anger would reverberate around the Chamber all afternoon. It was one of those rare mornings when everyone looked repeatedly at their watches, not out of impatience for lunch but counting the seconds until the curtain went up at 3.30. If they looked out of the window and saw Christopher and me shivering together on the Terrace, they must have assumed we had been driven mad by the excitement of it all.

In my case, they were right. Would a sane man in my position, holding most of the cards but still debating how best to play them, have shown his hand to his opponent's unreliable sidekick? It was pure folly, excused only by my sense that some good might somehow come of it. There were no rational grounds for the belief, but my hunch was a strong one and fatally insisted that no harm could result.

I told him the story from the beginning, as he had asked. In other circumstances, I might have teased him, sowing doubt in his mind whether particular incidents had really happened or were just mischievous embroidery by the narrator. But I wasn't in the mood for fooling, so I gave him a straight version of the facts, warts and all, and he believed me totally. A hell of a lot of emotions showed themselves on that most legible of faces, but doubt wasn't among them. If he asked me to repeat things, it was only because he wanted to have the facts clear in his head, where they quickly formed their own patterns and reinforced his burning sense of pain and betrayal.

By the end of my story, his cheeks were an angry shade of red. A beetroot is the normal comparison, I believe, although you would have to imagine a beetroot only half ripened to get the right colour. The slow transformation of his features from their usual consumptive pallor was clearly visible if, as I rather mawkishly was, you were looking for it. The first flush came when I told him about Carter's meeting in Wopsley with Mrs Wiseman – not, as he had lied to Christopher at the time, with the local party chairman. It was only a venial sin in my eyes, but worshippers of false idols take a more severe view of these things, and somehow that act of deception helped prepare him for the rest of the catalogue and soften its impact. He wasn't much shocked by my account of my meeting with Dr Trumper.

The Ball Committee escapade belonged to his hero's youth, and Carter's attempt to make honourable reparation brought a quiet smile to his face, as if that one act of penance redeemed all the rest. When the story moved on to Maidenhead, however, and I started drawing together all the deductive threads that pointed to Carter as the murderer, his smile disappeared completely and he held himself in a pose of shocked silence, not wanting to believe it but realising how perfectly it explained Carter's paranoid response to my investigations.

'It all adds up,' he muttered. 'It all adds up. He normally keeps his head while everyone around him – you know that silly expression – so I knew there had to be something pretty big behind all this, or he wouldn't be getting so desperate. But murder, John, murder! It seems so far-fetched. Couldn't he just have knocked this man Wiseman over by accident when he was drunk, and then been afraid to come forward?'

'One of his oldest friends? Someone who was trying to wreck his career by writing an incriminating book about him? I'm sorry, Chris, that's just wishful thinking.'

'Maybe it is wishful thinking, but I still think it's possible. If it was murder, it was a bloody silly way to kill someone.'

'Not all that silly. It made it look like an accident. What more do you want?'

'That's true. On the other hand –' He was clutching at straws, looking for a way to disprove a case which in his heart he accepted. 'On the other hand, he might have a perfectly good alibi. Had you thought of that?'

'Yes, I had thought of that, but he hasn't. He was visiting someone who lived only five miles from where the murder was committed.'

'How do you know?'

'Somebody told me.'

'Who?'

'Somebody pretty reliable.'

'Who, for Christ's sake?'

'It's not that important.'

'It might be. Who is it?'

I could have wriggled more, of course, and I should have. When I started telling my story, I hadn't meant to include the last chapter, however much he pressed me. Elementary decency warned that my promise to Sandra wasn't one of those flimsy bargains you struck with a Member to gain a temporary advantage, and then disregarded. I knew it was a more solemn compact, that the pain I had already caused Christopher would be quite dwarfed by this final revelation and that there was no knowing down what alleyways of vengeance or despair the pain would lead him. So, if my eyes were open when I did what I did, why did I do it? Was it just the accumulation of all my contempt for Christopher that made me want to wound him so deeply, or was my real target Carter? Did I want to make quite sure that his reputation would sink lowest where it had been highest and that nothing of that idiot boy's adoration of him would remain? I honestly can't say. We sometimes know why we do good, but never why we do evil. All I know, and know with shame, is that once Christopher had pressed me for the final piece of my jigsaw, I gave him the full works. In three brutally prosaic minutes, I described my visit to his wife and what she had told me. When I finished, he said he didn't believe a word of it and that I was making it all up. But that wasn't what he really thought, only the sort of rubbish people come out with when they want to stall for time, to delay the moment when the blow falls. And when, seconds later, the blow did fall, he didn't bother questioning me any more about the truth of my story. His beetroot face just crumpled and he fled from the Terrace in tears.

I say I felt ashamed of my behaviour. Now I do, but at the time that old elephant's skin of mine protected me from anything sharper than mild remorse. I was a journalist and therefore ideologically opposed to the concealment of painful truths. Christopher would have to toughen up, Sandra would have to toughen up, Carter would have to toughen up, they'd all have to toughen up. When I told the world my story, I didn't mean to write in euphemisms or pull my punches about the squalid episodes I'd uncovered. I meant to tell it like it was,

237

using exaggeration only where market forces demanded it, and Christopher would have to get used to the idea. If his revered emperor had no clothes and, while naked, had bedded his wife, then he should know about it. I was being tough but fair, as friends are supposed to be. Who did he think I was – a wet-nurse?

I had washed my hands of Christopher and his problems and was having lunch in the Press Cafeteria when a message reached me to ring a certain number urgently. Urgently, by definition, couldn't mean before finishing lunch, so I took my time over my meal and chin-wagged with some fellow hacks. The atmosphere was as charged as in the House itself and, because journalists aren't politicians and don't have to pretend to be deeply shocked by national calamities, the sense of unfettered joy was extraordinary. The Government was up Shit Creek, one head had already rolled, mud would be flying for weeks: it was a good time to be a lobby correspondent. If someone had started singing 'Happy days are here again', the whole room would have joined in spontaneously, knowing exactly why that song was appropriate. Only three months before, I thought wonderingly, drinking in the merry scene, I had been bored rigid with the House and everyone who worked there. Bored? I was now ecstatic, hugging myself for joy at the scoop I was incubating, which would make the chaos of the last few days seem like normality. The sweetness of anticipation was unbearable and I was grinning with the foolishest of pleasures when I made my telephone call after lunch.

'John Wellington speaking.' When a message is described as urgent, formality gives the other person a cue for seriousness, and I was surprised to hear 'You shit!' at the other end until I identified the speaker. A fear of Sandra's angry reprisals had been lurking at the back of my mind over lunch, for I felt guiltier towards her than towards Christopher, and I couldn't argue with her description.

'How could you do something like that?' Her mezzo-soprano voice shrieked out her indignation, soaring to registers I hadn't thought it possessed. 'Never mind me, what about Christ-

238

opher? He's young for his age, and sensitive, and you've just trampled all over him. You must be the cruellest, most deceitful man in London. I have never, ever . . .'

She laid into me bitterly, far more effectively than her husband, for mice have teeth and can use them. I wanted to hold the receiver away from my ear to lessen the impact, but it was a public telephone and there were people nearby, so I had to press it closer and take the full weight of her force-niner. She was right about my being a shit, but there must be a better man underneath, because a true shit would have hung up, while I listened meekly, almost penitently, to every word she said. From the abuse she hurled, I could reconstruct the whole marital explosion – his bitter recriminations, her shock that I had betrayed her secret, his tears, her tears, his despair, her despair – and I wondered how I had failed to anticipate it when I talked to Christopher. Had my middle-aged deviousness made me forget that young people are more direct with each other and exorcise their griefs by violent and open confront-ation? Or had I really guessed the whole scenario, but kidded myself I wasn't an actor in it?

I took my medicine from Sandra in silence and, in a few minutes, her angry denunciations had burned themselves out. Only then – how terrible the emotional upheaval that made her order her conversational priorities so badly! – did she tell me that Christopher had a gun.

'*What?*' I shouted. They must have heard me in the House of Lords. The world was going crazy, but why not, I thought savagely, why the hell not? Carter had used a grey Volvo and he was the sane one.

'I said, Christopher has a gun. He put it in his pocket before coming to the House, and he means to use it.'

'How did he get hold of it, for Christ's sake? They don't give gun licences to demented three-year-olds like him. It would be too dangerous. They'd be crazy to give him a licence. It must be a toy gun, a water-pistol or something.'

'No, it's a real gun. He's had it for some time. I don't know about the licence, but he was in the Army for two years, don't

239

forget.'

'Jesus Christ!' I had totally forgotten. Christopher's time in the Army had been mentioned in the mini-biographies of new MPs, but I hadn't thought it was significant, just a youthful career experiment which hadn't worked. Now it had a deadly significance. He not only had the gun, but knew how to use it. Lunch or no lunch, I swear there was a hole the size of a football in my stomach when I asked the next question.

'Do you know who he's after? Me?'

'No, not you.' She dropped to a whisper. '*Him.*'

'Are you sure?'

'Positive. He was completely beserk. You wouldn't have recognised him. It was terrifying. You've got to do something about it, you've got to. *Please.*'

'Of course, of course.' As she grew more desperate, I leapt at the chance to make good my reputation with her. 'I'll track him down right away and try to talk him out of whatever he's planning. OK?'

'OK. But don't tell the whole damned world about it this time.'

She rang off with a mixture of apprehension and tenderness, as if she knew I was the last person to count on in a crisis but treasured me because I was the best she had. God knows, she was right to doubt my reliability. In the seconds it took to replace the receiver, I had already done a rough calculation of the increased royalties if my scoop culminated with the assassination of the Chancellor of the Exchequer, and worked out where my self-interest lay. But there my cynicism ended. Sandra's plea for help had inspired me with a simple heroism, a chivalrous desire to track Christopher down and disarm him before he could strike. Eyes were turned in astonishment as I ran down the Committee Corridor in search of him, but I didn't mind being mistaken for a fitness fiend. As my Aunt Millie once observed in a different context, the game was afoot.

26

People forget how big the Palace of Westminster is. Because it's so congested and all its affairs are conducted in rabbit-hutches – no, not those affairs, the hutches aren't big enough – you quickly lose sight of the essential massiveness of Barry's nineteenth-century design. Probably nobody's been inside every room and most of us have only a few regular haunts: it's said there's a gymnasium, for example, but I've never located it. As soon as you're forced to widen your horizons and hunt for someone urgently, look everywhere, question everyone, leave no Pugin tile unturned, the enormity of your task is mind-boggling. You have to be ready to walk miles, and a 22-stone starting weight doesn't help.

I tried the obvious places, but without success. Christopher didn't answer his telephone and his secretary knew nothing about his whereabouts, except that he was in the House because his coat was hanging on the door. In the Members' Lobby, there was no sign of him. The attendants just shook their heads when I asked if he'd been sighted, so I moved on and did a rapid inspection of the watering holes on the principal floor: the famous Tea Room, the even more famous Smoking-Room, the Members' Dining-Room with Millais's portraits of Gladstone and Disraeli, and the adjacent Strangers' Dining-Room where Members bring their strange guests. Humble lobby correspondents are strictly forbidden in all these places and, as I was too antique and distinctively shaped to pose as the new Member for Staffordshire East, I had to make extravagant excuses to avoid being ejected by irate Members. 'Sorry chaps, just looking for a Member with a very urgent personal message. His mother's died. His father's died. His children and canaries have died. Terrible business, terrible business.' I invented stories shamelessly to gain admittance to the various joints, but had no luck. Not only wasn't Christopher there, there was nobody there who had seen him all day. He had become invisible.

I retraced my steps and tried the Library. This is also out of bounds for journalists, being a place of study, sobriety and silence, and a young official barred my way as I crossed the threshold.

'Excuse me, sir. Are you a Member?' The inquiry was polite, but the man obviously meant business. It wasn't the moment for half-measures, so I fixed him with a frosty stare and stuck my chest out a foot or two.

'Of course I'm a Member. Who do you think I am – a journalist?' Neat, very neat. That's exactly who he thought I was, but I'd successfully pre-empted him and was able to force my way into the Reference Room, where a young Member with his back to me was looking up his own entry in *Who's Who*. I checked that it wasn't Christopher, then went through to the reading-rooms, conscious of someone at my shoulder. It was the young man again, this time clutching *The Times Guide to the House of Commons*, the thinking man's rogue's gallery of Members.

'Excuse me, sir.' The politeness was draining away fast. 'Can I ask which is your constituency?'

'Of course you can't ask which is my constituency. I'm a Member of Parliament, not an answering-machine.'

'I'm sorry, sir. My job is to question people I don't recognise.'

'Are you saying you don't recognise *me*?'

'Yes, sir.'

'However long have you been working here?'

'Seven years, sir.'

'Well, it's a bloody disgrace. I shall put down a Question in the House about it. What's the point of having staff who don't do the job they're paid to do?'

That nailed him. He stopped and stepped back a couple of paces, plotting his next move with evident uncertainty. I was running out of time fast, so I rapidly scanned the faces in the reading-rooms, but didn't see the one I wanted. A few Members were scribbling out their speeches for the afternoon's debate, and one or two reclined in the green leather armchairs, nodding off to sleep. After a quick glance into the final room, I turned to leave. The anxious young man was blocking my way, so I reassured him that I was a Member, explained that I'd recently put on eight stone after a kidney operation, which was probably why he hadn't recognised me, and exited unscathed. Then I took the stairs down to the floor below and resumed my search.

The Strangers' and Members' Cafeterias and the Strangers' Bar, which adjoin each other next to the Terrace, were all bursting at the seams. They're always well patronised at lunchtime, but I'd never seen them like this. Everyone in the building seemed to have brought all the friends and relations along to enjoy the panic and, if someone had shouted 'Fire!', people would have slipped on the sea of chips and coffee on the floor and been trampled to death. There was no way through the crush, even for a sylph like me, so I just called out 'Chris!' a few times and, when various people of either sex who were doubtless charming but weren't the Chris I wanted had turned in astonishment to look at me, I gave up and left.

Annie's Bar was just as bad. It's a favourite place of consort between gossiping Members and gossip-hungry hacks, and there was no shortage of either that lunchtime. The congestion made the usual oh-so-discreet tête-à-têtes impossible, but a party to celebrate the Government's humiliation was in full swing when I arrived. Several people loudly offered me a drink and I wanted to say yes, as the people doing the offering were my friends – or they were when they were throwing their money round like this. I resisted temptation with difficulty and simply asked if anyone had seen Christopher. It was hard to strike the right casual note, as I was out of breath as well as excited, and I didn't fool anyone.

'What's up, Beef?' Bob Mumford asked, sliding off his bar-stool like a lizard. He knew Christopher was thick with the man of the moment, Carter, and probably thought I wanted some low-down from him. He had no idea how low, and I wasn't going to tell him, so I stonewalled.

'Just a small private transaction, Bob.'

'Come off it, Beef. You've been running. What is this? The Third World War?'

'Nothing earth-shattering, Bob.' Only about 250 on the Richter scale, Bob: there's nobody I lie to as determinedly as fellow hacks. 'It's quite trivial, I promise you. Hack's honour. If you see Christopher, just say I was looking for him.'

'What about?'

'Oh, nothing much. This and that.'

'What and what?'

'I can't tell you now, Bob; I'm in a hurry. Just say I wanted to talk to him. He'll understand.'

I slipped out quickly, seeing Bob's antennae starting to twitch violently, and took the corridor leading to the Harcourt Room. There's a row of private dining-rooms here which Members can hire to entertain visitors to the House – constituency workers, industrialists, pressure groups of all kinds. There was a chance Christopher had got caught up in one of these functions, so I stuck my head round all the doors in turn. Dining-Room A was taken by the Anglo-Japanese Society, Dining-Room B by what looked like the All-Party Wrestling Group, Dining-Room C by a lot of men in rugby-club ties, and Dining-Room D by a more varied group. I couldn't see any common denominator, then noticed that only vegetarian food was being consumed, so I shuddered and fled. Christopher was nowhere to be seen.

It was nearly 2.30, so I checked out the Harcourt Room, then panted up to the Central Lobby for the Speaker's Procession. I remembered Christopher's emotionally charged response to the spectacle in the summer and wondered if he took it every day like a drug, pumping himself up with the sense of belonging

244

to an ancient and venerable institution which meant so much to him. But he wasn't there; or, if he was, he was buried too far under the sea of tourists' faces to be visible. The Procession passed by at its usual stately pace, no faster or slower than it had moved when the pound had been worth nine cents more. When it reached the Chamber, the bells started ringing the Prayers and the start of the afternoon's sitting. I looked for Christopher among the Members waiting outside the Chamber while the Speaker's Chaplain conducted Prayers, then went up to the Press Gallery and studied the faces of the smaller, better dressed contingent who had attended them. I imagined that, even when Christopher had a gun in his pocket, he was the sort of person who prayed rather than didn't pray, but there was still no sign of him, so I left the Gallery to make more inquiries. Attendants expressed ignorance of his whereabouts, his secretary knew only that his coat was still on the back of the door, nobody had seen him anywhere. He had disappeared.

Back in the Chamber, Agriculture Questions, the monthly all-party Frog-bashing show, had got under way. It wouldn't normally have jammed the turnstiles, but by 2.45 the benches were packed and it was standing room only. The Members who weren't able to get emotional about the Common Agricultural Policy or fishing limits or gluten feed for pigs rhubarbed noisily in the background, making it hard for the Agriculture Minister, an uninspired performer with the chloroform touch at the despatch-box, to be heard at all. Everyone was waiting impatiently for Carter's statement at 3.30, as if he was teacher and a bag of flour had been put on top of the classroom door to greet him. It was so childish it was embarrassing. I saw someone on the Opposition front bench say something funny to his neighbour, which was then passed along the bench to the end and back along the row behind. Everyone enjoyed the joke hugely and was still chuckling when it had passed out of range. I asked the Press Association man next to me what it was and he asked the *Birmingham Mail* man next to him, who muttered something about Hutton's socks. I looked at the socks in question – Sydney Hutton was the most *gris* of the *éminences grises* on the Government backbenches – and saw that one was grey and the other red. Ha ha ha, I thought, how bloody hysterical. On an ordinary day, this would have given me material for a whole column and left me free to drink for the rest of the day, but now its triviality exasperated me. Why was everyone behaving like schoolchildren when a madman with a gun was loose in the House?

I glanced at my watch, then scoured the Government benches again. Three o'clock and still no sign of Christopher. If he was really out to get Carter, then I was running out of time, for Carter would be leaving Downing Street any minute and there would be no chance to warn him. In desperation, I left the Gallery and took up a position by a window overlooking Speaker's Court, the small courtyard where Government cars deposit Ministers on their way into the House. It was a good observation-post, although I was two storeys up and powerless to intervene if Christopher went up to Carter – and who the hell was going to stop him? – and took a pot-shot. At 3.08, Carter's car arrived in convoy with the Prime Minister's and the two of them entered one of the side-doors together. I held my breath and waited for a shot to ring out from some dark, unseen corner of the court, but nothing happened, so I scuttled back to the Gallery. Still no Christopher on the Government benches. I took out a handkerchief and wiped the sweat off my brow. I wished I couldn't hear my heart pounding so heavily and remembered Jenny's periodic lectures about cholesterol.

'Bladder problems, Beef?' asked the PA man quizzically, amused by my toing and froing. It was a Beef Wellington sort of comment, but its schoolboy humour irritated me and I told the man to get stuffed. Down in the Chamber, Carter and the Prime Minister hadn't yet taken their places on the front bench, so they were probably having a last-minute pep-talk in the Prime Minister's room near the back of the Chair. If I was quick, I could still get a message through, so I left the Gallery again and got on the telephone.

'Prime Minister's office,' said a starchy voice. I groaned at the prospect of having to instil urgency into such pompous

246

inertia, and tried to sound important.

'Listen carefully. This is Mr Wellington from the Press Gallery. Is Mr Carter there with the Prime Minister?'

My question obviously breached security or protocol or both, because there was a long, long pause before he said yes, or, to be precise, before he drawled, 'I believe he may be.'

'I have a message of extreme urgency which I must give to him personally before he makes his statement in the House. Will you please tell him that immediately?'

This was a blunder; I should never have said 'immediately' to a civil servant. He baulked and said, 'I'm sorry, sir. That's quite impossible. He's in conference with the PM.'

'Then you'll have to interrupt the conference. This is a matter of life and death.'

'Really, sir?'

'Yes.'

'I see.' There was another gargantuan pause, but I was slowly getting through to him, because he made his most helpful move yet. 'I'll certainly pass a message on to him, sir.'

I hesitated, then remembered my promise to Sandra not to bring everything into the open. 'No, I'm sorry. That's not good enough. This an urgent life-and-death message and I must deliver it to the Chancellor personally.'

'Very good, sir. I'll see what I can do.'

He left the telephone and I clenched my fist in excitement. Jerusalem had fallen, a civil servant had helped a journalist, I was winning. Then I heard Carter picking up the receiver.

'Beef?' I started to gabble my piece about Christopher, but I was too slow and he cut me dead. 'Just bugger off, will you. We'll talk later if you insist. This isn't the time.'

I heard the line go dead, thought of redialling the number, then rejected the idea. On your head be it, you bastard, I thought grimly, and I returned to the Press Gallery telling myself I had taken all reasonable steps to warn the victim. It was now 3.18 and Carter would be rising to deliver his statement at half past. If Christopher was perched somewhere with a gun pointed at him, he had only himself to blame.

247

27

For the sixth or seventh time, I ran my eyes along the Government benches. It's easy to miss someone in the uniform ranks of dark suits and pale faces, interspersed by only the odd woman and the even odder snappily dressed man, but I was certain Christopher wasn't there. He wasn't standing among the crush of Members at the Bar of the House, facing the Speaker, so, if he was in the Chamber at all, that only left the area behind the Speaker's Chair. This is a favourite loitering place when the benches are full and, from my point of view, had two dangers. It is directly underneath the Press Gallery and thus invisible from where I was sitting, and it is also the entrance to the Chamber which Ministers use when they take their seats on the front bench. If Christopher was lurking there, Carter would come face to face with him and I would miss it completely. The impotence of my position had me fidgeting with frustration and I started chewing a Biro to steady my nerves.

Finally, at 3.23, I spotted him. I hadn't thought of looking on the Opposition benches, but I glanced at a Member asking a supplementary and saw Christopher sitting right next to him. He was in the second row below the gangway, among a group of minor party Members, and was holding himself in such a still, anonymous posture, with his hands in his lap and his head slightly bowed, that nobody had noticed him. Strictly speaking, Members can sit anywhere they like in the Chamber, but for a Government Member to cross the floor in this way has an obvious dramatic symbolism which always provokes comment. It was as if Christopher was deliberately pushing himself into the limelight; either that, or he wanted to shoot Carter in the front rather than the back. I was baffled. Whatever was cooking in that lunatic young head?

A sudden murmur of derision greeted Carter's arrival with the Prime Minister into the Chamber. There were five minutes of Agriculture Questions left, but they squeezed their way over the outstretched legs of the other Ministers and took up their places near the despatch-box. Is there any other theatre in the world where the principal actors make such unimpressive entrances? They not only have to force their way through a packed crowd of extras, but must crouch double as they reach centre stage, to avoid the discourtesy of blocking the Speaker's view of the Member addressing the House. When they had crawled into their places, Carter put the folder containing his statement on the table and began whispering soft nothings to the Prime Minister. Any other Minister would have been anxiously studying his speech up to the last minute, reassuring the House that he was preparing himself properly for their questions, but Carter's confident, laid-back style made last-minute swotting anathema. Would he still be so laid-back when he saw Christopher on the benches opposite?

At 3.29, the Agriculture Minister mumbled his final Civil Service brief, bluffed his way through a couple of supplement-aries and sat down with relief. The digital clocks on the Clerks' table in front of the Speaker moved on to 3.30 and the Speaker called out, 'Statement, Mr Chancellor of the Exchequer', the cue for the next business. The Agriculture Minister and his junior colleagues lurched back to the pavilion to take off their pads, and Carter rose to his feet to cheers from his own side and assorted cat-calls from the Opposition. His own side didn't necessarily think all that much of him, and the Opposition held him in some respect, but the Mother of Parliaments has inane traditions as well as less inane ones and the vocal reception given to a ministerial debutant is pre-scripted. When the cheerers had tried to drown the cat-callers and the cat-callers had tried to drown the cheerers, and both had decided to call it

249

quits, Carter cleared his throat and began.

'As the House will be aware, the pound suffered heavy losses in foreign exchange dealings last Friday.' His tone was measured and authoritative and, although the Treasury brief was couched in the melodramatic language of war-reporting, he started well. He was three or four paragraphs in when he looked up from his notes and, quite by chance, glanced in Christopher's direction. To say he did a double-take would be an exaggeration, as Carter always expressed his emotions in miniature, preferring eyebrow movements to arm gestures and fractional inclinations of his head to emphatic shoulder-heaving. But he was obviously shaken. His body stiffened slightly and he went on with his statement twenty per cent faster. Twice he got sentences twisted and had to start them again, and you could see Members getting irritated by the pace of his delivery. After a couple of minutes of the accelerated tempo, the Prime Minister leant forward and whispered something, presumably an instruction to slow down, because he got a grip on himself and continued at a more measured pace.

Christopher sat impassively throughout. If he had crossed the floor just to unsettle Carter, he had succeeded totally, and I wondered if this ounce of flesh would satisfy him. His face gave no hint of a violent lust for revenge, and I was beginning to hope the danger had passed when he sent a nasty *frisson* right down my spinal column. Moving his hand very, very slowly so as not to draw attention to himself, he felt under his left armpit in the place where a gun would be carried. Reassured by the bulge, which in my racing imagination I could clearly see from where I was sitting, he replaced his hand in his lap and continued listening to Carter's statement. How he loved parliamentary democracy, I thought bitterly. He wasn't going to shoot his wife's lover until the House had heard the ministerial statement to which it was constitutionally entitled.

Time was running out for me fast. There aren't many things you can say about the pound, and Carter had said most of them twice already. Soon he would resume his seat and the barrage of

250

questions would begin. If Christopher meant to use his gun, the next half-hour was the obvious time. I thought of shouting 'Don't do it, Chris!', which would certainly have created more interest than the pound, even if I was chucked out by the door-keepers, but there was no guarantee it would have the desired effect and it might just panic Christopher into action. A discreeter plan was needed, so, seeing Jimmy Drummond sitting on Christopher's left, I decided to enlist him as an ally. Jimmy is a bullet-headed, copper-bottomed Scotsman who used to be a policeman, I think, before he came to the house. I say I think, because it's one of those popular myths which turn out to be inventions as often as not and may just have been a joke by his friends to explain his size 13 feet and his massively law-abiding appearance. He certainly *looked* the part, and I could visualise him grabbing football hooligans by the ear and swinging them round his head, so I put my faith in the myth and scribbled him a note: 'The Member on your right is carrying a gun which he may try to use. Stop the bastard if he tries anything. This is not, repeat not, a joke. Beef.' I went down behind the Speaker's Chair, told the policeman I would give him a winner at the next meeting at Sandown if the message was delivered urgently and returned to the Press Gallery in time to see it being passed along the benches to Jimmy.

As soon as he got it, I wished I'd chosen someone else. Jimmy's many qualities don't include the mastery of dead-pan expressions, and his eyes bulged like a cartoon character's when he read my note. It was the sort of melodramatic double-take that went out with silent films and it was noticed by his neighbours, who nudged each other, speculating what the note was about. Jimmy didn't realise he'd overdone it, of course. As far as he was concerned, he had kept a poker-face, and with the same face, which was actually an infringement of the rules of poker, he glanced at Christopher who fortunately was looking in the other direction. Then he looked up towards me in the Press Gallery and solemnly nodded his head. Keeping his arms folded, he swivelled round through about forty-five degrees to

251

keep Christopher covered. If a citizens's arrest had to be made, that burly frame proclaimed, then Jimmy Drummond was the man to make it.

At 3.40, Carter sat down to pallid cheers from his own backbenchers. He had performed passably, but not brilliantly, never quite finding the rhetorical verve to convince his colleagues there was nothing wrong with the pound after all. They knew the Government was right up against it, and they watched apprehensively as the Shadow Chancellor sprang to his feet to fire off the first volley of questions. He was a passionate man, one of those politicians who seems to use his brain only for tying his tie, and he couldn't have had a better chance to turn his passion to political advantage. Anywhere but the House of Commons, he could have gone straight in with both fists flailing, but there are parliamentary niceties which even the most splenetic Members have to observe, and his opening salvo was impeccably polite.

'I am sure that everyone on this side of the House would wish to join me in congratulating the Right Honourable gentleman upon his appointment to his new office.' Everyone did, that was the funny thing. Not a single heckler protested at this assumption of good will on their part. In the House of Commons, you open the door for your opponent, then kick him in the arse as he goes through. The boot went in swiftly on this occasion. 'I trust that his Chancellorship will be one of the shortest on record' (cheers) 'and that his Government will have the decency to resign as soon as possible' (cheers) 'and let someone else get the country out of the appalling shambles' (cheers) 'which their miserable,' (cheers) 'profligate,' (cheers) 'pig-headed' (cheers) 'and utterly incompetent' (cheers) 'policies have got this country into.' (Loud and prolonged cheers.) The cheering was cut short when an Opposition Member called Hugo Baxter-Walsh bounced to his feet on a point of order. Everyone shouted at him to sit down, but shouting at Hugo Baxter-Walsh to sit down has the same effect as shouting at anyone else to stand up and, despite the Speaker's plea to save his point of order until after the

252

Chancellor's statement, he insisted on being heard.

'I have just noticed, Mr Speaker, that a Member of the Government party is sitting on the Opposition benches. Is that in order?'

Everyone's eyes immediately scanned the Opposition benches and came to rest on Christopher, who sat still and said nothing. The Speaker stood up and said he was surprised to see the Honourable gentleman sitting where he was but, as the House well knew, there were no fixed seating places and any Member was entitled to sit where he chose; perhaps the House could now revert to questioning the Chancellor? He expressed the hope sanguinely, but obviously knew it was useless. The presence of a renegade on the Opposition benches was far too good a bone to be so quickly disposed of, and half a dozen Members rose with additional points of order. Was it reasonable for a Government Member to take up space on the Opposition benches while some Opposition Members were having to stand? Didn't the Honourable Member have a duty to explain his choice of seat? As the Chancellor's PPS, or former PPS, shouldn't he be sitting behind the Chancellor in the customary place, ferrying messages between the civil servants' box and the front bench? Wasn't it out of order –

'I have given my ruling,' said the Speaker testily, 'and I have no further guidance to offer the House. If, however, the Honourable Member himself wishes to say anything . . .'

It was a heavy hint and, since hints don't come any heavier than from the Speaker. Christopher was obliged as a good parliamentarian to fall in with it. He had sat impassively through the hullabaloo, but now rose to his feet to address the House.

'Certainly, Mr Speaker. I accept your ruling that I am entitled to sit where I choose, as I had always understood to be the case. If it is any assistance to the House, I have personal reasons for sitting where I am sitting today, and I may soon be in a position to make a statement about them.'

He sat down. Jimmy Drummond had been poised like a mating mongoose ready to pounce, but relaxed in his seat again. Once more the Speaker tried to get the Shadow Chancellor to resume his questions, and once more he failed. Christopher's intervention was so utterly mysterious that there were ten minutes' more points of order before the House was prepared to discuss the pound again. Normally, Carter should have been delighted that the serious business of roasting him alive had been interrupted, but he was the least relaxed man in the Chamber. A fiercer fire had been lit underneath him, and he knew it. He stared hard at Christopher, trying to fathom what lay behind his antics, then turned to look up into the Press Gallery where I was sitting. It was time to twist the knife, so I waved back insolently and had the satisfaction of bringing a flush of anger to his cheeks. When the points of order were exhausted and the Shadow Chancellor finally completed his list of questions, he answered them bitterly and crisply, dismissing the other man's points with contempt. His own side loved it, of course, and cheered him to the echo when he sat down. I think they thought it was his concern for the pound which made him so emotional and reckoned that was a fine patriotic thing to get emotional about.

The climax came sooner than I thought. Christopher's brooding impassivity trapped me into thinking he wasn't up to anything serious, and I took my eyes off him to concentrate on Carter, savouring the underlying desperation which was apparent in his performance if you knew what to look for. When he had dealt with the Shadow Chancellor's questions about a hundred other Members rose to catch the Speaker's eye, and I didn't immediately notice that Christopher was one of them. The Speaker called two or three questions from each side, then intoned in his familiar plummy voice; 'Mr Christopher *Jackson.*' There were immediately rumblings of protest on both sides of the House, for the Speaker traditionally calls Members from each side in turn and, having just called a Government backbencher, should have chosen an Opposition Member to follow. Had he made a mistake, or was Christopher deemed to belong to the Opposition while he was sitting on the Opposition benches? What were the precedents? Did Erskine May have any wisdom on the subject? There was a good hour's fun and games in prospect here for the proceduralists, and I could see one or two notorious points-of-order merchants about to leap to their feet in protest. But something about Christopher's posture restrained them. His eyes were gleaming brightly and there was a rare sense of purpose in his shoulders, as if here was a man with something to say, not just someone getting up on his hind legs for the sake of saying something. An expectant silence descended, stilling the baying and shouts of 'Answer!' which had accompanied the other questions, and I now saw why Christopher had drawn attention to himself by sitting on the Opposition benches: he wanted a captive audience and he had got one. I craned forward to listen and was relieved to see Jimmy Drummond still crouching purposefully on the edge of his seat. Christopher came straight to the point. He didn't bother to clear his throat or perform the ritual which all speakers in the House observe, of doing up the middle button of his jacket: he just threw a hand grenade into the middle of the room.

'Will the Chancellor tell the House about his role in the murder of Peter Wiseman on 8th May last year?'

The question was asked very slowly and very distinctly, then Christopher sat down. The silence that followed was incredible. For two or three seconds, I swear I could hear the remnants of my lunch filtering through my digestive tracts. All eyes swivelled to look at Carter and then at the Speaker. People in the Public Gallery asked each other if they'd really heard what they thought they had and leant forward in their seats, craning to see as much of the Chamber as possible. The Clerks at the Table conferred about precedents, and the Sergeant-at-Arms started nervously fingering his ceremonial sword. In the Press Gallery, hacks held their pens suspended in disbelief before scribbling down Christopher's words, as if there was any danger of forgetting them. On everyone's face you could see the same thought: all this was grossly disorderly; Christopher had abused the most basic rules of the House; Members were supposed to be questioning the Chancellor about sterling, not his private life. But there were no immediate cries of protest: everyone was much too shocked.

Carter sat calmly in his place. If Christopher expected him to give a guilty start – and I had no such illusions myself – he must have been disappointed. His nonchalance was so breath-taking that it sent a sharp flash of doubt through my head. Had I got it all wrong? Could Carter possibly have spent that evening in Slough and not driven to Maidenhead at all? I had been certain of my case, but my certainty wobbled as I watched Carter's cool, mildly aggrieved expression. Who was this deranged young man on the other side of the chamber, the expression said, and what was he shouting about? He stared at Christopher as if he was a lunatic selling balloons prophesying the end of the world, then looked at the Speaker for guidance. Surely Mr Speaker didn't expect him to respond to questions like that? This was the House of Commons, not the Old Bailey. I had never seen indignation so perfectly modulated. It was superb.

The Speaker tottered to his feet. You can't see his face from the Press Gallery, but you can tell how confident he is in his rulings by the vigour with which he shouts 'Order, Order!' He said it so hesitantly this time that I knew he was having to improvise frantically. In the circumstances, he did well.

'I have to tell the House that I have no knowledge of the matter to which the Honourable gentleman has referred, and that he gave me no prior notice of his intention to raise it. There is quite clearly no ministerial responsibility involved, however, and the question the Honourable Member has asked is therefore out of order.'

There were muted shouts of ''Ear! 'Ear!' from the Government side, but nobody thought that was the end of the matter and the Leader of the Opposition was on his feet on a point of order before the Speaker had sat down. What dreams of power must have been swimming round in the poor man's head at the sight of more mud flying round the Government's ears! Many more banana-skins like this, and he would be in Downing Street before the year was out. He was obviously terrified of his baser emotions showing through and spoke in the over-controlled voice of the politician who is determined not to sound cheap when he should be solemn.

'Nobody on this side of the House, Mr Speaker, would challenge your ruling that no ministerial responsibility is involved in the matter on which the Chancellor has just been questioned. Nevertheless, the implications of that question are so serious that I do not think the House will be satisfied unless some further explanation is forthcoming. What is the basis of the Honourable Member's question? If it has no basis, then he has abused his privileges as a Member of this House and should categorically withdraw it. If it has a basis, then the Chancellor should answer the allegation, either now or at an appropriate moment.'

This moderate and sensible intervention created exactly the senseless and immoderate mayhem intended, for the Opposition leader was a master of stirring up other people's emotions while keeping his own in check. The Government back-benchers bawled at Christopher to withdraw and the Opposition responded with concerted shouts of 'Answer!', directed at Carter. After the incomprehending silence a minute earlier, the uproar was deafening. As well as the ritual shouting-match and the waving of order papers, everyone was now talking excitedly to their neighbours. Who was Peter Wiseman? What was all this about? The man had said murder, hadn't he? The Press Gallery was in chaos. Someone said he thought Peter Wiseman had been one of the victims of the Essex Axeman, and the rumour fluttered from hack to hack like a pigeon with diarrhoea. A few people rushed out of the Gallery to ring their newspapers, but most stayed put, transfixed by the drama underneath. Bob Mumford forced his way across the Gallery and thumped me on the shoulder.

'What the hell's all this about, Beef?' How he hated me for knowing more than him, but how desperately he wanted to be my best friend in the world! I grinned frigidly.

'I'll let you know some time, Bob. It's a long story.'

'Who the fuck's Peter Wiseman?'

'He's dead.'

'I know he's bloody dead, but who was he?'

'A rather distinguished-looking man, with grey hair. His eyes –' I was about to be punched very hard on the nose when the action resumed below us. The shouting at Christopher to withdraw had outlasted the shouts at Carter to answer, and he rose to his feet to respond.

'I am quite happy to withdraw the question, Mr Speaker, but only on the basis of your ruling that no direct ministerial responsibility is involved. I still intend to ask my Right Honourable friend the question at the appropriate time, and I trust he will respond to it.'

Carter leapt angrily to his feet, his sang-froid finally punctured. The final goad was the demure way that Christopher, showing more irony than I had credited him with, referred to him as 'my Right Honourable friend'. This is the correct House of Commons terminology for a Privy Councillor of one's own party, but its deeper resonances obviously incensed Carter.

'I shall be happy to respond immediately,' he said, leaning aggressively on the despatch-box. 'I did not do so earlier because the Honourable Member's question was too absurd to be dignified with a reply. Yes, Mr Speaker, I am aware that Peter Wiseman died on 8 May last year, as he was a close and respected friend. I am not aware that he was murdered and therefore I accept no responsibility, ministerial or otherwise, for his death. The Honourable Member has been listening to idle gossip from overpaid, overweight lobby correspondents' (I blushed discreetly, although he was wrong about the first bit) 'and he really should know better. He has behaved naïvely and irresponsibly, and I think a few minutes under a cold shower would convince him of the fact.'

It was the last line that did it. If he'd listened to me earlier and known Christopher had a gun, he would never have said anything so cutting, so perfectly calculated to sting the other man into an angry response. I would have shouted out a warning, but everything happened too quickly. I had to rely on

258

ex-policeman Jimmy's viligance, and he didn't let me down. As soon as he saw Christopher reaching inside his jacket for his gun, he sprang on him and pinioned his arms behind his back. The two men rolled over together on the floor amid roars of protest from both sides of the house, and only with the muffled sound of the gun going off was the gravity of the situation appreciated. The bullet lodged itself in one of the benches opposite, grazing a former Foreign Secretary on the shin, and, as he let out a low cry, the Speaker suspended the sitting in chaos.

28

Carter resigned at six o'clock, after an emergency meeting of
the parliamentary party in Committee Room 14. Panic in the
ranks was now epidemic, although some speakers argued
passionately that he should stay. Christopher was obviously
insane, they said. Why should a distinguished career be ruined
just because a jumped up adolescent psychopath made a half-
baked allegation like that? No police charges were pending and
Carter's innocence should be presumed as a matter of simple
justice. It was a private matter, the excitement would die down
quickly, Christopher would be committed to an asylum, and
then the serious business of propping up the pound could be
resumed by the best man for the job.

Then they heard about Carter's affair with Christopher's
wife. A little birdie – all right, quite a big birdie, me to be
precise – told Hugh Paxton, the biggest gossip in the Party, and
the rest of the Party knew within minutes. I could see events
were coming to a climax and wanted them to accelerate rather
than run out of steam. There was much pious tut-tutting at the
meeting and sympathy switched from Carter to Christopher.
Poaching new Members' wives went further than the normal
run of discreet infidelities with discreet secretaries and
suggested that nice Mr Carter, the respectable face of the Party,
wasn't really the whole pound note. 'If sex is involved as well,'
one Member shouted, 'then he'll bloody well have to go. The
media will be at him for weeks.' There were murmurs of
agreement and, although loud cheers greeted the Member who
said they shouldn't hound Carter out of office just to pander to

the popular Press, the cheers rang hollow. The man was right, but most of their constituents read the popular Press.

At the end of the meeting, Carter made a short statement. The Press are excluded from these occasions, but the entire lobby had laid siege to the room and we extracted verbatim reports from obliging Members as they left. Carter apparently maintained that he was innocent of the murder charge and that his affair with Christopher's wife, which was anyway a private matter, was long since over. He had listened to the views of his colleagues, however, and believed it was right for the Party that he should offer his resignation to the Prime Minister. There was bound to be speculation for a number of days, and it would be better for everybody if someone else took over and concentrated on running the economy properly, without external distractions. This was greeted by loud desk-banging, which we could hear outside in the corridor and had no difficulty in interpreting. If Carter had chosen to brazen it out, the desks would have been banged mutedly, if at all, for politicians protect their own skins and want colleagues who attract bad publicity shunted off the stage as quickly as possible.

When the meeting broke, there was pandemonium. Party officials tried to shield Carter from jostling journalists, but the hounds closed in with fangs bared as he forced his way down the Committee Corridor. Would he definitely be resigning? Would he co-operate with police inquiries? How did he feel about Christoper? Was he going to get divorced? Did he think the pound would now fall further? Did sex help him concentrate on his work? Earnest and flippant, relevant and irrelevant, the questions rained down on him and, after barking 'no comment' a couple of times, he did all he could do, which was maintain a stoical silence. When he caught sight of me bulging self-importantly in the middle of the throng, he just stared right through me, as if my 22 stone didn't exist. Cold shoulders I can take, but not this concentrated, wordless malice, and I had to slink away to the Press Bar for a whisky to restore me. After that, I had another because I was feeling pleased with myself, and then a third for no particular reason. By eight o'clock I had

261

had half a dozen, and a befuddled smile took over my face as I held court to the swarms of hopeful drones around the honeypot. My fellow hacks knew I held the key to the story and the more naïve of them were buying me drinks to encourage indiscretions. I took the drinks, but gave away nothing. Events must follow their natural course, I said blithely; they could read the full story in the Sunday papers before the year was out, and that was all I could promise. Some of them got angry with me and they were all jealous, but I could forgive that. I was top of the pile for once and, whatever the pile consisted of, it felt just great.

In the Chamber, Members struggled to concentrate on the Local Government (Miscellaneous Provisions) Bill, but the proceedings had the verve of an undertakers' tea-party. Even the real addicts, the hard core of well-meaning cranks, exhibitionists and failed Ministers who have prolix views about everything, had been silenced by the day's events. People made repeated journeys to the telex-machines in search of news, and word-of-mouth rumours were passed round like marijuana at a pop-star's wedding. One excitement led to another all evening long. Carter's resignation at six was followed by intense speculation about his successor, and various would-be-Chancellors reportedly spent hours sitting in the Tea Room, hoping for a tide of backbench support in their favour. At seven, after complicated negotiations with the Speaker, Christopher agreed to face police questioning. I had no idea what he would tell them, but I expected to be interviewed myself soon and held myself drunkenly in readiness.

Away from the House, media activity was feverish. Extended news bulletins featured scenes outside the protagonists' homes, as first Sandra and then Sophie were mobbed by reporters asking facile questions about their private lives. Sophie remained dignified and silent, but Sandra lost her temper and punched a cameraman in the face, which the media loved, as it showed spunk and spunky women are the hottest news of all. The intensest speculation focused on Peter Wiseman's death. News film taken at the time was reshown and my friend

Inspector Popplewell, twitching nervously under the television lights, explained why it had been assumed that a drunken driver was responsible. He would naturally question Christopher about his allegations, he said, but it was too early to reach any conclusions and it was wrong to prejudge the issue. The warning was timely, because the issue was being prejudged right, left and centre and most of the commentators implied that Carter was guilty and his resignation proved it. My own working hypothesis was the same, of course, but the presumption of guilt irritated me. It was all right for me, because it was my bloody scoop and I'd sweated valuable pounds to get it. But now everyone was getting on the bandwagon; at this rate, I'd be lucky to get £100,000 out of it.

The biggest shock came in a short news flash at the end of the bulletin. A shrewder man might have anticipated it, but I had just blundered on like a clumsy bull, not looking where I was going or what tender human foliage I was trampling on. Anna Wiseman had given me whisky and cocoa and Dutch apple tart, and now I had betrayed her; it felt terrible. In the hushed voice of the newsreader, her suicide – it wasn't called that, but it was obvious – sounded as messy as her life: not a simple overdose and quiet descent into oblivion, but a violent wrist-slashing with a tiny, inefficient razor-blade. No note had been left behind, said the newsreader, and the motive for her action might never be known. Except by me and Carter, I thought blackly, shattered by the news; and, even then, did either of us really know what had been going on in that irrational head? Maybe if I'd listened to what she wanted to talk about, those soaring romantic fantasies I'd dismissed as mindless, I might have understood her better. But that just isn't my way. I can manage the visible, the tangible, the edible, the easily comprehensible and digestible, but give me a psychological riddle and I'm bored. I haven't the energy to explore the mysteries of the heart or the wit to understand them. I had thought Anna wanted Carter exposed and his career destroyed; all her anger had been directed to that end. But now she had her way, it seemed she had nothing left to live for. Why not, I asked bitterly, why the hell not? Was Carter everything in life? Of course not. Then why kill yourself over him? I hadn't the blindest idea; it seemed too senseless for words. I mourned Anna's passing with another whisky, a double, but cursed her for tearing yet more gilt off my gingerbread. If things went on like this, I'd be writing my best-seller in prison, with Carter and Christopher in neighbouring cells.

My anxiety bit deeper and deeper, and I hung around the House that night like someone reluctant to leave a good party for fear there won't be another one. I'm not normally a lingerer, one of those sad, compulsive alcoholics who stay till the last bar closes because home has nothing better to offer. I stay as long as duty calls, have one, maybe two, for the road, then go home happily to Jenny and sanity. But that night Jenny was at a party and would be back late herself. Home and sanity wouldn't be home and sanity at all till she got back, and I didn't want to be alone in my hour of, well, whatever my hour was of. So I stayed.

All evening long, in every crevice of the Palace, the arguments raged on. Should Carter have resigned or shouldn't he? The question was irrelevant – he had done it, it was ancient history – but Parliament wouldn't be Parliament if it lost its appetite for irrelevant argument, or wasn't fired by issues unconnected with the prosperity and security of the nation. Right versus wrong, good versus evil: the bigger and more abstract the underlying issue of principle, the more passionately politicians debate it, so the popular belief that they're small-minded contains a fallacy, though I've never pinpointed it. The only point of agreement that night was that it had been one hell of a day. Older Members conjured up the ghosts of earlier excitements, but they couldn't remember anything that had electrified the House in quite the same way. People felt privileged simply to have been there and, as always when events in the House capture the public imagination, there was unspoken gratitude that Parliament wasn't televised for public consumption. As one Member said to me, why go to a live match if you can watch it on the box with a can of beer in your hand? You can call it élitism, but the few hundred people who had seen the whole show were passionately grateful that history would know of it only through their own accounts. I'm a scoop-conscious journalist, so I understand the love of an exclusive, but I will admit it was tough on history. As I queued for a telephone in the Press Gallery, waiting to file my copy and listening to all the other scribes reeling off paragraph after paragraph of their purplest prose, it wasn't easy to marry their accounts to what had really happened. Like a game of Chinese whispers, truth had got lost early on and runaway fantasy taken its place.

Naturally, my own account was as camped-up as everyone else's. The tabloids couldn't discharge their escapist functions properly without abusing language, so I dictated a Beef Wellington special, confident of a front-page splash. Christopher's eyes 'blazed like an angry young dog's', the House 'roared its disapproval with a single voice', 'large beads of perspiration' formed on the Chancellor's forehead, the Prime Minister was 'as white as a polar bear's ghost', the Speaker (most ludicrously of all, for his face can't be seen from the Press Gallery) 'was ashen-faced, his craggy eyebrows pursed with anxiety'. My own metaphor record would have been broken had I not been saving my heavy artillery for the paperback version, but I'm a modest man underneath it all and I only blow my trumpet when the market for trumpets is at its peak. It would have been nice to have written, 'owing entirely to the vigilance of your correspondent, who anticipated the threat to the Chancellor and took steps to meet it . . .', but the time wasn't ripe. I had sworn Jimmy Drummond to secrecy, leaving him to attribute his razor-sharp reactions to a psychic suspicion that Christopher was armed (an improbable fiction, but one he played with relish), and kept my own role shadowy. I told the Editor I'd file a full report in due course, when we could discuss the appropriate way for a family newspaper to handle the story, and hung up on him. I imagine he had an apoplexy, but I didn't care; there was no way he was going to sack me now.

At ten o'clock, the House divided on the second reading of

the Local Government Bill almost as if nothing had happened. I say almost because the actual voting took twenty-five minutes rather than the usual fifteen, and Members were so deep in argument in the division lobbies that the Whips had difficulty shepherding them through. After that, everyone went home. The remaining business, some EEC secondary legislation, was uncontentious and not expected to last more than an hour, but still I hung around. Long after the centre of the drama had shifted away from the House, long after the white heat of excitement had faded to a satisfying afterglow, I sat with a few cronies in the Press Bar savouring the whole glorious confusion of it. I was drunk by now but not very drunk, for I was terrified of spilling any of my precious secrets. Let's just be old-fashioned and say I was pickled, with all the mellow, contented sogginess which that implies. I guzzled up the atmosphere like a pig at his favourite trough and, for all the odd bubbles of disquiet at the back of my mind, I was happy. How had I ever found the House of Commons, this great all-singing all-dancing circus, with acts for all the family, a source of boredom?

At half past eleven, I did something I hadn't done for years and wandered into the Gallery for the adjournment debate. This half-hour's epilogue to each day's proceedings in the House is a low-key affair, normally attended by only three Members: a junior Government Minister, a Government Whip and a backbencher. The backbencher initiates a debate on some issue of local concern – an aggrieved constituent maybe, or a hospital closure – and the Minister replies to the points raised. Don't ask me what the Whip does, but the show couldn't go on without him. Only rarely is there national Press coverage, for the debates take place too late at night to catch the morning editions, and the Public Gallery is deserted. But that doesn't make the exercise futile. Members prize it highly and people who revere the Mother of Parliaments – I'm not normally one of them, although that night I was – will cite the adjournment debate as a symbol of the House's determination to address small issues as well as great, listen to quiet protest as

266

well as soaring oratory and, not least, defer its bedtime for the convenience of a single backbencher. You will hear this view sentimentalised, but there's something in it.

That night a Member called Woodward had the adjournment debate. He was normally one of the House's journeymen, a willing bit of lobby fodder from the North-east, but he spoke energetically about the problems faced by council tenants in his constituency as a result of the inflexible policies of the council. He sounded angry and he may even have been angry, although it's possible he just had a lot of council tenants among his electors. I noticed he had made sure the reporter from his local paper was in the Gallery to report his anger, so perhaps my cynicism was justified. It was certainly justified in the Minister's case, for he spent fifteen minutes saying that something would be done but made sure the half hour would elapse before he could explain what. Altogether, it was a pretty shabby debate, now I think about it, but at the time I felt enormous warmth towards the two dancers in that political tango. A day so packed with drama required a diminishing close or we would think the world was turning upside down and the Thames was about to burst its banks and sweep the Houses of Parliament away. Because my own mood was restless and I needed some core of tranquillity to cling on to, I loved Woodward and the Minister for the tranquil way they brought the day's proceedings to a close. I stayed right to the end, heard the Speaker say 'usual time tomorrow' to the Serjeant-at-Arms, then listened as the policemen relayed the traditional cry of 'Who goes home?' echoing round the House. This ancient custom is now, quite literally, pointless. The policemen would be struck speechless if anyone answered their question, and it so embarrasses most of them to shout it that they use a truncated version, '*'goes*home?', as if it was a single word. But, point or no point, I was glad of the old tradition that night. Its antique irrelevance spoke to something in me that really did feel smaller and humbler than the cesspit of humanity it was my daily lot to chronicle. I might be baffled by Christopher's or Anna's boundless love for Carter, but I suddenly realised how little my feelings for that old whore, parliamentary democracy, differed intrinsically from theirs. If theirs could bring some light and hope to their lives, however fleetingly, then why shouldn't mine? I didn't whistle in the taxi home, but I did look in the driver's mirror and saw I was smiling.

29

The following afternoon at three o'clock, Jack Hayward walked into Maidenhead police station and asked to talk to Inspector Popplewell. He was a tall, stooping man with a sad moustache and an exaggerated nose, and he worked, he said, for Rose, Prendergast and Rose, a firm of Maidenhead solicitors. His wife stayed at home with their two young children, and most weekends they went down to Bristol where her parents lived. They weren't particularly well off, but they budgeted carefully and went on camping holidays in France every summer. Neither of them had ever been involved with police before. They were church-goers, Methodists, and were opposed to having any nuclear weapons on British soil.

Hayward told the desk sergeant all this, not because it was relevant or because the sergeant had shown much interest, but because he was agitated and agitated people will talk about anything to avoid the terrible ordeal of silence. The sergeant listened politely, for he was a gentle man who had never learnt to get rid of time-wasters efficiently, but all he wrote down on his pad was 'Hayward, solicitor'. The solicitor bit was important, because solicitors had to be treated with circumspection and Inspector Popplewell would expect to be warned of such a significant detail when he got back from lunch. The sergeant was used to explaining at three o'clock that the Inspector had taken a late lunch, just as he was used to telling callers at 12.30 that he was taking an early lunch. These little lies were all in a day's work and caused him no misgivings. If his superiors wanted to stretch their lunch-hours, that was their privilege.

He might do the same when he was their rank although, as he wasn't a mixer like Popplewell and didn't have a mistress in Twyford, he would find two and a half hours excessive.

When Popplewell returned, Hayward's agitation increased. He leapt to his feet too quickly and shook hands too vigorously to be credible as a level-headed professional man. He asked to speak to the Inspector alone and followed him into his inner sanctum, the same cramped office where I had talked to him the previous week. There he confessed to the killing of Peter Wiseman.

He had been visiting a friend in Henley, he said, and had been drinking, but not heavily. He didn't know what the limit was, but was fairly sure he hadn't exceeded it. Two glasses of wine he had had, maybe two and a half, but spread over two hours: nothing more than that. He wasn't a hard drinker, but he did have a poor head for the stuff and he bitterly regretted having drunk anything that evening, as he wasn't one hundred per cent in control of his car and knew it as soon as he put the key in the ignition. If he had thought he was a danger to the public, he wouldn't have tried to drive home, but he'd been proceeding very slowly and very carefully when he must have fallen asleep at the wheel. That was the only explanation he could think of. One minute he'd been driving along on the correct side of the dotted line, and the next there was a thud and a scream and he was almost in the ditch on the other side of the road. He knew he had hit a pedestrian, but was too terrified to stop and just drove on home, which was criminal, worse than criminal. It was *evil*, he said, stretching out his arms to the Inspector for benediction and bursting into tears. The sergeant in the outer office heard the tears and craned his neck to listen, but it was several minutes before Hayward said anything else.

Popplewell leant across the desk and, uncomfortable at the sight of tears, absent-mindedly patted the man's hand. He didn't say so when he talked on the telephone the next day, but I imagine he felt secretly pleased with himself. The police's mundane, boring, unimaginative theory had been proved right, and my wild, far-fetched fantasy wrong. He didn't use

270

those exact words, but he said something lugubrious about the dangers of jumping to conclusions and didn't sound impressed when I said I hadn't jumped, just made a series of gentle hops. So that nobody could accuse him of jumping to conclusions, he made Hayward sign a detailed 3,000-word statement. It was a fascinating document and, when I read it the following week, I couldn't put it down.

Hayward was a good man. You knew that immediately because of his passionate insistence that he was a bad one. He didn't have to say he had lost sleep over the killing because that lost sleep impregnated every sentence, and the logic that persuaded him not to confess earlier was the logic of a weakling, not of a hardened sophisticate. There was no bringing Peter Wiseman back, he had told himself, but great and undeserved suffering would fall on his own family if he gave himself up. He had told his priest about it but not his wife, even though it was the first secret he had ever kept from her. Having accepted the cross of his guilt, he had carried it alone.

The possibility of Carter's arrest had changed everything. He had never voted for Carter's party, indeed, reading between the lines, you could see he was the sort of man who never would. But Carter himself he had admired. He and his wife often watched political programmes on television and, when Carter had been made Chancellor, they had agreed he was the best man for the job, because of his integrity. Yes, *integrity*. I read that sentence twice, not believing that a man of real integrity would recognise the quality in Carter, but it was down there in black and white and left me as mystified as ever. Why did ordinary men attribute extraordinary qualities to other ordinary men, just because they were Members of Parliament and wore pin-striped suits on television? Hayward even spoke of his remorse that he had robbed the country of one of its promising young statesmen. He didn't know anything about Christopher and the name Beef Wellington meant nothing to him, but he thought there might be a conspiracy of people trying to destroy Carter for their own political ends. He was glad his confession would speed Carter's rehabilitation and,

271

although he didn't believe in his party's economic policies, he wished him well for the future. 'I have done great evil,' he said at the end, beating his breast sonorously for the last time, 'and I shall serve uncomplainingly whatever sentence the court imposes for my crime.'

The Maidenhead police function slowly and methodically, so news of Hayward's confession didn't reach the House until after six. By that time a new Chancellor had been installed, a man of so little imagination that the thought of having an affair with his friend's wife would never even occur to him, and a kind of normality had returned. The pound surged back two and a half cents on the day, in tribute to the spectacular dullness of the new incumbent at Number 11, and the morale of the parliamentary party was on the upswing. When Jill Appleby took her seat at 3.30, there were hearty jeers of derision from the Government benches. She was a nine-day wonder and would lose Wopsley at the General Election as sure as Tuesday followed Monday: that was what the jeering was about, and the cheers of welcome from Jill's own party weren't loud enough to drown it.

Neither Carter nor Christopher came in to the House. Christopher was still being questioned by the police and Carter was skulking in his tent, waiting to be questioned himself. Their absence reduced the temperature in the House, and there were broad smiles of relief on their colleagues' faces as if they had emerged from a dark wood into sunlight.

All day I waited impatiently for the wheels of justice to grind into action and for Carter to be arrested on a murder charge. That was the logical end of my campaign, the moment when I could come out in the open about my own heroic role and take soundings from the Sunday papers. My hard old head didn't dwell on Anna's suicide or the state of semi-insanity to which I had reduced Christopher. I spared no thoughts for the mouse Sandra or for Sophie, whose face appeared on television proclaiming – yes you guessed – her determination to stand by her husband. Nor did I doubt the eventual outcome. Didn't

272

Islington
Libraries

Carter's prompt resignation signal his guilt more clearly than anything? If he'd been an honourable man, he might have resigned even if he was innocent, to save the Party damaging publicity. But he wasn't an honourable man, therefore he was guilty, end of argument. Game, set, match and a world exclusive to Wellington. As you can guess, I was ambushed into fury by the news of Hayward's confession.

'I just don't believe it,' I snapped at Bob Mumford when he brought me the news in the Press Bar, barely concealing his pleasure. 'It must be some crank who supports the Government and wants to divert attention. Carter's guilty as hell.'

'Is he? Are you sure?'

'Of course I'm bloody sure. Who is this comedian Hayward?'

'A solicitor.'

'How bloody ridiculous! Can you see it? A solicitor! Ha bloody ha.'

'It's no more ridiculous than a Cabinet Minister.'

'Just bugger off, would you. It's a crank, a nutcase. You see.'

I sat and sulked and went on sulking for nearly two hours. The truth sunk in slowly but not slowly enough, for I didn't want it to sink in at all. I felt cheated because, whatever everyone would now say, I hadn't formed a wild hypothesis on flimsy evidence. I had greeted Anna Wiseman's allegations with professional scepticism and only taken them seriously when the corroborative evidence mounted. I had committed nothing to print, said nothing to the police, just leaked the story in a moment of cruelty to someone whose lack of dependability might be to my advantage. Was that so wrong? No, I thought as I sulked. Yes, I thought later.

In time, my colossal incompetence would become clearer; my bungling, haphazard style of investigation; my preoccupation with sexy news at the expense of hard facts; my blind certainty that Carter was a murderer, when his paranoia could have had so many other motives; my neglect of the boring bit of the story, his activities in the City; and my consequent failure to locate the true nerve-centre of his anxiety, a financial irregularity ten years before – the unauthorised use of company funds

273

for political purposes – which he feared would prove fatal. But all this was still to come. Now I felt only the pain and the bitterness of humiliation. I could already see the back-biters and mud-slingers turning their attention from Carter to me. Stern words would be spoken in the House about irresponsible journalism, early retirement suggested again by the Editor, committees of inquiry set up, the facts established, your correspondent lambasted by the Press Council. I would fight my corner, of course, throw damaging light on the private life of John Carter MP, be lionised at the nastier end of Fleet Street for my revelations. But to what end? I'm not an intellectual, but I hate appearing stupid more than anyone and I couldn't bear to contemplate the gloating I would see behind the sympathetic faces. 'Tough luck, Beef. It would have been nice if it had been him.' 'Great story, Beef. Pity it wasn't true.' As I left the House that night, homeward bound for Jenny and consolation, I didn't give a damn whether I ever came back. I hated politicians for being better than I wanted them to be and I hated myself for hating them. I was going on a diet.